Richard Cumberland

Calvary

The Death of Christ - A Poem in Eight Books

Richard Cumberland

Calvary
The Death of Christ - A Poem in Eight Books

ISBN/EAN: 9783744711272

Printed in Europe, USA, Canada, Australia, Japan

Cover: Foto ©Andreas Hilbeck / pixelio.de

More available books at **www.hansebooks.com**

CALVARY;

OR

THE DEATH OF CHRIST.

A POEM,

IN EIGHT BOOKS.

BY

RICHARD CUMBERLAND.

LONDON:

PRINTED FOR C. DILLY, IN THE POULTRY.

M.DCC.XCII.

C A L V A R Y;

O R

THE DEATH OF CHRIST.

B O O K I.

B

The ARGUMENT of the FIRST BOOK.

After a short introduction, which states the miraculous acts of Christ, and serves to mark the period at which the Poem commences, Satan goes forth by night into the wilderness, and finds himself in the very spot, where he had in vain practised his temptations upon Christ: Here he falls into meditation upon that unsuccessful interview, and vents himself in soliloquy: Indignant under disappointment and impatient to repair his defeat, he ascends to the summit of the mountain, from whence he had exhibited the kingdoms of the earth, and calls the Devils from all parts of the Heathen world: The whole host of Infernals assemble at his summons: The chief leaders are enumerated, their persons and attributes described: Satan addresses them, and proposes the subject matter for their consultation, namely, By what means to counteract the power of Christ upon earth: Baal delivers his sentiments by stating difficulties and objections without any decided opinion unless for seduction in the general: Moloch angrily resents what he considers as pointed at himself, and speaks disdainfully against the proposal of seduction, as not only desperate but disgraceful: Belial replies, and after much circumlocution suggests a temptation to be set on foot by Mammon: He is interrupted by Satan, who reproves him for certain digressions in his speech, but adopts his hint of employing Mammon, and calls upon that evil Spirit to attempt the fidelity of Judas Iscariot, whom he points out to him as the only one of the Disciples open to seduction: Mammon at first affects to excuse himself from the undertaking, but in conclusion accepts it, and taking wing in presence of the whole applauding host sets out upon his embassy, directing his course to the city of Jerusalem.

C A L V A R Y.

BOOK I.

THE ASSEMBLING OF THE DEVILS.

HAIL, awful CALVARY! forſaking now
    Aonian haunts and the unhallow'd Nine,
I viſit thy ſad mount, and thence invite
The mournful echoes to my deep-ton'd harp,
Hymning the whilſt in ſolemn numbers praiſe   5
To God for mercies purchas'd by the death
Of that myſterious Being, virgin-born,
Savior of loſt mankind, who on the croſs,
Lord though he be of life and one with God,
In mortal pangs expir'd; there to atone   10
For a degenerate world, by his pure blood
To waſh original corruption out,
And riſing victor from the grave diſpel
Sin and it's offspring Death, with all the train
Of idol gods, uſurping earth and heav'n.   15

Now

Now had the wond'rous acts by JESUS wrought
Spread wide his fame thro' all Judæa's realm ;
The leper cleans'd, the blind to fight reftor'd,
The fick to health and ev'n the dead to life,
Tho' warn'd to filence, for his modeft ear   20
Sought not the praife of men, fo much the more
Publifh'd his mercies ; Dæmons at his call
With horrid fhrieks, that teftified his power,
Came forth from men poffeft and fled ; his voice
Rebuk'd the feas and winds ; vaft was the throng   25
That follow'd where he led, and thoufands found
In the wafte wildernefs mirac'lous food :
They faw, they marvel'd, and of force confeft
Meffias in his power, not fo in form ;
For there no comelinefs, no outward grace,   30
No princely ftate appear'd : Slow to renounce
Illufions long indulg'd, their wavering minds
'Twixt two opinions halted, while in place
Of thefe bright vifions they beheld a man
Lowly and meek, a houfelefs wanderer,   35
That had not where on earth to lay his head :—
Such can our Ifrael's great Reftorer be,
Such our Meffias ?—Thus their troubled thoughts
Like meeting currents clafh'd ; when as he fpake
Truth flow'd refiftlefs from his lips, his eyes   40

Beam'd

Beam'd mercy, and his Father's glory fhone
Effulgent in his face; then every tongue
Was hufh'd to filence, every doubt difpell'd,
And every heart confefs'd him Lord and Chrift.

'Twas night, when SATAN, prince of darknefs call'd, 45
And fitly call'd, for evil hates the day,
Walk'd forth on hellifh meditation bent,
Prowling the wildernefs: Where'er he trode,
Earth quak'd beneath his foot; before him roll'd
Thick cloud and vapour, making night's dark fhade 50
More black and terrible; the beafts of prey,
Every wild thing that roams the favage wafte
And howling to the moon demands it's food,
Fled his approach; the lion and the pard
Scented the blaft and flunk into their dens; 55
For whilft his breaft with raging paffions boil'd,
Hatred, revenge and blafphemous defpight,
The fighs he vented from the hell within
Breath'd death into the air; his haggard eyes,
Which ftill in fpeechlefs agonies he roll'd, 60
Out-glar'd the hyæna's; other fires than their's
To light his difmal path he needed none.

Now, having ftretch'd athwart the fandy wild
Clear to its rocky verge, the Arch-fiend paus'd
And upward caft his eye, if haply there 65

Darkling

Darkling he might difcern what faucy mound
Dar'd to arreft his courfe; for yet there dwelt
Such vigor in his wing, nor depth, nor heighth,
Mountains nor feas might check his bold career,
Were he fo purpos'd; neither would he deign   70
To afk one charitable ftar for light,
Thoughtful of former glory, when he foar'd
Son of the morning far above their fpheres.

    Whereat he 'gan put forth his plumed vans
From either fhoulder ftretcht for flight, when foon   75
The fuel'd clouds to fierce encounter rufh'd,
Loud thunders bellow'd, and the lightning's flafh
Smote on the craggy cliff; at fight whereof
Confcious that now he prefs'd the fatal fpot,
Where late he commun'd with the Son of God,   80
Who for the fpace of forty days and nights
Foil'd ev'ry vain device, with fhame abafh'd
And pondering in his mind his foul defeat,
Down, down at once his flagging pinions fell
Clofe cow'ring to his ribs: As fome proud fhip   85
Between the tropics o'er th' Atlantic wave
Speeding amain to reach her deftin'd port,
If chance th' experienc'd mariner efpies
The gathering hurricane, no ftay, no ftop,
Quick to the yard each fwelling fail is furl'd,   90

                       The

The curl'd waves whitening as the torrent drives,
And foon her taunt and lofty topmaft lower'd
Strikes to the gale; fo he his towering heighth,
That to angelic ftature now had fwell'd,
Shrunk into human fize, nor other feem'd   95
Than pilgrim fqualid and with years and toil
Bending decrepit, when from his full heart
Words intermixt with groans thus forc'd their way.

   Yes, hateful wildernefs, detefted rocks,
Whom I would curfe, had Nature left one blade   100
On your bare ribs, which curfing I might blaft,
Full well I know you; deep, too deep engrav'd
On memory's tablet your rude horrors live.
And you, officious lightnings, hide your fires !
Come, Night, again; let central darknefs fhrowd   105
Scenes, whofe tormenting recollection ftabs
My unavenged foul.   Can I forget
This Son of Jofeph? Son of God henceforth
Of force I muft confefs him, for what lefs
Than god-like conftancy could have withftood   110
Temptations great and terrible as mine?
Something which man is not he needs muft be,
Virtue, that angels boaft not, he muft have,
Elfe had my fnares enclos'd him, elfe the world,
Which then was mine to give, had been a bribe   115
                        4

Too glorious not to dazzle every eye
But his, who made thofe glories what they are.
Still I muſt doubt the Father's love fincere,
Tho' loudly vouch'd by his own voice from heav'n:
Is this a father's love, is this his care,   120
Here to expofe him to this defart wild
Forty long fleeplefs nights and faſting days,
No Angel guard about him, loſt, forlorn,
Abandon'd to the elements, to beaſts
More fierce than this loud ſtorm ; nay, fiercer ſtill,   125
To me than all more terrible, to me,
Foe of his life inveterate and avow'd ?
Rare fample of God's love ! If here his CHRIST
Encounter'd aught of danger ; and if none,
What elfe could prompt him to this vain difplay   130
Of voluntary penance, but the love
Of flattery and a defpicable wiſh
To hear himfelf applauded ? In this ſpot,
Beneath the jutting roof of this rude cliff,
I firſt furpriz'd this wand'ring Son of God,   135
This Savior of the world : Fainting he feem'd
With thirſt and hunger, pale as death his cheek,
His hollow eyes deep funk, and from his brow
Big drops of fweat diſtill'd, as one o'erfpent
And finking to the earth there to expire :   140

A ready

A ready tale he had for pity's ear,
A melancholy lift of wants and woes ;
He had not tafted food, and fairly own'd
That Nature's cravings were intenfe ; when I,
Glad at the heart to find him thus befieg'd   145
With appetite fo eager, ftooping down,
From the diffever'd fragments, that here lie
About the bafe of this ftorm-beaten rock,
Chofe out a few fmooth ftones, and tempting faid,
If thou art hungry, eat ; convert thefe ftones,   150
If thou art God's own Son, to bread, and eat !
But he not fo beguil'd fpurn'd them away,
And filenc'd me with text of holy writ :
A nobler appetite I next affail'd,
Ambition ; to the mountain's top we foar'd ;   155
I fpread the kingdoms of the earth in fight,
Fit fight to whet the hunger of the mind ;
But mind and body he alike would ftarve,
Nor thank nor homage render back for food
Of my providing : One laft hope remain'd ;   160
Methought there was a godly pride about him,
Which with right holy flattery I might win :
Upon the temple's topmoft pinnacle
I plac'd this fcorner of an earthly crown,
And bade him be a God ; Caft thyfelf down ;   165

C   Behold,

Behold, quoth I, the Angels are on wing
To bear thee up unhurt: With ſtern rebuke,
Get thee behind me SATAN! he replied;
Some power unſeen control'd me, down I fell,
Down from the giddy eminence I plung'd,   170
And left him to his Angels, whilſt their hymns
And halelujahs echo'd through the air
His triumphs and my ſecond fall from heav'n.
And now if dark deſpair ſhall reach this heart,
Which of hell's tetrarchs can arraign their king,   175
Or fix on me his ſhare of public loſs
And overthrow ſuſtain'd in this attack?
None, for none dare. If I, till now ſupreme,
Great idol of the Gentile world, for whom
So many groves, ſo many altars blaze;   180
If I, to whom by various names ador'd
Thouſands of temples riſe, whilſt one alone,
One ſolitary pile on Sion's hill
Echoes the praiſe of God, neglected elſe
Of all; if I, if SATAN muſt ſubmit   185
To CHRIST, revenge to patience, war to peace,
And men muſt learn new maxims of forgiveneſs,
Maxims I neither practiſe nor inſtil,
Heroes and kings and conquerors, farewell!
Greater is he who ſerves than he who reigns: 190

                                      To

To suffer, to submit, to turn the cheek
To the proud smiter, these are virtues now ;
Hence with such virtues ! If these rules obtain,
If this tame doctrine shall unman the world,
Altars and groves and temples all must sink ;   195
Olympus and its synod, every Grace
And every Muse, all that the chissel wrought
In Greece or Rome, shall moulder into dust,
And CHRIST and Reason shall usurp the world.

He ceas'd, and now his swelling bosom heav'd   200
With indignation like the labouring earth,
Which subterranean vapors undermine,
Pent in it's sulph'rous entrails : Up he sprung
To that high mountain top whence he review'd
The kingdoms of the earth, whilst at his side   205
CHRIST's humble virtue stood, on other realms,
Realms of immortal happiness, intent :
Here, as a vulture, on the craggy peak
Of Caucasus or Hæmus left to watch,
Screams out his shrill alarm, at sound whereof   210
The carrion troop, upon the wing for prey,
Come flocking to the signal, SATAN thus
Stood eminent, and call'd his dark compeers ;
So loud he call'd, that to the farthest bounds
C 2

Of Pagan ifle or continent was heard   215
His voice re-echoing thro' the vault of heav'n.

   Heroes and demi-gods, Olympian powers,
Infernal princes of hell's dark abyfs,
Heav'n's exiles, fpirits of air, water, fire,
Or whatfoever element confines   220
Your incorporeal effences, Oh hear !
Hear and affemble ! 'tis your leader calls ;
It is your champion's voice, in happier hours
Heard and obey'd, now in extremeft need
Be prefent and affift our great divan.   225

   No more, for foon was heard the diftant found
Of wings that beat the air; from every point
Of the four winds the gathering fwarm came on ;
From Crete, from Cyprus and the Ionian coaft,
From Egypt, Afric and the Aufonian fhores,   230
Gods of all names, dimenfions and degrees.
Great was their fovereign's triumph to behold
This prompt obedience to his high command ;
For now defcending on the defart heath
To martial mufic, the infernal hoft   235
In bands and columns, by their chiefs arrang'd,
Stood firm ; if ever gleam of joy might reach
Heart fo accurs'd, the Arch-fiend had felt it here,

                                 As

As with a monarch's eye he now review'd
His armies, covering all the fwarthy plain. 240
    Come, Mufe, and to your fuppliant's eyes impart
One ray of that pure light, which late you pour'd
On the dark orbs of your immortal Bard
Eclips'd by drop ferene: Conduct me now,
Me from my better days of bold emprize 245
Far in decline, and with the hoary hand
Of Time hard ftricken, yet adventuring forth
O'er Nature's limits into worlds unfeen,
Peopled with fhadowy forms and phantoms dire :
Oh ! bear me on your pinions in this void, 250
Where weary foot ne'er refted ; and behold !
All hell burfts forth : Support me, or I fink.
    Now glimm'ring twilight ftreak'd the Eaftern fky,
For he, that on his forehead brings the morn,
Star-crowned PHOSPHORUS had heard the call, 255
And with the foremoft ftood. Befide him one
Of towering ftature and majeftic port,
Himfelf a hoft ; his black and curling locks
Down his herculean fhoulders copious flow'd ;
In glittering brafs upon his fhield he bore 260
A kingly eagle, enfign of command,
BAAL his name, fecond to none in ftate
Save only his great chieftain ; worfhipp'd long

In

In Babylon, till Daniel drove him thence
With all his gluttonous priefts ; exalted fince   265.
High above all the idol gods of Greece,
Thron'd on Olympus, and his impious hand
Arm'd with the thunder; yet he ru'd the zeal
Of furious Jehu, and that mournful day,
When he beheld his altars ftream with blood,   270
His prophets and his priefts by hundreds flain
Upon Mount Carmel.   MOLOCH in the van,
Mail'd at all points for war, with fpear and helm
And plumed creft and garments roll'd in blood,
Flam'd like a meteor : Him with horrid joy   275
SATAN awhile furvey'd, then fighing cried,
Oh ! worthy of command, had all like thee
So bravely fought, heav'n never had been loft.
Thence as he glanc'd his eye, far other form
And much unfit for war he next efpied,   280
CHEMOS, the fin of Moab; power obfcène,
Emafculate and foft, in loofe attire
A fenfual deity; his glory 'twas
In arts of bafe feduction to excel,
And leagu'd with harlots to have turn'd the heart   285
Of that wife king, and drawn him from his God
To bend his aged knees at idol fhrines.
Clofe at his fide ftood one, in whofe foft eyes

                                             Enfnaring

Enfnaring fmiles and beauteous ruin lurk'd ;
Oh ! that fuch grace fhould be allied to fin ;   290
Zidonian goddefs, ASHTORETH her name ;
Heav'n would not quite deftroy fo fair a work,
But wantonnefs ufurp'd an angel face,
And with her innocence had chang'd her fex :
Yet let that fex beware, for in their fouls,   295
When once fhe enters, peace no longer dwells ;
Witnefs that Magdalen, whofe frantic breaft,
Till by CHRIST's mercy heal'd, fev'n dæmons rent,
All fin-begotten, all her brood accurft.
But SATAN, whofe ftern heart, ftranger to love,   300
All weaknefs tho' in fhape of fin difdain'd,
And only priz'd fpirits more like himfelf,
Indignant turn'd afide, and bent his eye
Where DAGON, giant god, amidft the ranks,
Like Teneriff or Ætna, proudly tower'd :   305
DAGON of Gath and Afkalon the boaft
In that fad flight, when on Gilboa's mount
The fhield of Saul was vilely thrown away,
And Ifrael's beauty perifh'd : Him awhile
With fcowling eye the infernal king furvey'd,   310
Then taunting cried, O DAGON, vaft in fize,
In foul diminutive, had that huge mafs
Valour proportionate, heav'n had been our's ;
                                            But

But fitter thou, dull fpirit, to people hell
Than re-affault God's throne: Where was thy pride,   315
When overthrown in Gaza by the ftrength
Of that uxorious Danite? Humbled now
I know thy nightly haunts, and how thou driv'ft
Wretches poffeft to hide themfelves in tombs,
Whence I beheld thee 'midft the herd unclean   320
Scour down the fteep and plunge into the fea.
But now a fairer form arrefts the eye
Of hell's defpotic lord; his radiant veft
Of Tyrian purple, ftudded thick with gems,
Flow'd graceful: He for courts was form'd, for feafts,   325
For ladies chambers and for amorous fports;
He lov'd not camps nor the rude toils of war;
BELIAL his name; around his temples twin'd
A wreath of rofes, and, where'er he pafs'd,
His garments fann'd a breeze of rich perfume: 330
No ear had he for the fhrill-toned trump,
Him the foft warble of the Lydian flute
Delighted rather, the love-foothing harp,
Sappho's loofe fong and the Aonian Maids
And zonelefs Graces floating in the dance;   335
Yet from his lips fweet eloquence diftill'd,
As honey from the bee, but ftill his voice
Ne'er counfell'd aught but cunning and deceit,

Mean

Mean truce and bafe capitulating terms;
Therefore by SATAN held in flight account,   340
For devils affect a dignity in fin.
Laft in the field, and from the reft apart,
Was MAMMON; cautious was his ftep and flow,
His eye ftill watchful to prevent furprize,
Squalid his vefture and his locks uncomb'd;   345
For gain and ufury engrofs'd his foul,
Nor other care had he but to amafs
Wealth unenjoy'd, and gloat upon his hoard:
Had there been only happinefs in heav'n
And gold in hell, MAMMON had fpurn'd the blifs,   350
And hugg'd the treafure cheaply earn'd with pain.
    His princes thus review'd, from the hill top
SATAN fwift-glancing flew, and in the midft
Rofe like a meteor; whereat all the hoft
Sent up a general fhout: he with his hand   355
Gave fign, and wheel'd the Stygian phalanx round,
Horrible fight! A theatre of fiends,
And each the foe of man; idols and imps,
Wizzards, familiars, fprites, phantafmas, dreams,
Sorrows and pains and deaths in every fhape   360
Cover'd the blafted heath: Th' infernal king,
Tho' in his heart, by mutinous paffions torn,
Thought clafh'd with thought, and all was anarchy,

D   Yet

Yet with affum'd compofure beck'ning forth
His princes, whilft th' inferior throng ftood off,   365
And mute attention reign'd, in few thus fpake:
    Friends and confederates, welcome! for this proof
Of your affiance, thanks! On every call,
Whether we need your counfel or your arms,
Joyful I fee your ready zeal difplays   370
Virtues, which hell itfelf cannot corrupt.
I mean not to declame: The occafion told
Speaks its own import, and the time's difpatch
All wafte of words forbids.   God's Son on earth,
CHRIST, the reveal'd Meffias, how to oppofe   375
Is now the queftion; by what force, or power—
Temptations have been tried, I name not them—
Or dark confpiracy, we may pull down
This fun of righteoufnefs from his bright fphere
Declare, who can: I paufe for a reply.   380
    Silence enfu'd, whilft every eye was turn'd
Inftinctively on BAAL; he of all
Hell's magi fill'd the feat of wifdom chief:
Experienc'd long in craft, and nothing apt
To give ftrait counfel, flow of fpeech he was;   385
To hint, propound, dilate, and fo entice
Other opinions forth, them to refute,

                                        And

And thereon build his own, was all his art.
After long paufe and hefitation feign'd,
Stale trick of orators, he thus began :   390
  Why thus on me, as I were worthy, me,
Loft being like yourfelves, as I alone
Cou'd compafs this high argument, on me,
Leaft in your fapient conclave, why you point
Thefe fcrutinizing looks, I mufe; and aw'd   395
By this your expectation fain wou'd fhrink
From the great tafk to filence, had you not
O'er thefe poor faculties fuch full controul,
As to put by all pleas, and call them forth
In heav'n or earth, or hell's profound abyfs,   400
Your's in all ufes, prefent at all hours.
Our kingly chief hath told us we are met
To combat CHRIST on earth : Be't fo! We yet
May try our fortune in another field ;
Worfe fortune than in heav'n befell our arms,   405
Worfe downfall than to hell, we cannot prove.
But with the fcene our action too muft change :
How ? to what warfare ? Circumvention, fraud,
Seduction ; thefe are earthly weapons, thefe
As man to man oppofes, fo muft we   410
To CHRIST incarnate. There be fome, who cry,
Hence with fuch daftard arts ! War, open war !

D 2

I honor

I honor fuch bold counfellors, and yield
All that I can, my praife; till one be found,
One that may rival God's own Son in power,   415
And miracle to miracle oppofe,
More than my praife I cannot, my affent
I will not give; 'twere madnefs: And how war
With God? what arms may we employ 'gainft him,
Whofe very prophets can call down heaven's fires   420
Upon our priefts and altars? For myfelf,
What powers I had I fhall not foon forget;
What I have left I know, and for your ufe
Shall hufband as I may, not vainly rifque
Where they muft furely fail.   The Jews pretend   425
That CHRIST colludes with Belzebub; the Jews
As far miftake my nature as my name:
The fallacy, O peers, confutes itfelf,
Forg'd to difparage CHRIST, not honor me:
Oh! that I had his wonder-working powers;   430
I'm not that fool to turn them on myfelf:
No, my brave friends, I've yet too much to lofe;
Though Babylon's proud fhrines are laid in duft,
Rome's capitol furvives, and thro' the world
Where'er her eagles fly, upon their wings   435
They bear my thunder and they fpread my fame:
Therefore no more of Belzebub and CHRIST;

No

No league, no compact can we hold together.
What then enfues? Defpair? Perifh the thought!
The brave renounce it, and the wife prevent;   440
You are both wife and brave.   Our leader fays
Temptations have been tried, and tried in vain,
Himfelf the tempter.   Who will tread that ground,
Where he was foil'd? For Adam a mere toy,
An apple ferv'd; CHRIST is not brib'd by worlds: 445
So much the fecond Man exceeds the firft
In ftrength and glory.   But tho' CHRIST himfelf
Will not be tempted, thofe who hear him may:
Jews may be urg'd to envy, to revenge,
To murder; a rebellious race of old,   450
To kill a prophet or betray his God
What Jew was ever found to need the fpur?
Wift ye not what a train this preacher hath,
What followers, what difciples? Thefe are men,
Mere men, frail fons of Adam, born in fin.   455
Here is our hope.   I leave it to your thoughts.

   He ceas'd, but neither murmur nor applaufe
Follow'd his fpeech, for MOLOCH, whofe fell heart
Ill ftomach'd this tame counfel, leaft of all
Taunts thinly cover'd under mafk of praife,   460
Sprung forth impetuous, and with fcowling brow
And accent acrimonious thus replied:

                                 My

My thoughts it feems are known before I fpeak;
War, open war is all my note : I rife
To thank the prophet, who thus reads my heart,   465
Where honefty fhou'd wear it, in my face ;
That face from danger I did never hide,
How then from him ? Nor am I by his praife
More honor'd than by his diffenting voice :
For whilft he counfels circumvention, fraud,   470
Seduction,—if my memory wrongs his words
I yield it to correction,—we ftand off
Wide as the poles apart.   Much I had hop'd
When the great Tempter fail'd and in your ears
Sung his own honor's dirge, we had heard the laft   475
Of plots and mean temptations; mean I call them,
For great names cannot fanctify mean deeds :
SATAN himfelf knows I oppos'd the attempt,
Appeal'd, protefted ; my thrice-honor'd chief
Knows it full well and blufhes for th' event.   480
And are we now caballing how to outwit
A few poor harmlefs fifhermen, for fuch
Are CHRIST's difciples; how to gull and cheat
Their fimple hearts of honefty ? Oh peers,
For fhame, if not for pity, leave them that,   485
That beggar's virtue : And is this the theme,
The mighty theme, which now employs the thoughts

6

Of

Of your immortal fynod? Shame, Oh fhame!
Princes, Dominions, Arch-angelic Thrones,
Imperial Lords! thefe were your titles once,   490
By thefe names ye were known above the ftars,
Shame not your antient dignities, nor fink
Beneath the vileft of the fons of men,
Whifperers, informers, fpies. If CHRIST be God,
Fight, as becometh you to fight, with God: 495
If man, and fure his birth befpeaks no more,
Why all this preparation, this confult,
Thefe mighty machinations and cabals?
Off with your foe at once, difmifs him hence
Where all his brother prophets have been fent;   500
Where his precurfor John is gone before,
Whofe voice ftill echoes thro' this wildernefs :—
" Repent ye, for God's kingdom is at hand!
" Prepare ye the Lord's way!"—It is prepar'd;
It leads to death, it marfhals him the road   505
To that oblivious bourne, whence none return :
Herod yet lives; another royal feaft,
Another wanton dance, and he, for whom
So many innocents were flain, fhall fall.
Once vanquifh'd, are we therefore to defpair?   510
In heav'n unequal battle we provok'd;
Tho' vaft our hoft, the million was with God:

                                                            On

On earth enquire of all the nations round
Whom they will ferve, with one voice they reply,
We are their gods; they feed us with their blood,   515
Their fons and daughters they make pafs through fire
To do us grace; if their own flefh they give,
Shall they with-hold to facrifice a foe?
Twelve tribes were all Jehovah had on earth,
And ten are loft; of this fmall remnant few   520
And wretched are the friends that league with Heav'n.
And where is now CHRIST's promis'd reign on earth?
When God's own fervants rife againft his Son,
And thofe, to whom the promifes were giv'n,
Revolt from their Meffias, can we wifh   525
Greater revenge? What need have we to tempt
Them, who have hearts rebellious as our own,
As prompt to malice, no lefs prone to vex
God's righteous fpirit? And let come what may,
It comes not to our lofs, rather our gain.   530
Let God arife to vengeance; let him pour
Deftruction on his temple, whofe proud heighth
Our chief can witnefs, meafur'd by his fall:
Let him not leave one ftone upon another,
As his rafh Son hath menac'd; let his wrath   535
Thro' all the inhofpitable earth difperfe
His fcatter'd tribes; fuch ever be the fate

Of

Of all his worſhippers ! May ſcorn, contempt,
Deriſion be their lot, and may their God
Never recall his curſe ! Are we, O peers,   540
To mourn for his Jeruſalem ? Our joy
Springs from confuſion ; enmity 'twixt God
And man is our beſt triumph : For myſelf,
War is my harveſt, then my altars blaze
Brighteſt, when human victims feed the flame.   545
    Breathleſs he paus'd, ſo rapid was the pulſe
Of his high-beating heart he ſtood as one
Choak'd and convuls'd with rage ; when as he ceas'd,
He ſmote his mailed habergeon ſo loud,
Hell's armed legions heard, and ſhook their ſpears   550
Betok'ning war : Frowning he look'd around,
Whilſt from his fiery eyes ſuch terror glanc'd,
It ſeem'd as if his pride meant to abaſh
And ſilence all oppoſers : Yet not long
His triumph, for now BELIAL from the ranks   555
Graceful advanc'd, and as he put aſide
His purple robe in act to ſpeak, the throng,
Such was the dazzling beauty of his form,
Fell back a ſpace ; then ſtood all eyes and ears
In expectation mute as death : Though hell   560
Own'd not a ſpirit more falſe, ſenſual and baſe,
Yet ever as he ſpake ſuch action grac'd
               E

His

His words, so musically soft they flow'd,
Who most despis'd the pleader prais'd the speech:
When thus with mild insinuating looks,   565
Masking his rancorous heart, the Fiend began.
    After so many peaceful ages past
Since first emerging from hell's dark abyss,
Rous'd by our Arch-angelic Chief, we sprung
Up to this middle region, and here seiz'd   570
On this terrestrial globe, created first
For man, our vassal now, where at full ease,
Lords of the elements and gods ador'd,
We reign and revel undisturb'd of Heav'n,
If God, whose jealousy be sure ill brooks   575
That this fair world should be so long possess'd
Of us his exil'd angels, and his name
Pent up in Palestine, should now arouse
His slumb'ring wrath, and his best strength put forth
To wrestle for lost empire, and our earth,   580
As we in evil hour his heav'n, assail,
Who of this mighty synod but must own
The provocation warrants the retort?
If then the Maker of mankind hath cause
To meditate their rescue, we no less   585
Have cause to oppose th' attempt, and hold them fast
To their allegiance in despite of Heav'n.
    5

Much then we owe to our great Leader's care,
Which, ever watchful o'er the public weal,
Calls us to this full council, here to meet   590
In grave confult how beft we may repair
Paft difappointments, and repel the fpite
Of this new Champion, levell'd at our fhrines.
Great is the trouble of my thoughts, O peers,
And much perplex'd am I with doubts, what name,   595
Nature and office to afcribe to CHRIST;
In form the lowlieft of the fons of men,
In miracles omnipotent as God;
Whofe voice controuls the ftouteft of our hoft,
Bids the graves open and their dead come forth;   600
Whofe very touch is health; who with a glance
Pervades each heart, abfolves it or condemns;
Whofe virgin birth credulity fcarce owns,
And Nature difavows.   Prais'd to all time,
Immortal as himfelf be the renown   605
Of that wife fpirit, who fhall devife the means
By force or fraud to overthrow the power
Of this myfterious foe, what fhall I fay?—
Prieft, Prophet, King, Meffias, Son of God.
Yet how God's unity, which well we know   610
Endures no fecond, fhould adopt a Son
And effence indivifible divide,

E 2   Baffles

Baffles my weak conjecture: Let that pafs!
To fuch hard doctrines I fubfcribe no faith:
I'll call him man infpir'd, and wait till death   615
Gives fentence of mortality upon him.
Meanwhile let circumfpection on our part
Fill all the anxious interim; alarm
Rome's jealoufy, ftir up the captious fpleen
Of the proud Pharifee, befet him round   620
With fnares to catch him, urge the envious priefts,
For envy ftill beneath the altar lurks,
And note the man he trufts.   MAMMON could tell,
Though MAMMON boafts not of his own fuccefs,
How few of human mould have yet withftood   625
His glittering, golden lures.   The fword can kill
Man's body, gold deftroys his very foul:
Yet mark me well, I counfel not to tempt
The Mafter; poverty can do no more
Than his own mortifying penance does,   630
Hunger and thirft and obftinately ftarve,   .
When his mere wifh could make the rock a fpring
And its hard fragments bread: Yet fure I am
All are not CHRIST's in heart, who with their lips
Confefs him; thefe are men, and therefore frail,.   635
Frail and corruptible: And let none fay,
Fear prompts this counfel; I difclaim all fear

                                                                    But

But for the general caufe : In every heart
Nature hath built my altar; every fect,
Nation and language with one voice confefs   640
Pleafure the fovereign good : The Stoic churl,
The dogged Cynic fnarling in his tub,
And all the ragged moralizing crew
Are hypocrites ; philofophy itfelf
Is but my votary beneath a cloak :   645
It harms not me, though every idol God
Were tumbled from his bafe; alike I fcorn
Sampfon's ftrong nerve and Daniel's flaming zeal :
And let CHRIST preach his mortifying rules,.
Let him go forth through all the Gentile world,   650
And on the ruin of our fanes erect
His church triumphant o'er the gates of hell;
Still, ftill man's heart will draw the fecret figh
For pleafures unenjoy'd ; the gloomy cell
And melancholy faft, the midnight prayer   655
And pale contrition weeping o'er her lamp
Are penances, from which the fenfe revolts,
Fines, that compounding fuperftition pays
For pleafures paft, or bribes for more to come.

    Enough of this vain boaft, here SATAN cried;   660
More than enough of thefe voluptuous ftrains,
Which, tho' they lull the ear, difarm the foul

                            Of

Of its beſt attribute : Not gaudy flowers
Are cull'd for med'cine, but the humble weed ;
True wiſdom, ever frugal of her ſpeech,   665
Gives ſage advice in plain and homely words.
The ſum of all our reaſoning ends in this,
That nothing but the death of CHRIST can ſolve
The myſtery of his nature ; till he falls
Scarce can I ſay we ſtand : All voices then,   670
Though varying in the means, conſpire his death ;
Some cautiouſly as BAAL ; ſome with zeal
Precipitate as MOLOCH, whoſe ſwift thought
Vaults over all impediments to ſeize
The goal of his ambition.   But, O peers,   675
Our's is no trivial care ; direct your fight
Along the ranks of that redeemed hoſt ;
On us hangs all their ſafety : Night and day
My anxious thoughts are labouring in their cauſe,
And whilſt CHRIST walks the earth I take no reſt,   680
A watchful ſpy for ever at his ſide,
Noting each word and deed ; ſometimes I mix
With the ſelected Twelve that page his ſteps ;
Of theſe, though ſome have waver'd, none is falſe
Save one alone, ISCARIOT he by name ;   685
The taint of avarice hath touch'd his heart;
I've mark'd him for my own.   Hear, princes, hear !

                                                      This

This night the priefts and elders will convene
Their fecret conclave : I am in their hearts ;
Burning with envy, malice and revenge,   690
Their only thought is how to tangle CHRIST,
In whom of force I own no guile is found,
But gentlenefs inftead and perfect truth,
A lamb in nature without fpot and pure,
Fit victim therefore for their Pafchal rites,   695
Which now are near at hand ; apt is the hour,
Apt are the inftruments.   What now remains
But to fend forth a tempter to perfuade
ISCARIOT to betray his Mafter's life,
And damn himfelf for gold? Speak, is there one,   700
One in this patriot circle, whom all eyes
Point out for this emprize? Moft fure there is ;
BELIAL hath well predicted of our choice :
MAMMON, ftand forth ! On thee th' election lights.

    He fpake, and all approv'd, for choice fo fit   705
None could oppofe ; when MAMMON thus replied.

    Prince of this world ! To whom thefe armies owe,
Loft but for thee in everlafting night,
The glorious profpect of yon rifing fun,
'Tis not to evade the labor, but prevent   710
The failure of your hopes, that I befeech
Your wifdom to correct it's choice, and lodge

                                        This

This arduous embaſſy in abler hands :
Nathleſs if ſuch your will, and my compeers
Adjudge me to this ſervice, I ſubmit : 715.
In me is no repugnance, no delay ;
For ever what theſe toiling hands could do,
Or patient thoughts deviſe, that I have done ;
Whether in heav'n ordain'd to undermine
God's adamantine throne, or doom'd to dig 720
The ſolid ſulphur of hell's burning ſoil,
Fearleſs I wrought, and, were there no tongues elſe
To vouch my ſervices, theſe ſcars would ſpeak.
How many daintier ſpirits do I ſee
Fair as in heav'n and in freſh bloom of youth, 725
Whilſt I, with ſhrivel'd ſinews cramp'd and ſcorch'd
'Midſt peſtilential damps and fiery blaſts,
Drag as you ſee a miſerable load,
Age-ſtruck without the laſt reſource of death :
This for myſelf, no more. You're not to know 730
The ſnares which I employ are golden ſnares ;
Theſe are my arts, and like the crafty ſlave,
Who in Rome's Circus hurls the fatal net
Over his fierce purſuer, ſo oft times
Have I entangled the proud hearts of men, 735
And made their courage ſtoop to ſhameful bribes,
Paid for diſhoneſt deeds, perjuries and plots,

That

That draw them off from God, who elfe had fill'd
His courts ere now with guefts and peopled heav'n.
Thefe weapons and thefe hands you ftill command ;   740
So dear I hold the general caufe at heart,
So difciplin'd am I in duty's fchool,
That recklefs of all hazard I prefent
Myfelf your fervant, or, if fo fate wills,
Your facrifice ; for though from mortal man   745
Difcomfiture I dread not, yet if CHRIST,
Whom the great Tempter foil'd not, fhall ftand forth
The champion of his follower, witnefs for me,
You my brave peers and this angelic hoft,
I fought not this bold heighth, whence if I fall,   750
I do but fall where SATAN could not ftand.

    Go then, exclaim'd th' Arch-Enemy of man,
Go, brave adventurer, go where glory calls :
Aufpicious thoughts engender in my breaft,
And now prophetic vifions burft upon me :   755
I fee the traitor JUDAS with a band
Of midnight ruffians feize his peaceful Lord :
They drag him to the bar, accufe, condemn ;
He bleeds, he dies ! Darknefs involves the reft.
Afcend the air, brave fpirit, and 'midft the fhout   760
Of grateful myriads wing thy courfe to fame.

F

He

He faid, and pointing to the facred towers
Of God's high temple, wav'd his fceptred hand,
Whereat the infernal armies gave a fhout
That fhook the rocky defart to its bafe :   765
Meanwhile the fiend, ambaffador of hell,
Exulting heard his high election crown'd
With thefe applauding voices, and the call
Of his great Chieftain echo'd to the fkies :
Pride fwell'd his confcious breaft; no longer now   770
Crouching with age and pain, but nerv'd anew,
As with a fpell transform'd, erect he ftood
With towering ftature talleft of the throng,
And looks of high fupremacy and ftate.
And now from either fhoulder he unfurl'd   775
His wide-ftretch'd pinions, and uprifing fwift
Tower'd in mid-air; the hoft with loud acclaim
Hail'd his afcent; he on the well-pois'd wing
Hover'd awhile, till from his cloudy heighth
Sweeping the wide horizon he defcried   :   780
Far in the weft the holy city, of God,
His deftin'd port, then to the orient fun
Turn'd his broad vans, and plied their utmoft fpeed.

END OF THE FIRST BOOK.

CALVARY;

OR

THE DEATH OF CHRIST.

BOOK II.

The ARGUMENT of the SECOND BOOK.

Mammon, alighting on the Holy Mount, assumes the form and character of a Levite, and under that appearance goes in search of Judas Iscariot. He meets that disciple most opportunely for his purpose in a solitary place, and entering into conversation with him, pretends a commission from the priests and elders for engaging him in their service with the promise of a reward, and urges many insidious arguments for detaching him from his Master: They separate with a promise on the part of Judas to report his final answer to the priests that evening. Christ is now brought to view sitting in the midst of his disciples at his Last Supper: He addresses them in those solemn and affecting terms recorded in the Gospel of Saint John, washes their feet, foretells his death, and points out to them his betrayer in the person of Judas then present: The traitor, perceiving himself discovered, hastily departs. Christ, pitying the affliction of his disciples, tenderly consoles them with the promise of his support under their future tribulations, and concludes with an aweful invocation to the Father in their behalf: whereupon, warning them that his hour is come, he goes forth to the garden. A reflection, naturally springing from the subject, addressed to unbelievers, closes the book.

C A L V A R Y.

BOOK II.

THE LAST SUPPER.

NOW on the confecrated Mount of God
    MAMMON, invifible to mortal eye,
Stooping the wing from his aerial heighth
With feet unhallow'd lands ; a direful peft,
Fartheft from heav'n of all that outcaft crew,   5
Who fell from blifs ; fit meffenger was he,
And fatal was their choice, who fent him forth
To work corruption's purpofe in man's heart ;
For in his pow'r excelling he can take
The femblance of each virtue, fhift each form,   10
And turn and turn new faces on the world,
Till he hath fnar'd a foul ; then he appears
In nature as he is, loathfome, obfcene,
Rapacious as thofe filthy monfters feign'd
By fabling poets of amphibious breed,   15

Harpies,

Harpies, of earth and ocean the foul fpawn,
Half brute, half human, with cadaverous face
Horribly pale, and hollow hungry eye,
Glaring aghaft, with wings outftretch'd to chace
And talons crook'd to pounce their mangled prey.   20
And now by dev'lifh fpell transform'd he feems
A reverend Levite, bearded to the waift;
Hypocrify ne'er wore a graver mafk:
And ftill with wolf-like watch he prowls around,
If haply in thofe haunts he might furprize   25
Occafion to put forth his damning arts,
And from the flock of their good Shepherd cull
One tainted ftraggler, one, whofe fordid foul
Avarice might tempt to take the price of blood,
And facrifice the Son of God for gold: 30
Of CHRIST no care had he, but to elude
His vigilance, which ftill was all his dread;
Nor of the Twelve, fave JUDAS, was there one
Whom to affail; on him alone, on him,
Son of perdition, refted all the hopes   35
Of SATAN and his legions.   Now the fiend
With ineffectual fearch had coafted all
The facred region round, and in the fhade
Beneath the temple porch awhile repos'd,
Lift'ning the converfe of the idle crowd,   40

The

The fun then high at noon; and much they talk'd
Of CHRIST and his great miracles, of fome
Elias deem'd, of fome the Baptift John
Ris'n from the dead, but by all tongues confeft
A prophet mighty both in word and deed :   45
Silent the whilft in fecret mufings wrapt
The wizard fpirit ftood, when all at once
Loud voices ftrike his ear, and ftrait comes one
Leaping and bounding 'midft the fhouting throng,
A cripple new reftor'd; the very bed,   50
Which from his birth the palfied wretch had prefs'd,
Now in it's turn was carried, and to all
Triumphantly expos'd : Behold, he cried,
The token of my cure; I am the man
Whom ye all knew, and this the doleful bed,   55
On which, faft bound in mifery and pain,
Helplefs before your charitable gates
I laid and begg'd for pity and relief :
Lo! I am free! Mark how thefe new-found limbs
Nimbly the health-reftoring voice obey !   60
CHRIST gave the word; he fpake and I am whole.
    This whilft he heard, conviction fmote the fiend;
His confcious heart a fudden tremor feiz'd
And off he flunk abafh'd : A winding path
Led down the mount, and here as he purfued   65
In

In gloomy thought his folitary way,
Behold by happy chance the man he fought,
ISCARIOT and alone : Joy flufh'd the cheek
Of the incarnate dæmon, thus to find
His labour in aufpicious moment crown'd.   70

    Hail, fon of Simon ! peace be to thee, friend !
Fairly encounter'd art thou in good hour,
The prieft-like Tempter cried ; thy worth is known
To all our Levites, from whofe tribe I come
With friendly greeting charg'd : This night they meet   75
In fpecial conclave ; our chief pontiff there
Will in the holy convocation move
Points of high import to our antient law,
Queftions it much importeth thee to hear,
And well accepted fhalt thou be of all,   80
Who with large recompence and honors due
Will greet thee fo complying : I have faid.

    Grave Sir, I know thee not, JUDAS replied ;
Yet for thy greeting thanks, and peace for peace,
As holy men becomes.   To him the fiend.   85

    Unknown I well may be, who night and day
Serving God's altar rarely ftir abroad,
And little commerce hold with this great world ;
But thee I know one of that Teacher's train,
Who walks at large, nor fhuns the haunts impure   90

                          Of

Of finners and of publicans : Alas !
That one of thy wife bearing fhould be feen
In fuch bafe fellowfhip, paging his fteps,
Calling him Lord and Mafter, whom the world
In mere derifion fuffers to grow up   95
To full-blown vanity, at once to crufh.
But good report is pregnant with thy name,
As one exempted from the general fcorn ;
And fure I am thou wilt not fo abafe
And lower thy nobler thoughts to one fo mean,   100
Vile and mechanic ; to the driv'ling crew
Of children and of women leave that tafk,
To Peter and his brethren of the net :
Fine reas'ning we fhall have, and well be fchool'd,
When fifhermen turn preachers and inftill   105
Doctrines and laws, which Mofes never taught.
Woe to our fcribes ! Rare mockery of the world
And the world's wifdom, if thefe fimple folk,
Lur'd from their daily drudgery, fhould fet up
Fifhers of men ; the fynagogue, to them   110
A barren element, will never yield
Such gainful earnings as the fea affords.
And what is CHRIST, that JUDAS fo fhould court
His ftarving fervice ? What fo tempting lure
Hath this deceiver to beguile thy hopes ?   115

G   Not

Not of this world my kingdom, he hath faid ;
Yet of this world are we, in this alone
We live and move, here only we expect
Or pain or pleafure, all that lies beyond
In the unknown abyfs is dark as death.   120
And wherefore carrieft thou that bag about ?
A beggar needs no treafurer, and thy Lord
Feeds but by miracle : Alas for him,
Who ferves a mafter, that keeps Sabbath fafts
Forty long days in the bare wildernefs,   125
Makes poverty his paffport into heav'n,
And bids us throw away life's prefent means
For doubtful chance of intereft after life :
And art thou of all reafon fo bereft
As to account profperity a crime,   130
Or think none bleft but him, whofe every ftep
Through mifery's thorny path is mark'd with blood ?
O fon of Simon, take thy laft refolve ;
Either refign thy body to the worm,
And die with CHRIST, or him renounce, and live   135
Rich, honor'd, profperous, and enjoy the world.
    The Fiend now paus'd, well pleas'd that he had gain'd
Audience fo large ; when JUDAS, in whofe foul
The pois'nous inftillation 'gan to work,
Thus to corruption's advocate replied.   140

                                        That

That CHRIST, rejected and defpis'd of men,
Hath in this world no part I freely grant;
Therefore if we his followers, who renounce
Things prefent, build our hopes upon a dream
Of what fhall never come, we are of all   145
Moft miferable; if we, who bid farewel
To all that Nature holds moft dear to fhare
Sorrows and pains and poverty with CHRIST,
Find not thofe blifsful manfions in the heav'n
Which he hath promis'd; if, when all is paft   150
And this fad fcene concludes, no reck'ning comes,
No grateful compenfation after death,
Hard is our fate, and much hath he abus'd
Our weak credulity; but ftill thefe hopes
Of an expected glory, though with doubt   155
And darknefs clouded, faint yet not extinct,
Yield not to words; words made them what they are,
CHRIST's words, and furely man ne'er fpake like him;
Wherefore if thefe your doctors of the law
Invite me to their conclave but to hear   160
A railing accufation, I hold off
From their affembly, and to CHRIST adhere,
As to the better reas'ner; and though poor
The fervant, equal is the Mafter's lot,
Poor as the pooreft, houfelefs and forlorn,   165

G 2   A man

A man of forrows ; nor can we complain,
Whilft he of all we fuffer ftill partakes,
Firft in all labours, penances and pains.
You afk, and bid me take my laft refolve,
If I will give this body to the worm   170
And die with CHRIST : To die is Nature's dread ;
Inftinctively fhe loaths the gloomy grave,
And turns a longing eye to light and life ;.
But fortune gives to all things their degrees ;
To them, who bafk in funfhine thro' the day,   175.
Night comes with double fadnefs, whilft to me,
Who toil from morn to noon, from noon to eve,
Yet nothing but a dim horizon fee
Low'ring in clouds, darknefs is nothing ftrange,
Nor death a terror : Wealth prefents no dower   180
To wed me to the world ; no pleafures cling
Around my heart ; no foft affections woo
My longer ftay on earth, there to prefer
Brief joys poffefs'd to hope of future blifs.

    Thus whilft he 'plain'd the fubtle Tempter's ear   185.
Caught the foft murmur that betrays the foul,
The figh capitulating virtue breathes,
When from her laft defences fhe retreats ;
Whereat a bolder tone he now affum'd,
And thus the wav'ring falfe difciple plied.   190

                                      All

All joys that gold can purchafe wait your choice ;
Rich to your heart's ambition you fhall be,
Nor only rich, but refcued from a doom
So dreadful, had you all the wealth in ftore,
Which the fea covers or the earth contains, 195
'Twere well beftow'd to purchafe your redemption.
With CHRIST impending death, with me you meet
Life with encircling pleafures. Throw afide
That beggar's purfe, your ftarving office fpurn ;
Serve God's high prieft, whofe treafury is full ; 200
Caft thofe few mites away, the fcanty dole
Of fome contaminating leper's hand,
For which you bid God heal him and pafs on ;
Whilft he, good cred'lous foul, cries out amain,
As powerful fancy works, Lo ! I am clean ; 205
Behold a miracle ! But gold performs
Greater and happier miracles than this :
Gold with a touch can heal the mind's difeafe,
Quicken the flow-pac'd blood, and make it dance
In tides of rapture through each thrilling vein ; 210
Caft out that worft of dæmons, poverty,
And with a fpell exorcife the fad heart,
Haunted with fpectres of defpair and fpleen.
If then this prize can tempt thee, if thy foul
Still thirfts for life, for riches, for repofe, 215

If

If in thy breaſt there dwells that manly ſcorn,
Which ſlighted merit feels, when envious pride
Thruſts it aſide to build th' unworthy up,
Now, now aſſert it; from a Maſter turn,
Who turns from thee, who before thee exalts   220
Thy meaner brethren, Peter, James and John :
On them his partial ſmile for ever beams,
They have his love, his confidence, his heart;
Of them revolting he might well complain,
Of thee he cannot; thine were juſt revenge :   225
He is no traitor, who reſents a wrong;
Who ſhares no confidence, can break no truſt.
Bid conſcience then be ſtill, let no weak qualms
Damp thy reviving ſpirit ; but when night
Wraps her dark curtain round this buſy world,   230
Come thou to CAIAPHAS ; there will be found
Our prieſts and ſcribes in council to attaint
And bring to judgment this preſumptuous man,
Who boaſts himſelf Meſſias Son of God.
If thou, to whom his midnight haunts are known,   235
His ſecret incantations and his ſpells,
By which he does thoſe feats that cheat our ſight,
Wilt to thoſe guilty haunts conduct our guard,
And render up his perſon to the law,
Much praiſe and large reward ſhalt thou receive;   240

3

If thou wilt not—But wherefore ſhould I doubt ?
I would perſuade, not threaten : Know withal
It is not thou, 'tis juſtice gives the blow ;
The law will have its victim.   Thinkeſt thou
That we, to whom the cuſtody is given   245
Of God's prophetic oracles, ordain'd
To guard his worſhip and expound his laws,
Will let this innovating Teacher ſpurn
Our holy order, mock our ancient rites,
Prophane our Sabbaths, and himſelf exalt   250
Co-equal with Jehovah, to confound
His unity, and claim divided power ?
No, let death arbitrate 'twixt him and us ;
If he be very CHRIST, death ſhall not dare
To aim his dart at immortality ;   255
His incorruption ſhall defy the grave :
If man, blaſpheming man, he juſtly dies.
Living or dying thus his fate diſpells
All myſtery ; truth ſtarts of force to light,
And God is glorified in either caſe.   260
     He ceas'd, and on the Traitor fix'd a look,
Which, like the ſerpent's faſcinating eye,
Gaz'd motion's power away ; ſullen he ſtood,
As with a ſpell entranc'd ; the aweful ſenſe
Of his great Maſter's virtue and the dread   265
                                                          Of

Of an hereafter terrible to thought,
No longer ferv'd to hold the wizard fiend
And his fell arts at bay : The word of truth,
Sown on the furface of his ftony heart,
Had perifh'd without root ; religion's lamp,   270
Faint and more faint as MAMMON's crafty breath
Blew up the ftorm of paffion, now expir'd
In his benighted foul ; there rankling pride,
Malicious envy, avarice and revenge,
Leagu'd with hell's minifter and uncontroul'd   275
Their impious orgies held.   At length the wretch,
To calm deliberate treachery refign'd,
With all th' unrighteous Mammon in his heart
And vile prevarication on his lips,
Thus with confent in dubious phrafe implied   280
The grand feducer of mankind difmifs'd.

   Great is the peril of the attempt you urge,
For great the power of him you would deftroy ;
Therefore if I demand fome paufe for thought,
Deem it not much.   Your offers fhall be weigh'd ;   285
But now no more : Occafions call me hence ;
This night the Mafter hath convok'd the Twelve
To keep the facred feaft, ordain'd of God
With bread unleaven'd and the Pafchal lamb :
Thither, tho' laft and in his favor leaft,   290
                                    I go,

I go, a cited gueſt: There whilſt I ſit
Unnotic'd at his table's loweſt foot,
My meditations ſhall recall your words,
And ponder them apart.   Say to your prieſts,
Thoſe conſervators of our ancient law,   295
This night they may expect my laſt reſolve.
And now behold the length'ning ſhadow marks
The ev'ning hour, that warns me hence: Farewell!
   This ſaid, their conf'rence ended, they embrace
As friends, who plight their faith: Upon the touch,   300
So quick th' infection ran, ſo dire the blight,
The pois'nous ferment on the inſtant reach'd
Iscariot's tainted heart, and now he burnt
With the fell luſt of gold.   Joy ſeiz'd the Fiend;
For well he knew how mortal to the ſoul   305
That deadly aconite, the growth of hell.
Oh! wretch for ever loſt, for ever curſt,
Whom Mammon thus embraces! Who ſhall wake
Thy conſcience from its lethargy? Who now
Shall ſtop the courſes of that baneful drug,   310
And ſtem the ſwift deſtruction? 'Tis too late:
Better for thee hadſt thou ne'er ſeen the light,
Or loſt it ere this fatal hour had birth.
Thy doom is ſeal'd; hell hath its hour of joy,
Thou, traitor, an eternity of woe: 315

H   The

The meditation of thy heart fhall hurl
Thee to perdition and thy Lord to death.

 Now JUDAS down the mountain turn'd his fteps ;
Not fo the Tempter ; he from the high rock,
Exalted where he ftood, his impious eye   320
Glanc'd o'er the city' of God full in his view
From Eaft to Weft in moony crefcent ftretch'd.
Here yet JEHOVAH was ador'd, here reign'd;
All elfe to SATAN and his idol.gods
Thro' earth's wide range belong'd; to their dire names 325
Each temple echo'd, every knee was bow'd :
How oft, ev'n here upon his holy hill,
Did Judah's kings with their polluted groves
Affront God's houfe, and pagan altars raife
To Chemos, Milcom, Afhtaroth and all   330
The hoft of heav'n within his facred courts !
Witnefs that impious king, who pafs'd his fon
Through fire to Moloch, homicidal God,
Which rous'd th' Almighty's vengeance, and entail'd
Mournful captivity on all his race.   335
Hither, as to the delug'd world of old,
In promis'd time the dove of peace was fent;
Upon this Ararat, his facred mount,
He refted; hence falvation dawn'd on man :
Him to deftroy the Tempter now afpir'd.   340

          Secure

Secure of his new convert firmly leagu'd
In his dire plot and to perdition feal'd :
Nor refted on that mount the darkling Fiend,
Nor further need had he of prieftly garb,
Than till he faw Iscariot join the train   345
Of Christ and his difciples; then at once
To his own airy properties diffolv'd
A fpi'rit invifible, with eager fpeed
To hell's affembled chiefs he wing'd his flight.

    The fun had funk beneath the Weftern hills,   350
And now at ev'ning hour the Jews prepare
To celebrate their Paffover, ordain'd
T' eternize their deliv'rance, when God's wrath
Smote ev'ry firft-born male in Mizraim's coaft,
Save where the blood of lamb piacular,   355
Sprinkling the confecrated door, was found
Of the deftroying angel : To this feaft,
Prelufive of his own pure facrifice
And type of his blood-fhedding, Jesus came :
The guefts were prefent and the table fpread;   360
With loins begirt, as men upon the march,
And ftaff in hand, they fnatch a hafty meal :
This done, in penfive meditation rapt,
The Savior, confcious of impending death,
Sate in the midft; to his all-prefent mind   365

The

The treafon and the traitor ftood confeft.
Low'ring, abafh'd and from the reft apart,
ISCARIOT at the table's loweft foot
Took poft, where beft he might efcape that glance,
From whofe intelligence no heart could hide   370
Its guilty meditations: All eyes elfe
Were center'd on the Savior's face divine,
Which with the brightnefs of the Godhead mix'd
Traces of human forrow, and difplay'd
The workings of a mind, where mercy feem'd   375
Struggling to reconcile fome mortal wrong
To pardon and forbearance: Such a look
Made filence facred, every tongue was mute;
Ev'n PETER'S zeal forbore the vent of words,
Or fpent itfelf in murmurs half fuppreft.   380
At length the meek REDEEMER rais'd his eyes,
Where gentle refignation, tempering grief,
Beam'd grace ineffable on all around,
And with thefe words the awful filence broke.

    Mufe not if I am fad, nor ftand aghaft   385
As doubtful of my conftancy; thefe pangs
And more which I muft fuffer were forefeen;
The hour now coming comes not by furprize,
It is the confummation of my charge,
And fills the meafure of atonement up.   390

Shall

Shall I then fay, Father, avert this hour,
And fave me from thefe agonies? Not fo.
With heart prepar'd to fuffer and fubmit
I meet my doom forewarn'd : Yet ere we part
Take this laft office from your Mafter's hands ; 395
And when you fee me ftoop to wafh your feet,
As foon as you fhall, remember 'tis your Lord,
Your dying Lord this legacy bequeaths,
And edify by his humility.

    This faid, his feamlefs mantle he threw off, 400
And girt his tunic clofe about his waift;
And now with mute amazement they beheld
The Son of God in fervant-like attire
Prepar'd to execute his menial tafk.
All gaz'd, all wonder'd, but no voice oppos'd ; 405
None dar'd to pray forbearance of the deed,
Till he, whofe heart was ever on his lips,
PETER, in warm expoftulation cried :

    Lord, doft thou wafh my feet, thy fervant's feet,
Mean as the duft he treads on? Never, Lord, 410
Never fhalt thou do that for one fo vile,
So all-unworthy : That be far from thee !
Such homage ill befeemeth thee to pay,
Me to receive.—To him the Lord replied :

PETER,

PETER, as yet thou know'ft not what I do,　　　415
Hereafter thou fhalt know; therefore no more:
Ceafe to oppofe, for if I wafh thee not,
With me thou haft no part.—Struck to the foul
With horror at the thought, his eager words,
Wing'd with the flame of rhapfody, burft forth:　　　420

　　Oh! not my feet alone, my hands, my head,
Wafh me all o'er, and fanctify each part.

　　There needs not this, the meek REDEEMER cried,
Enough is done; thus wafh'd, though but in part,
Thou fhalt be clean throughout: Yet I'll not fay　　　425
Ye are all clean: Spite of the Shepherd's care
The taint hath touch'd his flock. Alas! for him
On whom the foul contamination lights;
Woe to that wretch that ever he was born!
And do ye need a comment to expound　　　430
This leffon of humility and love?
Ye call me Lord and Mafter; well ye fay,
For fuch in truth I am; if then your Lord
Be meek and lowly, will not ye renounce
Pride and contention? If the Mafter ftoops　　　435
To wafh his feet who ferves, fhall ye do lefs
To thefe your equal brethren? Learn of me,
And each with other deal, as I with you:

　　　　　　　　　　　　　　　　Write

Write on your hearts my words; the time draws nigh
When I fhall fpeak no more with you on earth :   440
Ye have all heard; how bleft if ye obey !
I fpeak not of you all : Whilft here ye fit
In feeming fellowfhip around my board,
Sharing this focial meal, my laft on earth,
Doubt not but I can fearch into your breafts,   445
And fee whofe hearts are loyal, whofe is falfe;
And mark me well, I fall not by man's wiles,
Not unpredicted is the trait'rous act,
And well I know the wretch, whofe faithlefs hand
Dips with me in the difh, fhall foon be dy'd   450
With my devoted blood. Betray'd I am,
Deceiv'd I cannot be.——This when they heard,
Each with the other interchang'd a look
Of queftion and fufpect; fpeechlefs they ftar'd,
Confounded and aghaft : As men drawn forth   455
For decimation tremble to unfold
The lot of life or death, fo thefe in doubt
On whom the word of prophecy might light,
Curious yet fearful to enquire of CHRIST;
Search'd their own hearts in filence. All perceiv'd   460
Omnifcience, which to God alone belongs,
Familiar with their thoughts, and every foul,
Save that dire wretch whom confcience inly fmote,

6   Trembled

Trembled left unpremeditated guilt
Might be denounc'd upon him, or the sin   465
Of one man, as of Korah, move the Lord
With the whole congregation to be wroth.
But PETER, in whofe ever-anxious mind
Thefe terrors undifpell'd long could not dwell,
To the belov'd Difciple, on the breaft   470
Of CHRIST reclining, now gave fign to afk
The fearful queftion, in what traitor's heart
Plot fo accurs'd could harbour. Thus befought,
Though much his humble nature fear'd offence,
In accent foft, with fupplicating eye   475
Turn'd on the Mafter, the meek fuitor faid:
Lord, fhew thy true and faithful fervants grace,
And let us know the traitor.—He it is,
JESUS replied, on whom I fhall beftow
This fop, when I have dipp'd it in my cup.   480

     He faid, and as he plung'd the morfel in,
All eyes were fix'd upon the fatal work,
Wond'ring on whom he would beftow the fpell;
And foon with filent horror they beheld
The faturated fop to JUDAS giv'n,   485
Pledge of perdition; he with greedy hafte
Devour'd it, by the fiend within him urg'd;
For MAMMON to the dark divan had told

                                        The

The joyful tidings, and had pofted back
Swift as the magic whirlwind conjur'd up   490.
By all hell's wizard imps could drive him on,
And now fate neftling in the traitor's heart,
Brooding his filthy fpawn : Great was the joy
Of the infernal tempter, thus to find
That guardian Pow'r, whofe providence he fear'd,   495
By thefe fymbolic elements withdrawn,
And his apoftate victim now caft out
From the Lord's Supper, alien from God's grace,
And foul-furrender'd to hell's gloomy realm.

 Now, as the fpell within him 'gan to work,   500
The traitor's vifage, like the troubled fea
Uptorn and furrow'd with tempeftuous winds,
Shifted it's hues, now deadly pale, aghaft
And horror-ftruck, now fiery red, deform'd
With hellifh rage, and from man's femblance chang'd   505
To very dæmon, terrible to fight.
Oh ! what a fall from heav'n to deeper hell
Than thought can fathom, horrors worfe than heart
Of man, unlefs abandon'd of his God,
Can fuffer or conceive ! Words do but fail   510
To paint that unreveal'd abyfs, thofe depths
Of the immeafu'rable profound, where groans,

I

Wailings

Wailings and woes and toffings amidft fires
Unquenchable await the wretch condemn'd !
　　Meanwhile in cloudlefs majefty and mild　　　　515
The Savior's face divine on all around
Effulgent beam'd; about his temples fhone
A radiant glory : This when JUDAS faw,
Whom now the fpi'rit of darknefs had poffefs'd,
And none fuch in the fphere of that pure light　　520
Long could abide, he ftarted from his couch
Prepar'd for flight, when thus in few the Lord—
Go then ! and what thou haft in hand to do,
Do quickly ; fo depart !—The word of power,
Though gentle yet commanding, JUDAS heard,　　525
And inftantly the fpirit took him thence ;
Nor could he not obey, for fo rebuk'd
The prince of hell, SATAN himfelf, had fled.
The faithful remnant fate in mute fufpenfe,
Pondering what this difmiffion might import.　　530
The Mafter with a glance difcern'd their thoughts ;
He faw them in profound conjecture loft,
Humbled in heart and fad, their honor ftain'd
By bafe defection, and their faith convuls'd :
When thus, at once to ftrengthen and confole　　335
Their wav'ring minds, thefe healing words he fpake.

　　　　　　　　　　　　　　　　　　　　　Let

Let not your heart be troubled : Ye believe
In God, believe also in me his Son.
Doubt not but in the compass of the heav'ns
My Father will provide for all his Saints   540
Manfions of peace, feats of eternal blifs,
Where fpi'rits made perfect after death fhall dwell,
And reft from earthly toils : Thither I go
To feal your fure election, and prepare
For you my faithful fervants an abode ;   545
That, as in forrow here, fo there in blifs
With me your Lord, now dying for your fakes,
Ye may furmount the grave, and ever live
In heavenly communion undifturb'd.
Lament not therefore if I now depart,   550
Your provident precurfor, for ye know
Whither I go, and alfo know the way.

   Lord, we are ignorant and dim-fighted men,
THOMAS replied, we fee not what thou fee'ft ;
And as it ftands not in our reach to guefs   555
Whither thou go'ft, how fhould we know the way ?

   I am the way, th' infpired Teacher cried,
I am the Truth, the Life : None can approach
The Father but by me ; me had ye known,
This blindnefs had been done away, and now   560
Behold Him prefent !—Where ? ftill doubting cried

One of th' aftonifh'd number; Oh! impart
That intellectual vifion to difcern
And fee the Father; fet Him in our view
In form demonftrative; we afk no more.   565
    Say'ft thou? refum'd the Lord, and have I been
So long familiar yet fo little known?
Will not the works, O PHILIP, I have done,
Done in thy fight, inftruct thee whence I am,
And what my power? Doth there need light for this?   570
'Midft the broad blaze of proofs that fhines about thee
Can'ft thou not fee God's prefence in his power?
Of this mortality which ye behold,
This flefhly felf, I fpeak not; 'tis the Spirit,
The virtue of my Father, which is in me,   575
In act how vifible, in voice how ftrong,
Clear and exprefs! And can you fee and hear
And yet withhold belief? Oh, flow of faith!
If words cannot perfuade, let works convince:
If miracles, which only God can do,   580
Are done before your eyes, how fay you then,
Shew us the Father? Sanctify your hearts
From fear and terror; though the hour comes on,
When to the filent manfions of the dead
From this impeni'tent world I muft withdraw,   585
Mourn not, but let your grief be turn'd to joy;

                                    For

For as in me the Father, fo in Him
I live and move ; my Spirit, though unfeen
Still prefent, fhall protect and hover o'er you.
I will not leave you comfortlefs ; my name   590
Shall be your tower of refuge ; with my peace
Now dying I endow you ; of that peace
The powers of this world never fhall defpoil you,
And in my Name whatever ye fhall afk
Believing, ye fhall have : By faith in me   595
Ye fhall command the elements, uplift
The everlafting mountains by their roots,
And whelm them in the centre of the fea :.
This in my Name potential ye fhall do,
And greater works than this : By faith in me   600
Ye fhall confront th' oppreffor ; 'midft the fhock
Of tribulations and the angry fcorn
Of a malignant world, abhorr'd, defpis'd,
Thruft from their fynagogues, ye fhall poffefs
Your fouls in patience, glorying to endure   605
Like tribulation with your martyr'd Lord.
Defpair not therefore, for before that day
A Comforter fhall come, whom I will fend,
And he fhall teach you all things. When ye ftand
Before the judgment feat of impious men   610
Friendlefs, accus'd, environ'd with a throng,

Of

Of perjur'd witneffes athirft for blood,
Your Guardian Spirit fhall provide a voice,
Action and eloquence, and prompt your lips
With untaught languages to found my Name   615
With tongue miraculous through all the world.
Wars then and rumors and portentous figns,
Famine and earthquakes and difaftrous plagues
Shall vex the nations; prophets fhall arife
With lying divinations to confound   620
The weak, pervert the wavering and perplex
The very Saints themfelves.   Await the time;
Thefe are but harbingers of mightier woes;
The day of terror is but in it's dawn:
The powers of earth and heav'n muft undergo   625
Direful convulfion; this majeftic pile,
This temple, fhall become fo mere a wreck,
That not one ftone fhall reft upon another:
Then fhall your hour of tribulation come;
Then to confefs my Name fhall be your crime   630
By torture and by death to be aton'd:
The tyrants of the world fhall then let loofe
Their perfecuting rage, and great fhall be
The falling-off of many; rocks and caves
Shall be your hiding-places, yet from thence   635
Your found fhall echo to the fartheft ends

.5   Of

Of the redeemed earth ; from thofe dark cells
The beams of revelation fhall break forth,
Maugre the pow'rs of hell; and bleft is he,
Whofe faith unfhaken fhall abide the time,   640
Till the great end and confummation comes
My peace and my falvation to enfure.
Few are the moments now and paffing fwift,
Which thus converfing we have yet in hand.
Servants no more, henceforth I call you friends;   645
Therefore, as friends and children, let your love
Each to the other knit your hearts together
In brotherly communion ; this command,
New to the world, I give you : Let good will,
And peace and concord harmonize your fouls,   650
And mark you as the followers of him,
Whofe every act was charity, whofe life
Was fpent and clos'd expiring for your fakes :
And ftronger proof of love what man can give,
Than to yield up his body to the grave,   655
And die, as fhortly I fhall, for his friends ?
Time was that I have fhadow'd out my fpeech
In proverbs and allufions ; time now is
To caft obfcurity afide and fhew
Th' unveiled glories of the Father to you.   660
Henceforward ye fhall afk of Him and have ;

My

My Name for your petitions fhall fuffice;
My prayers ye need not, for the Father's love
Without an interceffor fhall protect
Mine, as you love me, and prevent your wants.   665
From Him I came into this world, to Him,
This world now leaving, I again return.

    This faid, conviction fmote their glowing hearts
With faith, and hope's bright image new infpir'd,
And fcenes of future glory beaming on them: 670
When thus with voices join'd in loud acclaim
CHRIST in the Godhead manifeft they hail'd.

    Now, Lord, we hear and underftand thy words,
Plain words and not in parables involv'd:
Now are we fure all knowledge is reveal'd,   675
All pow'r committed to thee from above,
And without further queftion we believe
And henceforth know thou cameft forth from God.

    Do ye at length believe? the Mafter cried;
Behold, the hour comes on, yea now is come,   680
When your ftrong faith fhall ftagger at the fcene
Of thefe impending horrors, and fhrink back
Confounded and appall'd; to the four winds,
Wide as your fears can fpread you, all fhall fly,
And leave me ftruggling with a ftorm of woes   685
Unfriended and alone; what did I fay?

                                    Alone

Alone I cannot be, for in me dwells
The Father ever prefent.: Let this thought
Arm you with conftancy to meet the fhock
Of tribulation, and withftand the powers   690
Of this brief world; for to your comfort know,
I have o'ercome the world.   This faid, he paus'd,
And fate, whilft all were hufh'd, as one entranc'd,
So faft the heav'nly vifion pour'd upon him :
Then with uplifted eyes and heaving breaft,   695
Full of his God, this folemn pray'r breath'd forth.

    O Father ! give thy glory to the Son,
As he hath glorified thy Name on earth,
And thefe, whom thou haft giv'n him, taught to know
Thee, the true God alone, and JESUS CHRIST   700
Thy meffenger and advocate with thee
For loft mankind.   Father ! To me reftore
That glory, which was mine before all time,
Or e'er the world was made and man fell off
Fróm his obedience, now at length redeem'd   705
From fin by my atonement, and made heir
Of life eternal, purchas'd with my blood.
The act of mediation is complete ;
Thy work is finifh'd and thy Name gone forth
To thefe of thine election : Thine they were,   710

                    K   To

To me thou gav'ft them, and they have receiv'd
And kept as faithful witneffes thy Word. .
For them I pray :. The world, which now I leave,
Hath no more part in me ; for them alone,
Not for the world, I pray ; they muft abide,   715
I fhall depart and be at peace with Thee.
O holy Father ! keep them in thy Name
Whole and entire, link'd in the bond of faith,
Firm as I hold them. 'One alone is loft,
Son of perdition ; him the prophets faw   720
In their profpective vifions, and foretold
That fo thy Son fhould fuffer ; but for thefe,
They are unftain'd, they ftand not in the guilt
And condemnation of that wretch accurft.
I pray thee not to take them from the world,   725
Through which I fend them forth as fhining lights
To draw men's eyes and hearts, and guide their fearch
To the bright fource, whence thy falvation beams.
Thefe are my minifters, as I am thine :
Oh ! fanctify them through thy truth ! For them,   730
And all through them converted to thy word,
Father ! I pray.   Tranflate them in thy time
From this unquiet world to that high ftate
Of heav'nly blifs, where they may dwell with me

§   And

And fee my glory : So fhall they receive   735
Thy love, through me transfus'd into their hearts,
And reft from all their forrows in thy peace.
   So fpake the Lord, and with thefe gracious words
His faithful remnant cheer'd, for foft they fell
As heav'n's bleft dew upon the thirfty hills,   740
And fweet the healing balm, which they diftill'd
On forrow-wounded fouls.—Now treach'rous eve
Crept filent on, and threw her dufky veil
O'er Nature's face; mafking the deeds of men :
The Savior rofe, for in his confcious breaft   745
A warning voice had whifper'd, Up, arife,
Go forth to death ! One folemn act remains;
One facrifice ; 'tis now God's wrath demands
Atonement, a whole world's redemption now
Hangs on the minute's point. Behold him then,   750
A voluntary victim, leading forth
His fad difciples to the fatal fpot,
Where treafon lurk'd in ambufh for his life,
Where ftood the prince of darknefs and his pow'rs
Arm'd with commiffion'd terrors to affail   755
Him fingle, him forfaken, him oppos'd
To myriads, whilft Heav'n's angels foar'd aloof
Trembling fpectators of th' unequal ftrife.
Who now fo comfortlefs as God's own Son ?

    His

His foul in woes unutterable whelm'd,   760
All commerce with its native heav'n denied,
Prefs'd down to earth; nor other ftrength had he,
Than in his human nature might be found,
To combat more than human agonies,
Accumulated pangs, which all the fins   765
Of all the world, from lofs of Paradife
By man's firft fall to the laft damning page
Of heav'n's black regifter, had pil'd upon him,
The mafs of ages.   Oh! what tongue can fpeak
The love of our REDEEMER? And yet man,   770
Ingrateful impious man, hourly reviles
His Benefactor's name, affects the ftyle
Of fophiftry and metaphyfic pride
To quibble with falvation, and renounce
Thofe guides, that lead us by the hand to heav'n.   775
This they call reafon, this man's natural right
To queftion his Creator, and in pride
Of independant dignity reject
Salvation, rather than confent to own
God's privilege to fave him by fuch means   780
As to God's wifdom beft and meeteft feem'd.
Such monfters doth this teeming earth produce:
Impious audacity! which dares to fay—
I need no Mediator, I difclaim

                                          CHRIST

CHRIST and his offer'd peace; 'twixt God and me   785
I want no advocate to plead my caufe,
By my own rectitude I ftand or fall:
The Evangelic Volumes I regard
As fabricated tales of juggling tricks,
Witnefs'd by none but partners in the craft: 790
Deep read in pagan ftory I confront
The facred records with the filent page
Of thofe, who regifter no ftrange eclipfe,
No noon–day darknefs, not one friendly groan
Of fympathifing Nature to atteft   795
CHRIST's dying hour.——Shut, fhut the Book of Life
Go to the Jews, the Pagans, for thy creed,
Go to the duft, blafphemer! In the ear
Of Death whifper thy doubts, and learn of him
Thy folly's confutation and thy doom   800
In thofe fad realms, to which he fhall conduct
Thy trembling foul, when the Arch-angel's trump
Hath fummon'd thee to judgment, and fet ope
The grave, thy rafhnefs deem'd for ever clos'd.

END OF THE SECOND BOOK.

CALVARY;

OR

THE DEATH OF CHRIST.

BOOK III.

The ARGUMENT of the THIRD BOOK.

Iscariot, having separated himself from Christ, wanders through the streets of the city in a disconsolate manner, and at length arrives at the brook Cedron without the gates. Here he breaks forth into soliloquy, in which, after reviewing his past situation, he affects to justify his present motives for betraying his Master to the priests. Christ and his disciples, proceeding to the Mount of Olives, are discovered by him as they are passing the brook in their way thither, and Judas resolves upon availing himself of the opportunity for delivering Christ into the hands of his enemies. In the mean time the priests and elders assemble in the palace of Caiaphas, and there hold a council upon the measures to be pursued for the apprehension of Christ: The high priest harangues the assembly to this immediate purport: In the interim Judas is announced, and being admitted makes his proposal to the council; this produces some observations on the part of Caiaphas, and is objected to by Nicodemus, who after delivering his opinion quits the assembly. Caiaphas then takes up the matter afresh, controverts the sentiments of Nicodemus, and with the approbation of all present closes with the proposals of Judas, and sends out a company with that traiterous disciple to the Mount of Olives, there to apprehend the person of Christ. The assembly breaks up, and the hall is no sooner evacuated by the priests and elders, than their seats are filled by Satan and his infernal spirits. Satan addresses to them a congratulatory speech on the success of Mammon's temptation, on whom he bestows many high encomiums; an ovation takes place in honor of that dæmon, when Chemos appears wounded by the spear of Gabriel, whom he had encountered on the Mount of Olives, where he had been posted as a spy upon the motions of Christ and his disciples. Satan, enraged at the account, sallies forth with a resolution to revenge the attack by punishing the temerity of Gabriel, arms himself for the occasion, and after much proud vaunting of his superior prowess disappears, and the infernal spirits disperse.

C A L V A R Y.

B O O K III.

THE TREASON OF JUDAS.

D A R K came the ev'ning on, and the pale moon,
 Now faintly glimm'ring through a wint'ry cloud,
Shed her dim horrors o'er the fhadowy earth;
Whilft through the filent ftreets with ftep difturb'd,
And heart by hellifh meditations rent,   5
The Outcaft of the Lord purfued his way,
ISCARIOT, name for evermore accurft.
Onward he went unqueftion'd, unobferv'd,
For all upon this folemn night kept houfe,
Nor ftopp'd till forth the city gates he came 10
To Cedron's brook, whofe bubbling current laves
The olive-crowned Mount, favor'd of CHRIST
For its umbrageous groves and filent haunts,
For pray'r and contemplation fit retreat.
Here firft, as one awaken'd to new thoughts, 15

L   Starting

Starting he check'd his ſtep, and with a groan,
That rent his lab'ring boſom, thus broke forth.
    Oh, my torn heart! Oh, ſoul-tormenting ſcenes!
Can I forget the bliſsful hours I've paſs'd
Beneath your ſhades liſt'ning the Maſter's words?   20
When as he ſpake of heav'n and heav'nly joys,
Of righteouſneſs and the bleſt Spi'rits with God,
Such life in his deſcription glow'd, methought
All Paradiſe was preſent to my view
And courted me to enter.   Heav'n and earth!   25
Muſt I remember? Never man like him
Could with ſuch magic eloquence entrance
The ſenſes of his hearers, lift the ſoul
To heav'nly contemplations and tranſport
To thoughts beyond itſelf; thence to look down   30
Upon this lower world and all it's cares,
It's pains, it's perſecutions with contempt:
Sometimes envelop'd in myſterious ſchemes
And parables he couch'd the moral truth,
Which painted on the memory left it's tints   35
Indelible: But when with tongue inſpir'd
The fall of nations he foretold, and drew
The curtain of futurity aſide;
When in the pomp of numbers he deſcrib'd
Jeruſalem beleaguer'd with a hoſt   40
                                         Of

Of Gentile foes and trodden down to duft,
Her matrons and her virgins whelm'd in blood,
Or dragg'd to violation, fhame and bondage
By ruffian fpoilers ; when his foaring flight,
Spurning the world's wide compafs, fcal'd the fkies,   45
And there amidft the empyrean fields,
As in his proper region, fhook the fpheres
Of fun, moon, ftars, as with a mafter's hand,
And fhew'd them falling in prophetic awe
Of his own glorious coming in a cloud   50
With pow'r and ftate fupernal, then our hearts
With fympathetic raptures burnt within us,
And we vain mortals faw, or thought we faw,
Our own vile bodies glorified to fhare
In his triumphant entry, and ourfelves   55
To dignities and thrones and ftarry fpheres
Exalted, loftieft in the realms of light.
But now thefe bright illufions are no more ;
Vanifh'd thefe glitt'ring fcenes, my claims on heav'n
All cancell'd, and my hopes a bankrupt's dream,   60
Mocking the haunted fancy with a pile
Of vifionary wealth.   Behold me fham'd,
Banifh'd his board, detected, and my thoughts
Turn'd outward to provoke my brethren's fcorn,
And blazon forth his prefcience : Let that pafs !   65

L 2   Traitor

Traitor pronounc'd, a traitor I will be;
That prophecy at leaft fhall be fulfill'd.
Though mafter of my will I could refute
And dafh his bold prediction, yet my heart
Ponders revenge more fuited to it's wrongs,   70
Greater than fuch flight triumph can beftow,
And not lefs terrible than death itfelf.
This night, the laft that he fhall walk at large,
This night fhall be his triumph or his fall.
If thefe grave elders, who confpire his death,   75
Thefe reverend priefts revolt not from the deed,
That cafts on them, their function and their tribe
The peril of his blood, why fhould my heart
Shrink from it's purpofe? What have I to fear
In act fubordinate, in caufe fupreme,   80
Traitor prejudg'd, of uncommitted crimes
Arraign'd, and thrown upon the world condemn'd?

　　More he had faid, but, like a ferpent coil'd,
With fudden ftart he fhrunk into himfelf,
And lift'ning held his breath to catch the found   85
Of fteps, that echoing o'er the flinty foil
Befpoke a company in near approach:
With thefe the Mafter's well-known voice he heard;
Whereat, like murd'rous Cain when call'd of God,
The cow'ring confcious outcaft flunk afide,   90

　　　　　　　　　　　　　　　　　　　　　And

And wrapp'd his ruffet cloak about his head,
Then darkling ftood ; the holy troop meanwhile
Forded the fhallow brook and held their way
Strait to the Olive Mount, their wonted haunt.
Forth fprung the lurking caitiff from his watch :   95
· The greedy Mammon rufh'd upon his heart,
Glorying that now he held them in his net,
Darknefs confpiring with occafions apt
Of hour and place to make his vengeance fure. '
Remorfe was dead within him, every fenfe   100
Of virtue loft, yet in his coward breaft
Such languor, dread and cold repugnance dwelt,
Scarce could the breath of hell's worft fiend fuffice
To blow it into flame : Now fudden rage
Impell'd him onward, now with palfied fear   105
Struck back, he reel'd and fhook in ev'ry joint.
This SATAN faw, and evermore at hand
To drive the wav'ring finner to his doom,
Breath'd all his fpi'rit upon him ; direr blaft
Cocytus never vented, the full tide   110
Of aconite engender'd with his blood,
His brain, fet ev'ry fev'rifh nerve in play,
And fcrew'd his heated fancy to the pitch
Of daring and defiance ; yet the wretch,
Not lefs a traitor to himfelf than CHRIST,   115

Or

Or e'er the acting of the dreadful deed
Thus strove by sophistry to glofs it o'er.
   Why do I doubt ? What horrors shake my mind ?
Why should not my affronted honor stir
Me to betray, as their insulted law   120
Provokes our elders to destroy their foe ?
For Moses they, I for myself oppose ;
And where's the wrong, if he, who knows my heart
And all it's meditations, will not deign
To turn it from it's purpose, and divert   125
The danger he foreknows ; nay rather helps
To lure the embryo treason into birth ?
Either his own free will makes death it's choice,
And so becomes accomplice in the deed,
Or else, foredoom'd to die, he knows his hour,   130
And thus, not acting of ourselves but rul'd
By strong neceffity, we stand abfolv'd,
Mere guiltlefs tools and instruments of fate.
What then ? Why let the Scriptures be fulfill'd,
Let prophecies, which are the voice of God,   135
Sound out his knell ; we fight not against Heav'n.
Let CHRIST, if glory waits him in the grave,
Descend into the dust and seek it there :
If his foul covets to make league with death,
And dwell in confort with corruption's worm,   140

9   What

What time more apt for death than this dark hour,
Image of death itſelf? And who ſo fit
As God's high-prieſt, the temple's miniſter,
To put life's intervening veil aſide,
And uſher him to glory? I meanwhile,   145
His humble harbinger, will go before
T' announce his coming, and make clear the road
That leads to death, the goal of his ambition.
Yet how if all this tame indifference
Be but a feint to draw the world about him,   150
And then amaze them with ſome grand diſplay
Of wonder-working power? And who can tell
How far his hand miraculous may ſtretch,
Who from the tomb pluck'd forth the feſt'ring corpſe
Of ſhrowded Lazarus, three days in earth,   155
And bade him live again? Stupendous act!
This we beheld and hail'd him Lord of Life;
But ſtill the unconverted Jews ſtood off,
And deem'd us witneſſes of ſlight account,
Weak cred'lous men, firſt dup'd and thence become 160
Aſſociates in impoſture. What remains
But inſtantly to put my thoughts in act,
And yield him up to thoſe, who in th' attempt
Succeeding vindicate their diſbelief,
Failing abide the ſhame of their defeat?   165

In

In this or that opinion there muſt be
A dangerous error; to perſiſt were fatal:
This night diſpells all doubt: If he be CHRIST,
He lives confeſt and triumphs over death;
If man, he falls unpitied and abjur'd.   170

    Thus for foul deeds pretending fair excuſe,
The caitiff wretch on trait'rous errand bent,
Back through the city gates purſu'd his way,
And to his nightly aſſignation hied.

    Perch'd on the ſummit of the ſacred Mount,   175
Should'ring God's temple, a proud palace ſtood:
There dwelt the ſovereign pontiff, and this night
Held ſolemn convocation and conſult,
Not for God's glory, other cares had they,
Cares nearer to their ſelfiſh hearts, concerns   180
Heav'n had no part in, impious dire cabals
How to prevent the day-ſpring from on high,
Now by CHRIST's revelation and his acts
Miraculous juſt dawning on the world,
Aforetime wrapt in darkneſs black as death,   185
Beſt veil for their hypocriſy and craft.
In their great hall of council, there in ranks,
Precedencies and dignities diſpos'd,
Doctors and long-rob'd phariſees and ſcribes
And bearded elders met; ſenate, to whom   190

For

For machinations, plots and fecret wiles
Rome's purple conclave ftoops.   High over all
On throne pontifical in robes of ftate,
With facred ephod girt of various hues,
And breaft-plate glitt'ring bright with myftic gems,   195
Mitre-crown'd CAIAPHAS, the temple's chief,
Exalted fate : The fanhedrim was full.
All came, whom luft of power, or bigot zeal,
Or enmity to CHRIST rous'd to the call ;
Mouth-worfhippers of God, agents of hell   200
In heart, and hypocrites abhorr'd of CHRIST,
To public fcorn held up and pictur'd out
As rebel hufbandmen, who bafely flew
Their Lord's commiffion'd Son.   Scarce was there one,
Whofe galled confcience had not felt the fting   205
Of fome keen truth extorted from the lips
Of the elfe-humble JESUS, meek to all
But the proud Pharifee or cavi'lling Scribe,
To knaves, who thought by cunning to outwit
Wifdom itfelf, and fnare him in his talk ;   210
To hypocrites, who fafted oft with fad
And woe-worn faces to be feen of men,
Or fuch as made long pray'rs for a difplay
Of rightcoufnefs, and vaunted their good deeds,
Mocking their confcience and infulting Heav'n :   215

M   To

To thefe in all the majefty of truth
Frowning he fpake, nor fpar'd he for rebuke
Severe, indignant; many a time and oft
To their whole fect he had denounced woe,
Woe trebled on their heads : What wonder then,   220
If thus combin'd by intereft to oppofe
His fpreading glories, their envenom'd hearts
Rankled with envy, hatred and revenge ?
Nor were there wanting to their great divan
Thofe, who can work unfeen within the heart,   225
Dark minifters, who know to touch the fprings
And cords, whofe movements can convulfe the foul
With furious paffions, burfting from their mine,
Like fulph'rous fires that tear the quaking earth :
SATAN himfelf was there, for at this hour   230
He and his hoft had furlough upon earth,
Dæmons of blood, ambition, envy, ftrife
Rang'd the vex'd world at large : Loud were their tongues,
And fiery hot their zeal againft the Lord,
Whofe miracles, refounding through the land,   235
Rung in their ears the downfall of their pow'r,
Ill-omen'd knell.—Brethren ! 'tis time to roufe,
Cried CAIAPHAS, and ftarted from his throne
Furious as Korah, when at his tent door
With his rebellious company he ftood,   240

And

And waving high his cenfer call'd aloud
To mutiny 'gainft Mofes : So now call'd
With voice as loud, and deeper plung'd in crime
Than thefe who funk outright, this fecond prieft,
This worfe revolter againft God himfelf   245
In his own Son reflected ; from his ftate,
High o'er their heads exalted, he look'd down
On all beneath ; then with uplifted eyes
And hands extended, as in act to rend
His robes pontifical—Yes, facred feers,   250
Again he cried, yes, venerable priefts,
Elders, and reverend fages of our law,
'Tis more than time to call your vengeance up ;
Awake ! ye fleep too long : For me, your flave,
Servant of fervants, me, by how much more   255
In place exalted fo much more in heart
Abas'd, as meritlefs of fuch high ftate,
I were content to caft thefe robes afide,
Pluck off this beard, and on this mitred head,
Unworthy of fuch honors, fcatter duft   260
And afhes, might fuch penitence avert
The fhame, that for my fins is falling on you,
And quell the mad'ning faction now afloat,
Since this bold Bethlemite hath ftarted up
To mock the church of God.   Shall it be faid,   265

M 2   That

That for my punifhment thefe evils light
On you the righteous? that in my day rofe
This innovator to confpire your fall,
To broach new doctrines and unhinge the faith
Of the ftill wavering multitude? If I,   270
If I am in the crime, if in your thoughts
My negligence hath fofter'd this revolt,
Make me your facrifice, thruft me from hence,
For this high place unfit; fet up your crofs,
And there exalt me: But if I am clear,   275
And this your looks encourage me to hope,
If CHRIST not CAIAPHAS deferves the death,
Why do ye paufe? What terror holds you back?
Time-honor'd rabbi, elders, fages, guides
And mafters of our Ifrael! ye, by whom   280
Our fynagogues are taught, of God's own law
Interpreters ordain'd, which of your grave
And reverend council will at once unfold
To my yet faithlefs ears the mighty fpell
By which this JESUS works? Who will expound   285
This prodigy, that fets the crowd agape,
This more than man, of whom the people bruit
Thefe more than human doings? You are dumb;
None offers a reply; for none will fay
This wifdom and thefe mighty works accord   290

With

With one fo mean of birth, with Jofeph's fon,

A bafe mechanic: Fitter tafk for him

To ufe his father craft, and humbly ply

The workman's tools, than in the temple fit

Difputing with our doctors; or withdrawn, 295

A's late the Baptift, to fome defart mount,

There fit in fullen dignity enthron'd,

And from his rocky theatre declaim

To lift'ning thoufands.   Here be fome have heard

His doctrines, many have endur'd his taunts, 300

And though in wife and well-pois'd minds like your's

Such meteors breed no terror, yet they draw

The gazing vulgar, and fo rank a taint

Runs through th' infected fold, that much I doubt

If half the flock of Ifrael be not touch'd; 305

So diligent is he to fpread the plague,

So carelefs we to ftem it.   If his word

Be fuffer'd thus to overturn our law,

The monument of ages, then alas!

We've feen the laft of thefe folemnities: 310

Before this night returns there'll not be found

Or lamb to facrifice, or prieft to flay,

Or temple to receive our Pafchal rites;

Rome, whofe ambition grafps the conquer'd world,

Shall

Shall plant her eagles on our holy mount,   315
And Jupiter ufurp JEHOVAH's fhrine.
    He paus'd, yet ftood as one in act to fpeak,
Struggling for words, which furious paffion choak'd
And ftifled on his tongue; a ftormy cloud
Hung on his brow, his vifage ghaftly pale,   320
Mad'ning with rage he ftampt and fhook his robe:
As when the Delphic prophetefs, convuls'd
And foaming on her tripod, fets aghaft
The fcar'd enthufiafts, who believe her fill'd
And fighting with the God oracular;   325
So through the hall of council filence reign'd,
Whilft expectation turn'd all eyes and ears
On their rapt prophet; till the word being giv'n,
That one of CHRIST's difciples ftood without
And inftant audience crav'd, that awful name   330
Their fpell-bound faculties at once fet free;
Inftant loud murmurs fill'd the vaulted roof,
Like the deep roar of fubterranean tides,
Whofe eddies undermine the cavern'd fhores
Of fea-girt Mona or Bermuda's ifle: 335
This paft, the fenate's chief refum'd his throne;
Whence from his ftate inclining he gave fign
For filence and commanded to admit

·X   Their

Their unexpected fuitor ; at the word
Wide flew the doors apart, and there behold   340
With cloak to' the knee tuck'd up and ſtaff in hand
IsCARIOT, caitiff viler than the worſt
That e'er wore pilgrim's fanctimonious garb
In after-times, when fierce crufading zeal
Sent forth it's wand'ring eremites to put   345
The murd'rous fword in meek Religion's hand,
The crofs, on which our patient Lord expir'd,
Their badge of victory, and fignal made
For their deſtroying armies, lur'd to war
With pardons earnt in fields of carnage, fought   350
For God's pretended glory', as if, dire hope !
Rivers of blood could waft their fouls to heav'n.
Founder of thefe, and prototype of all,
Who dy'd the crofs with blood, IsCARIOT ſtood
Full of the fiend, and caſt around on all   355
His haggard eyes, that augur'd vengeful ire
And fraud deep brooding in his treach'rous heart :
When after paufe now fummon'd to expound
His purpofe, whether by his Maſter fent,
Or felf-impell'd, thus MAMMON's convert fpake.   360
    Fathers of Iſrael, patrons of our law,
And chiefly thou, great prieſt, vicar of God,
And faithful ſhepherd of the remnant fav'd

                                        From

From Abraham's ſcatter'd flock ! I muſe not, lords,
That you are caſt in wonder to behold   365
Me ſtanding in this place, me, to your cauſe
Unfriendly deem'd, and, which to all is known
Nor on my part denied, one of the Twelve,
And follower of JESUS.   But, grave ſirs,
I do adjure you by your love to truth,   370
No longer wear this jealous eye upon me,
Than to your patient ears I ſhall unfold,
Why hither I am come, not as a thief
To ſteal into your councils, ſpy them out
And after blazon them, but in fair faith   375
And plain ſincerity with no double heart
To make confeſſion ſure, and give my life
A pledge into your hands.   Stand not amaz'd,
As if it were a thing impoſſible
That CHRIST's diſciple ſhould not be his friend.   380
Mine hath been toilſome huſbandry, my lords,
And none but bitter fruits have I reap'd from it,
Fruits of repentance : Weary days and nights
I've miniſter'd to him without reward,
And weary miles full many travel'd o'er,   385
Fainting and pinch'd with hunger; then at night,
When the wild creatures of the earth find reſt
And covert in their holes, houſeleſs have watch'd

                                        Amidſt

Amidſt the ſhock of elements, and brav'd
Storms, which the mail'd rhinoceros did not dare   390
Unſhelter'd to abide : Sometimes on ſea
Laſh'd by the ſurging waves I've toil'd for life,
Whilſt he ſate ſleeping, reckleſs of the gale :
Reſcu'd from theſe, for I of force confeſs
His pow'r is abſolute, and ſafe on ſhore,   395
My labors ceas'd not with the ſcene ; new toils,
New taſks ſucceeded : Now to rocks and caves,
To ſandy wilds, or whereſoever elſe
The Spirit led and deſolation reign'd,
His wand'ring ſteps I follow'd, yes, his ſteps,   400
But at what diſtance from his heart he held me,
Bear witneſs, mem'ry ! Others had his heart,
Peter and James and John, to them he breath'd
The ſecrets of his ſoul, on them he ſhower'd
His promiſes ; of theſe he made no thrift,   405
Theſe he abounded in ; to me he gave
What he had leaſt in ſtore, a barren purſe,
And bade me bear it ; no hard taſk I own,
For it was light as beggary could make it,
But office moſt ignoble.   Here perchance   410
Your wiſdom would demand of me a cauſe,
Why I endur'd theſe ſlights year after year,
And ſtill toil'd on in ſuch a thankleſs ſervice ;

N

What

What fafcination and what fpell, you'll afk,

Doth this man work with, fo to charm the mind   415

And lure it on through mortifying toils,

Sorrows and pains, and, worfe than thefe, contempts,

Yet hold it ftill enchain'd flave to his will?

Moft equal judges, I muft here fubmit

My weaknefs to your cenfure, and refer   420

My caufe to mercy, or in felf-defence

Conjure you for a moment to defcend

From your high ftate, and to my humble place

And peafant thoughts accord your own great minds:

My lords, I neither mean to varnifh o'er   425

My own too feeble nature, nor to fmooth

The rough fincerity of truth through fear

Or flattery of thofe, 'fore whom I fpeak:

If JESUS works by fpells, I know them not;

Pray'rs but not incantations I have heard;   430

If thefe be charms, they are no charms for devils,

Yet fuch he's charg'd withal: Neither by league

With Beelzebub, as fome have gravely urg'd,

Nor art Samaritan, nor elfe by imp

Or genius, as the heathen loudly vouch   435

Of their fam'd Socrates, do I believe

His miracles are wrought: Alas, alas!

Which of hell's minifters will be fuborn'd

4

To work his own confusion ? No, they shriek,
They tremble, at his bidding they come forth   440
From men possest, they vanish to the winds,
They sink into the pit from whence they sprung.
I am a man, my lords, not over-prone
To rash credulity, nor apt to veer
With ev'ry breath of doctrine, and I've heard   445
A voice, that sways the elements, commands
The springs of health, making maim'd nature whole,
Nay, life itself return into the trunk
Which it had left, and give a second pulse
To the cold heart of death : This to have seen,   450
And not to stand in reverence of the pow'r
That wrought these miracles, were a degree
Of apathy above my nature's reach.

   No more ! cried CAIAPHAS, no more of this !
You much abuse our patience with this talk.   455
Here is no place to sound CHRIST's praises forth ;
We are not met to recognize his pow'r
And back his daring claims, but to chastise
Imposture, to assert our sacred law,
And vindicate the majesty of Heav'n.   460
You tell us you are wearied with the tasks
Of a hard Master ; quit him then and earn
A better service, earn a rich reward

By

By yielding him to juftice. You well know
His haunts, his privacies, his darkling hours,   465
When without hazard of a public brawl
We may make lawful feizure for the ftate
Of his attainted perfon : On this point,
So you will order your difcourfe aright,
You may fpeak freely; of his praife no more.   470

    To him th' Apoftate : If from my forc'd lips,
Unwilling witneffes although they be,
Truth wrings this praife, the laft which they will utter,
Suffer thus far in candor, and let pafs
Thefe words in juftice to a Mafter's fame,   475
Whom I renounce and with an oath devote
To wrath, to punifhment, to death itfelf,
If death you doom. But oh ! moft reverend lords,
It is not as a falfe and juggling cheat,
A dealer with familiars I prefent him   480
To your juft judgment : Wretches vile as thefe
Would but difgrace your wrath and my revenge.
But take him as a victim from my hands
Richer than hecatombs of vulgar blood,
A facrifice for God's high prieft to make,   485
Whilft all earth's fcepter'd monarchs ftood around
To gaze upon the work. Be not deceiv'd :
I know the jeopardy in which I ftand,

                          Yet

Yet I will on; in me is no delay:
This night, this hour, this inftant I am your's   490
To trace him to his haunts, to be your guide
And marfhal you to vengeance.   But beware!
Let them be chofen men you fend, approv'd
And conftant, though the heav'ns fhall rain down fire,
And the earth rock beneath them: He, who call'd   495
The dead anatomy to life, can well
Make corpfes of the living.—Here the voice
Of one, who neareft to the throne had place,
Cut fhort the traitor's fpeech: Of high renown
Was he now rifing, NICODEMUS, known   500
To after-ages as the nightly gueft
Of JESUS, and his converfe with our Lord
In holy writ recorded: Grave he was,
A Pharifee and ruler of the Jews,
Yet not of foul vindictive like the reft,   505
Nor afpect arrogant; when thus he fpake.

 I call the time mifpent, that is beftow'd
On loud-tongu'd orators, whofe art it is
To launch their hearers upon paffion's tide,
And drive them on by gufts of windy words   510
A giddy defperate courfe to rocks and fhoals,
Which fteer'd by fage experience they had fhunn'd.
Such fhipwreck of our wifdom we might make,

         Should

Should we our better fenfes now permit
To take improv'ident counfel of our ears,   515
By this high-ton'd declaimer thus affail'd.
I pray you, therefore, carry back your thoughts
To times foregone, when prophets have arofe
And boafted mighty works, which, being done
Of man's device and cunning, came to nought :   520
So will it be with JESUS, if his fpirit
Be not of God ; time will o'ertake deceit,
If time be let to run ; but cut it fhort
By death's rafh ftroke, you cover him with glory,
And from his afhes raife a mightier name,   525
Than living he had reach'd with all the aids
Of artifice to back him.   Give me, Heav'n!
That tolerating policy, which fhews
No bitternefs in fpeculative points :
Difdaining from my heart what this man fays,   530
A traitor fays, who comes to fell his Mafter,
My fentence never fhall affect the life
Of this or any other man accus'd
On vague prefumptions, nor will I fay, Die!
Till I have that in proof, which merits death :   535
For if this JESUS vaunts himfelf to be
What he is not, God will confute his pride;
But if with pow'r divine he acts and fpeaks,

                                          Commiffion'd

Commiffion'd to fome awful unfeen end,

Shall man contend with God? Vain ftrife! fhall we   540

Fall off from our great origin, the faith

Of our bleft father Abraham? Shall we,

Sore fmitten for our trefpaffes, cut fhort

And wafted to a remnant, we, on whom

The guiltlefs blood of all the prophets refts,   545

Send this man up to heav'n to cry againft us,

And to a burthen heavier than enough

Add more and weightier guilt than all the reft?

Heav'n's grace forefend! You have my confcience, lords;

I leave it to your thoughts: I ftand abfolv'd.   550

    He faid, and confcious that his words were loft

Upon obdurate hearts, departed thence,

So warn'd of God, and from the gulph efcap'd

Of that night's dire perdition, wherein all

Save him alone were loft.   So in the wreck   555

Of fome great admiral, full fraught for war,

When his tall veffel fplits, and the bold crew

Plunge quick into th' abyfs, Heav'n fometimes deigns

By wond'rous providence to fnatch one life

From the devouring waves, and waft him home   560

A folitary relick, there to tell

God's mercies and his fad companions' fate.

                              Him

Him thus departing the proud pontiff ey'd
With look malign, and to thefe taunts gave vent.
    Weak is that caufe, whofe advocate flies from it: 565
I paufe to fee if any here will follow.
None moves, none fpeaks, none feconds his appeal:
'Tis well! One only convert to our foe,
One patron of his caufe this fenate held,
And holds no longer: Vanifh'd, flown, efcap'd!   570
One heart, one mind, one voice now rules the whole.
For me, I nor opinion fhift nor place,
Faithful I fhrink from neither.   You have heard
What this wife elder counfels; he hath left
His confcience as a legacy behind him: 575
Let him, who loves the giver, take the gift;
I, for fuch part as to my fhare may fall,
Scorn to engraft that fcyon on my heart,
Which, if admitted, might impart the feeds
Of treafon and apoftacy like his.   580
Till cold and hot agree, till felfifh fear
And temporifing maxims coalefce
With patriot zeal for Ifrael and firm faith
In God's reveal'd decrees, his thoughts and mine
Will never mix, and the attempt to join   585
Their jarring elements could only ferve

                             To

To make this breaſt a field of mental war.
Mark, brethren, mark how this man contravenes
Your antient juſt retaliating law.
Moſes ſaid—Eye for eye, and tooth for tooth!   590
So is revenge a virtue : By this rule
JESUS muſt die; for who puts out the law,
Puts out the light of Iſrael, ſtabs the life,
And life for life is juſtice upon record.
This ordinance our abſent elder ſpurns;   595
He holds at nought our antient equity,
And ſets new doctrines forth ; tells us forſooth,
That we muſt wait the time, wait till the light
Of Iſrael be extinct, and leave redreſs
For thoſe, who without eyes can ſpy it out :   600
Such councils would make cowards of us all,
Rebels to God, deſerters from the faith,
Traitors to Iſrael.   Can I wear theſe robes,
And wear a heart within ſo vile, ſo baſe ?
Tear them away, uncover me to ſhame,   605
Make me the ſcorn of men, if, thus array'd
And trickt in outſide honors, I am found
Falſe to that King, whoſe ſtandard I ſupport.
No, venerable ſages, if your rule
Were ſhort to teach us what our duty is,   610
The very heathen would inform us of it :

O   The

The Roman foldier, who deferts his poft,
Or fleeping fuffers a furprize, fhall die;
But we, with God's own armies in our charge,
We, whofe commander is the Lord of Hofts,   615
Should we be found thus criminal, what death,
What doom, more terrible than death itfelf,
Can recompenfe fuch treafon? Forth then, lords!
Draw out an armed band and fend them forth.
Behold a ready leader! Time yet ferves;   620
This night no ftir, no ftragglers in our ftreets
To fhake the city's peace: JESUS fecur'd
And hither brought, a largefs I decree
To all concern'd; to JUDAS a reward
Befitting us to give, him to receive.   625

    No more; loud acclamations fhook the hall:
'Th' affembly rofe, the traitor bow'd affent,
A band of ruffians arm'd with fwords and ftaves
Forth iffued with ISCARIOT at their head,
And to the Olive Mountain bent their courfe.   630

    Oh, hour accurft! Oh, all ye ftars of heav'n!
And thou pale waining moon, etherial lights,
Firft-born of Nature, look not, ye chafte fires,
Upon this monfter-breeding earth, but quench
Your confcious lamps and whelm this murd'rous crew   635
In darknefs black as their own damning plot.

                        And

And thou, conductor of this Stygian band,
Vile hypocrite, what fiend infpir'd the thought
To hail thy Mafter with the kifs of peace,
And fo betray him ? Wretch, the time will come, 640
When rack'd with horror, and to all hope loft,
Thine agonizing foul fhall rue this deed,
Curfe its birth-hour, and whilft thy Mafter foars
To heav'n, triumphant over death and fin,
Thou fhalt fink howling to the depths of hell. 645

Now break your fynod up, ye envious priefts,
Elders and fcribes ! prepare your harden'd hearts
To judge the Lord of Life, convene your fpies
To forge falfe witnefs, and make fmooth the way
To man's redemption by the blood of CHRIST, 650
The very Pafchal Lamb, whom by the type
Of this night's facrifice ye fhadow'd forth,
Blind unbelieving prophets as ye are.
Fit hour ye chofe, ye murd'rers, to embrue
Your curfed hands in that pure Victim's blood, 655
Peace-offering for the fins of loft mankind.
Hence to your homes ! there meditate new plots ;
The fiends fhall be your helpers, to your thoughts
Prefent, though not to fight, they fwarm around,
Now here, now there, now hovering over head, 660
Where, as your enmity to CHRIST breaks forth,

O 2

And

And your blafpheming voices fill the roof,
Like fteaming vapors from fulphureous lakes,
Joyous they catch the welcome founds, and fan
With clapping wings the peftilential air,   665
Applauding as they foar.   Now clear the hall ;
Yield up your feats, ye fubftituted fiends ;
Hence, minor dæmons ! give your mafters place !
    And hark ! the King of Terrors fpeaks the word,
He calls his fhadowy princes, they ftart forth,   670
Expand themfelves to fight and throng the hall,
A fynod of infernals : Forms more dire
Imagination fhapes not, when the wretch,
Whom confcience haunts, in the dead hour of night,
Whilft all is dark and filent round his bed,   675
Sees hideous phantoms in his fev'rifh dream,
That ftare him into madnefs with fix'd eyes
And threat'ning faces floating in his brain.
The ghoftly monarch mounts the vacant throne ;
Gives fign for order, the fuperiors fit,   680
Each as his ftellar attribute gives rank
And place peculiar, the untitled ftand
Circling their LUCIFER, their fallen fun :
He of his ftate more jealous, as in heart
Confcious of faded glory, in the midft   685
Now rifing, after many a hard effay

                                                    To

To wreathe his war-worn face into a fmile,
Semblance at leaft of joy, at length with voice
Screw'd to the pitch of triumph vaunting cries.

     Pow'rs and Dominions, Lords by victory's right   690
Of earth and man, now from his Maker won
By overthrow of Heav'n's laft champion giv'n
In God's own city, battle fairly gain'd
On hoftile ground, his Sion's facred mount,
Warriors, your king applauds you: Thanks, brave friends;
Now fhall your temples with loud pæans ring,   696
Your vindicated altars and your groves
Exhale rich clouds of incenfe, fteaming forth
From od'rous gums; your ftatues gaily crown'd
With garlands, every trophy, that the art   700
Of painting or of fculpture can beftow;
Shall be hung round to decorate your fhrines;
Your oracles henceforth fhall find a voice,
Which future CHRISTS fhall never put to filence,
And nations from your lips fhall afk their fate: 705
This day to all pofterity fhall be
Sacred to games, proceffions, triumphs, feafts,
And laurel-crowned bards fhall hymn your praife.
But fure no fpirit of etherial mould,
For fuch of right ye are, will fo forget   710
His native dignity as to repine,

                                 Or

Or gloat with envy, if I now demand
Your tribute of efpecial praife to him,
Whom your joint fuffrages deputed firft
To this important embaffy; a fpirit　　　　　715
Our fubterranean empire cannot mate
For high authority and potent fway
O'er man's fubjected heart : MAMMON, ftand forth !
Stand forth, thou profp'rous, rich, perfuafive pow'r,
·Worfhipp'd of all, great idol of the world ;　　　720
May fortune on thy patient labors fmile,
Thou perfevering deity ! Purfue
Thy darling metal through earth's central veins,
Ranfack her womb for mines, fend forth thy flaves
To undifcover'd realms and bid them fap　　　725.
Potofi's glittering mountains for their ore ;
Pull down her golden temples, ftrip her kings,
Rack them with tortures, wring their fecrets out
By flow-confuming fires, lay Nature wafte,
Let nothing mortal breathe upon the foil　　　730
That covers gold : All hell applauds thy zeal,
And all hell's engines fhall affift thy fearch.

　　He faid, and lo ! from either fide the throne
Upon the fignal a feraphic choir
In equal bands came forth ; the minftrels ftrike　　　735
Their golden harps ; fwift o'er the founding ftrings

　　5　　　　　　　　　　　　　　　　　　Their

Their flying fingers fweep, whilft to the ftrain
Melodious voices, though to heav'nly airs
Attun'd no longer, ftill in fweet accord
Echo the feftive fong, now full combin'd   740
Pouring the choral torrent on the ear,
In parts refponfive now warbling by turns
Their fprightly quick divifions, fwelling now
Through all the compafs of their tuneful throats
Their varying cadences, as fancy prompts.   745
Whereat the Stygian herd, like them of old
Lull'd by the Theban minftrel, ftood at gaze
Mute and appeas'd, for mufic hath a voice,
Which ev'n the devils obey, and for a while
Sweet founds fhall lay their turbid hearts afleep,   750
Charm'd into fweet oblivion and repofe.
The praife of MAMMON the rapt feraphs fung
And Gold's almighty pow'r; free flow'd the verfe;
No need to call the Mufe, for all were there,
Apollo and the Heliconian Maids,   755
And all that pagan poet e'er invok'd
Were prefent to the fong.   Above the flight
Of bold Alcæus, Tifias bard divine,
Or Pindar's ftrain Olympic, high it foar'd
In dithyrambic majefty fublime.   760
At the right hand of hell's terrific Lord

MAMMON

MAMMON exalted fate, and as the choir
Chanted their hymn, his fwelling bofom throbb'd
In concert with the ftrain; pride flufh'd his cheek
Furrow'd with care and toil, his eyes, now rais'd   765
From earth, their proper center, fparkling gleam'd
Malicious triumph, whilft ovations loud
And thund'ring plaudits fhook the trembling roof.

The fong was clos'd, and, order now refum'd,
MAMMON ftood forth to fpeak; when ere the words   770
From his flow lips found way, the infernal King,
With eager action ftarting from his throne,
Gave figri for filence and thus interpos'd.

Paufe, worthy fpi'rit, awhile! my mind forebodes
Cares more immediate, for amid the throng   775
I fpy our faithful CHEMOS; well I know
'Tis not on flight occafion he hath left
The poft affign'd him; and behold! his looks
Augur important tidings. Fall back, friends,
And give our gallant centinel accefs.   780

Obedient to the word the opening files
Fell back and let him pafs; he to the throne
Low rev'rence made, and thus his chief addrefs'd.

Imperial Lord of this feraphic hoft,
As I kept ftation on the faithlefs Mount,   785
Where once my altar blaz'd, revolted now

From

From it's allegiance and with olive crown'd
In token of God's peace, I thence defcried
By glimpfe of the pale moon a vagrant train,
With JESUS at their head, fording the brook,   790
As thither bound: I couch'd upon the watch,
So bidd'n, and to their talk gave heedful ear.
A melancholy theme the Mafter chofe:
Sadly he warns them of his own death's hour
Now near impending, and how all fhall fly,   795
Like fcatter'd fheep, and their lone Shepherd leave
Forlorn, abandon'd: This the fiery zeal
Of PETER, to our chief well known, difclaims,
Who boldly vouches, though all elfe fhould fwerve,
His own unfhaken conftancy; when CHRIST,   800
Severe though not with railing, him reproves,
And folemnly dénounces triple breach
Of this vain boaft, and inftant, for this night,
Or e'er the cock's fhrill trumpet twice fhall found,
So CHRIST predicts, he fhall be thrice denied   805
Of this felf-vaunting man: All this I heard,
And held it for my duty to report;
What more enfu'd imperfectly I learn;
For now the Mafter taketh three apart,
And much difturb'd in foul and fore amaz'd   810
Wills them ftand off and watch, whilft he retires

        P   And

And vents his grief in pray'r: I faw him fall
Proftrate to earth, and vent fuch heart-felt groans,
That were I other than I am, lefs wrong'd,
Lefs hoftile to the tyranny of Heaven,   815
Whence I am exil'd, I had then let fall
Weak pity's tear and been my nature's fool.
But, lords, I cannot fo forget your caufe,
Or my own wrongs, nor would I wear a heart
Made of fuch melting ftuff. With noifelefs tread   820
The kneeling Supplicant I approach'd, and mark'd
His agony of foul, whilft from his brow
I faw large drops and gouttes of bloody fweat
Incarnardine the duft, on which they fell.
Bear witnefs, my revenge, 'twas there, ev'n there,   825
The very fpot, on which he knelt and pray'd,
Where now his blood, wrung out by agony
As in atonement, dropt, on which my fhrine,
Rear'd by the wives of the uxorious king,
Deck'd out with blazing tapers proudly fhone,   830
And front to front of God's own temple ftood,
Till Afa's parricidal hand pluck'd up
Maacha's groves and burnt my fhrine to duft.
Now hear the fequel : As I ftood at gaze,
Noting his pray'r, one of the heav'nly band   835
And of the higheft, GABRIEL, with his fpear

8   Couch'd

Couch'd as for combat, ftarted forth to view,
And frowning bade me take my flight with fpeed,
Nor trouble that juft perfon : Valiant peers!
I am not one to back at his proud bidding,   840
Nor ever did I turn my face to flight
Save in our army's univerfal rout,
When all from heav'n fell headlong to the gulph :
Such weapon as I had, this trenchant fword
Of adamantine proof, forthwith I drew ;   845
But ere my arm could wield it, fwift as thought
I felt his fpear's fharp point with forceful thruft
Deep plung'd into my fide : Staggering, amaz'd,
I gave back fo compell'd ; he ftill advanc'd
Arm'd for a fecond onfet, when my ftrength   850
Foil'd, though immortal, and my fight grown dim,
My wound the whilft fore rankling, I took wing
And hither came on painful pinions borne,
Your faithful fervant, whether to attempt
Frefh battle, or my prefent lofs repair.   855

    This faid, he put his azure tunic by,
And bar'd his wounded fide, where GABRIEL's fpear
Had lodg'd it's maffy fluke, a ghaftly chafm
Trench'd by the force of arch-angelic arm,
And to aught elfe than deathlefs fpirit death.   860

Fir'd

Fir'd at the fight with eyes that fparkling blaz'd
SATAN uprofe, and thus infuriate fpake.

    GABRIEL in arms ! Hah ! warriors, we are brav'd :
CHRIST hath his guard about him and defies us.
If this immortal fpirit could not ftand,   865
What fhall ISCARIOT do ? Myfelf will forth ;
We fhall then fee who wields the ftronger lance,
SATAN or GABRIEL : In the fields of heaven,
In the mid-air, on earth, in deepeft hell
He knows my might fuperior, and fhall rue   870
His daftardly affault.   Why not with me,
The fender rather than the fent, this ftrife ?
So might he boaft the conteft, though fubdued.
The fcars by this fharp fword in battle dealt
Are the beft honors GABRIEL hath to vaunt ;   875
The brighteft laurels on his brow are thofe
I planted when in equal fight I deign'd
To meafure fpears with fuch inferior foe.
Doth GABRIEL think God's favour can reverfe
Immutable pre-eminence, and raife   880
His menial fphere to that, in which I fhone
Son of the morning ? Doth he vainly hope
Exil'd from heav'n we left our courage there,
Or loft it in our fall, or that hell's fires

                                Have

Have parch'd and wither'd our fhrunk finews up?   885
Delufive hope ! the warrior's nerve is ftrung
By exercife, by pain, by glorious toil :
The torrid clime of hell, it's burning rock,
It's gulph of liquid flames, in which we roll'd,
Have calcin'd our ftrong hearts, breath'd their own fires 890
Into our veins, and forg'd thofe nerves to fteel,
Which heav'n's calm æther, her voluptuous fkies
And frequent adorations well nigh fmooth'd
To the foft flexibility of flaves,
Till bold rebellion fhook it's fetters off,   895
And with their clangor rais'd fo brave a ftorm,
That God's eternal throne rock'd to it's bafe.
Now break we up this council : Each difperfe
Or to his poft, his pleafure or purfuit ;
Sufficeth for this tafk my fingle arm :   900
CHEMOS fhall be reveng'd ; the public zeal
Of MAMMON ftill fhall be our theme of praife ;
Nor fhall ISCARIOT's nightly plot be foil'd
By intervening angels, nor thefe priefts,
Whofe feats we fill and whofe allies we are,   905
Fail of their victim, or find us remifs
To fecond them in this our common league
And joint emprize againft the pow'rs of Heav'n.

'Twas

'Twas faid, the princes of th' affembly rofe
In reverence to his will; the legion round   910
Smote on their fhields the fignal of affent.
Tow'ring he ftood, the Majefty of Hell,
Dark o'er his brows thick clouds of vengeance roll'd,
Thunder was in his voice, his eye fhot fire,
And loud he call'd for buckler and for fpear;   915
Thefe bold AZAZEL bore, enormous weight,
For Atlantean fpirit proper charge:
With eager grafp he feiz'd the towering maft,
And fhook it like a twig; then with a frown,
That aw'd the ftouteft heart, gave fign for all   920
Strait to difperfe, and vanifh'd from their fight.

END OF THE THIRD BOOK.

C A L V A R Y;

O R

THE DEATH OF CHRIST.

B O O K IV.

THE ARGUMENT OF THE FOURTH BOOK.

A general review of Chrift's agony in the garden: His difciples, who are ordered to watch, fall afleep ; Chrift prays apart ; he wakens them, and warns them to watch left they enter into temptation. Satan arrives, and takes poft near the fpot where Chrift is praying in his agony: He is difcovered by Gabriel, the fupporting angel; their interview defcribed: Chrift approaches, and reproving Satan, by the word of power cafts him to the ground difabled and in torments. Judas now advances with an armed company; betrays his Mafter with a kifs ; Chrift is feized and carried away to the palace of the high prieft. Satan, unable to rife, laments over his difconfolate condition : He is difcovered by Mammon, who confoles him and affifts in raifing him from the ground: Satan teftifies to the power and divinity of Chrift, feels a prefentiment of his impending doom, and having delivered his laft injunctions to Mammon, is lifted from the earth by a ftormy guft and carried through the air out of fight of that evil fpirit, who terrified by the fate of his chief turns to flight and efcapes.

BOOK IV.

THE AGONY IN THE GARDEN.

O MOUNT of Agony! water'd with tears
    From my Redeemer's eyes, and by his knees,
Preffing thy turf, made facred as the ground,
Where ev'n the Chofen Shepherd might not ftand
But with unfandal'd feet, Ah! where is now   5.
That purifying Angel me to cleanfe
From this vile world, that fo I may approach,
Though but in thought, with a right fpi'rit renew'd,
Thy hallow'd folitude? Lo! where the Lord
Sorrowing retires apart: Where are the Three   10
Station'd to guard his facred privacy?
Stand they aloof, as their forefathers ftood,
When from the midft of darknefs, cloud and fire,
JEHOVAH thunder'd out of Sinai's mount?
Ah, no! within that olive grove they lie   15

Q   Stretch'd

Stretch'd on the ground, a drowfy flumb'ring guard.
And could ye not, ye fleepers, watch one hour
For fuch a Mafter? Oh! what heart could tafte
Of reft or peace, whilft his was rack'd with pain?
Was it the fighs his fuffering virtue breath'd   20
Into the air of fad Gethfemane,
That fo entranc'd your fenfes? Or was he,
The ftrength'ning Angel, fent from Heav'n to fhield
The Savior's anguifh from all human eyes,
And veil the myftery of that awful hour?   25
Then was that angry cup, full mix'd and red
From God's right hand, prefented to his lips:
The bitter effence of origi'nal fin,
With every life-deftroying extract, drawn
From man's corruption fince, were there infus'd,   30
Compounded and refolved into that draught,
Mix'd by the hand of Death and drugg'd in hell.
The coward, fhrinking under fortune's blows,
With defperate lip hath oft-times drank and died;
'Tis refuge, 'tis defertion from a poft   35
He dare defend no longer, 'tis the hope,
Falfe fruitlefs hope, of a perpetual fleep,
When he hath bottom'd that Lethæan cup:
But our Redeemer's potion was not fuch;
Horrors and heart-diffolving woes and pangs,   40

8   That

That mock imagination's scope, and stretch
The heart's strong cordage, till it bursts asunder
And leaves the mind a wreck, these were the drugs,
That brew'd that cup of agony, which God
Now tender'd as the wrath-atoning draught   45
For a revolted world ! Mysterious act !
The Father sacrifice the Son belov'd !
The just to spare the unjust lay the rod
Upon the guiltless head ! Shall all offend,
And One atone for all ? One Victim bear   50
The accumulated load of punishment,
The mass of vengeance, that amazing whole,
Which each particu'lar sin had pil'd in store,
And that devoted sacrifice a Lamb
Pure, without spot or blemish ? O my soul !   55
Beware, nor to that tabernacle press,
Where clouds and darkness canopy thy God.
    Lo ! where the Savior kneels ; he looks around
For some to succour, to support, some friend,
Whose sympathising eye might beam upon him,   60
And with a moment's glance of pity chear
His desolated spirit. All around
Is vacant horror, solitary, dark ;
The partners of his heart, the chosen few,
The friends, who should have watch'd, are wrapt in sleep, 65

Infenfible, fupine, oblivious fleep ;
Woes multiplied by woe, and that the worft,
Ingratitude, the fharpeft fang that gnaws
Man's bleeding bofom. In this fad extreme,
His foul revolting from the noifome draught, 70
With eyes to Heav'n uplifted, and a figh,
Which fhew'd that human weaknefs then o'erpower'd
His foul's diviner part—Abba ! he cries,
Father, all things are poffible to Thee,
Remove this cup !—Then bows his patient head 75
And qualifies the pray'r—Yet not my will,
But Thine be done !—No voice from Heav'n replies :
All Nature fleeps in filence ftill as death,
As if the planets in their fpheres had paus'd
To watch the trembling balance, on whofe point 80
The fortunes of this globe fufpended hung,
It's ruin or redemption, death or life.

'Twas then the ftrength'ning Angel dealt the blow,
That put the hovering fpy of hell to flight,
Seen of our Lord in ambufh where he lay. 85
And now the Mourner rifes from the earth,
On which he knelt, and a few paces moves
Penfive and flow to find his ftation'd friends :
He finds them not as friends upon the watch,
Not as God's faithful foldiers fhould be found, 90

But

But at their length ſtretch'd out in lazy ſleep
With folded arms ſupine. Rous'd by his voice
They ſtare, they ſtart confounded and amaz'd.
Could ye not watch one hour? the Sufferer cries:
Watch, for the foe of man is near at hand;   95
Pray, leſt ye fall into the Tempter's ſnare: ..
The ſpi'rit is ready, but the fleſh is weak.
 So warn'd, he leaves them with this mild rebuke:
A ſecond time he ſeeks the diſmal dell,
Again he prays remiſſion of his woe,   100
And deprecates the agonizing cup:
Meanwhile his drowſy centinels perceive
A languor, which their ſenſes muſt obey,
And down they ſink, their leaden eye-balls clos'd
As in a death-like trance. Again he comes, 105
Again he calls, a ſecond warning gives,
And ſo departs.——Now SATAN on the wing
Swift as a fiery meteor rides the air,
With ſhield and ſpear arm'd at all points for war:
Then down at once with huge Titanian bulk, 110
Plumb down he lights upon the ſolid ſoil,
Hard by th' angelic poſt: Earth felt the ſhock,
And trembling to her center inly groan'd.
Nor did his haughty courage deign to crouch,

           Or

Or lurk with lion watch, but firm of foot   115
Erect and confident in arms he ſtood,
As one, whoſe prowefs all advantage ſcorn'd
And mean ſurprize of an unguarded foe:
Such arts to weaker ſpirits he reſign'd;
He of his former ſelf felt no decay,   120
Or feeling ſcorn'd confeſſion, for his pride
Still deem'd that heav'n, though loft, contain'd no peer
To mate with him in hardihood and proof,
Save only the Almighty; to ſuch heighth
Of arrogance had pow'r long time uſurp'd   125
Over the Gentile nations, and the ſight
Of God's own Son, now, as he falſely deem'd,
Vanquiſh'd and proſtrate, ſwell'd his impious heart.
    Our bleſſed Lord meanwhile having preferr'd
For the laft time his interceding prayer,   130
Summon'd his ſtrength, and conſcious that the hour
Was come, which finiſh'd or revok'd the taſk
Of man's redemption from the powers of hell,
Whoſe repreſentative hard by at hand
Stood eager to arreft the forfeit prize,   135
Put forth his hand, and as he took the cup,
SATAN, who ſtood ſpectator of the deed,
Started aghaft; cold tremor ſhook his joints,

                                                             His

His threat'ning fpear now droop'd, and his broad fhield,
So proudly borne aloft, weigh'd down his arm   140
Slack and unnerv'd; confufion feiz'd his heart,
And his high courage quail'd. This GABRIEL faw,
Yet left he not his poft till CHRIST had drain'd
The cup myfterious; to its loweft dregs
He drank it; now convulfion fhook the fiend,   145
Death fhriek'd amain and through his hollow ribs
Drove his own ebon dart with defp'rate rage.
Bitter the draught and hateful to the tafte,
But Immortality had crown'd the cup,
And Light and Life on phœnix wings fprung forth   150
From the foul dregs in new-born glories bright.

GABRIEL, who knew that by this folemn act
Thus happily perform'd his charge expir'd,
Now turn'd away in fearch of that fierce fpi'rit,
Whom thro' the darkling covert he had feen,   155
Whilft by the fide of God's afflicted Son
Minift'ring he ftood: Right well he knew the form
And towering port of hell's terrific King;
Nor had the dire confufion and difmay
Of that fell dæmon fcap'd th' angelic glance.   160
Him now within a gloomy dell retir'd
To further diftance, wrapt as it fhould feem
In penfive thought, the Guardian Seraph fpied.

In

In the fame moment SATAN's ghaftly eye
Glanc'd on his foe : bright in cærulean arms   165
Heav'n's champion fhone, high o'er his crefted helm
The arch-angelic plume triformed wav'd,
Enfign of throned ftate and high command.
The grifly monarch gnafh'd his teeth with fpite
To find himfelf encounter'd at fuch odds ;   170
His foe frefh blooming in immortal youth,
Vigorous, in heav'nly-temper'd armor brac'd ;
Himfelf at this ill hour furpriz'd, his ftrength
As by enchantment blafted, and that voice,
Which in the ears of all hell's princes vouch'd   175
Such bold atchievements, fhrunk from it's high pitch
To feeble murmurs and weak whining fighs.
     So when on Zama's plain the rival chiefs,
Rome's conful and the Punic captain, met
To parley in mid-way 'twixt either camp,   180
The war-worn veteran, blighted and defac'd
By wint'ry marches over noifome fens
And fnows on mountains pil'd, with envious eye,
Sole relick of his toil, furvey'd the form
And blooming features of his youthful foe ;   185
Then to his mind recalling glories paft,
When his proud menace aw'd immortal Rome,
Sigh'd to reflect how far in the decline

     §   From

From that bright morn his evening fun had funk;
Then ey'd the youth again, and in his face,   190
Shadow'd by fate, faw Carthage doom'd to fall,
And his own glories to a foe transferr'd
Lefs than his equal once, his conqu'ror now.
   But 'twas not long that SATAN fo endur'd,
For now the confcious fenfe of former deeds   195
Bold, though unbleft, and high innate difdain
Of mean capitulation and demur
Rous'd his proud heart, like a hot courfer fpurr'd,
To chafe and lafh his languid courage up:
Red'ning he fwell'd, and gnaw'd his nether lip   200
For vengeance that it would not give him words
To hurl defiance on th' advancing foe:
When GABRIEL, noting his diforder'd mien
And haggard afpect, ftrait befpoke the fiend.
   Thus ever may the foe of CHRIST be found   205
Speechlefs, abafh'd, ftruck down of Heav'n and quell'd!
How long, malicious Spi'rit, wilt thou perfift
To trouble this vex'd earth? How long to haunt
This righteous perfon, whofe ftrong virtue mocks
Thy faint attempts? Warn'd by this fhame, avaunt!   210
Hence, baffled Tempter! roaming thus at large,
Thou doft but fhew by melancholy proof,
That a tormented confcience never refts.

R

As

As the fierce panther, through the ribs transfix'd,
Writhes round the bloody weapon in his fide,   215
And tugs it to and·fro with foamy teeth,
Mad'ning with pain and gnafhing at his wound;
So 'gainft himfelf and foe alike enrag'd,
Hell's gloomy Lord, by this deferved taunt
Cut to the heart, with many a hard effay   220
Struggled for voice; at length collecting breath,
Thefe words difdainful, though of their full tone
And energy abated, found their way.

GABRIEL, the brave in danger earn renown;
True valor fpares the weak, but thou, more wife   225
Than valiant, ftudieft well the fafer hour,
When to come forth and wage inglorious war
'Gainft unprovided foes; if CHEMOS then,
Or fome flight Cherub, crofs thy wary path,
Woe to the ftraggler! if thy barbed fpear   230
Can make fafe tilt at his unweapon'd fide.
But I, who day and night have pac'd this globe,
Found in all quarters, I, who never fhun'd,
Rather have fought, thy walk, am left to roam
Free and of thee unqueftion'd from the hour,   235
When on the confines of this new-made world
We parlied under Eden's fhady fence,
To th' inftant now, when faint and ill at eafe,

4   ·   Unwarlike

Unwarlike Angel, thou haſt found me here
Nervelefs, and little more than match for thee. 240
    To whom th' indignant Virtue thus reply'd :
If SATAN here is found in evil plight,
He's found of me unfought. Thine own dark wiles,
Degen'rate Spi'rit, and Heav'n's all-ruling hand
Have caſt thee in my way. Muſt I turn off 245
From duty's road direct becaufe forfooth
A wounded adder hiffes in my path ?
Why didſt thou prefs into this place of prayer,
This hallow'd folitude, where CHRIST hath breath'd
A charm, that withers up thy blaſted ſtrength ? 250
Could'ſt thou not learn, by late experience taught,
There is a fphere about the Son of God,
In which no fpi'rit like thee accurſt can draw
His breath blafpheming ? At a word begone !
Though with my foot I could have fpurn'd thee hence, 255
I tread not on the fall'n ; nor do I vaunt
Conqueſt of thee ; that to a mightier arm,
Rebel to God, to God's own Son thou ow'ſt,
To CHRIST, not GABRIEL : Nor ſhalt thou alone
Stoop to his name, but every idol God, 260
And ev'ry pow'r of darknefs with their prince,
And Sin hell-born, and thy foul offspring Death.

        Whereto

Whereto, by thefe prophetic words appall'd,
Satan with taunting argument replied.

Since this angelic form, from death exempt,   265
Sometimes fhall yield to aches and tranfient pains
And natural ailments for awhile endur'd,
What wonder, if etherial fpi'rit like me,
Pent in this atmofphere and fain to breathe
The lazy fogs of this unwholefome earth,   270
Pine for his native clime? What, if he droop,
Worn out with care and toil? Wert thou as I
Driv'n to and fro, and by God's thunder hurl'd
From Heav'n's high ramparts, would that filken form
Abide the toffing on hell's fiery lake?   275
Hadft thou like me travers'd the vaft profound
Of antient Night, and beat the weary wing
Through ftormy Chaos, voyage rude as this.
Wou'd ruffle thofe fine plumes.   I've kept my courfe
Through hurricanes, the leaft of which let loofe   280
On this firm globe would winnow it to duft,
Snap like a weaver's thread the mighty chain,
That links it to heav'n's adamantine floor,
And whirl it through the Infinite of Space.
And what haft thou, foft Cherub, done the whilft?   285
What are thy labors? What haft thou atchiev'd?

                                              Heav'n

Heav'n knows no winter, there no tempefts howl;
To breathe perpetual fpring, to fleep fupine
On flowery beds of amaranth and rofe,
Voluptuous flavery, was GABRIEL's choice :   290
His bofom never drew th' indignant figh,
That rent my heart, when call'd to morning hymn
I paid compulfive homage at God's throne,
Warbling feign'd hallelujahs to his praife.
Spirits of abject mould, and fuch art thou,   295
May call this eafy fervice, for they love
Ignoble eafe ; to me the fulfome tafk
Was bittereft flavery, and though I fell,
I fell oppofing ; exil'd both from heav'n
Freedom and I fhar'd the fame glorious fall.   300
Go back then to thy drudgery of praife,
Practife new canticles and tune thy throat
To flattery's fawning pitch ; leave me my groans,
Leave me to teach thefe echoes how to curfe ;
Here let me lie and make this rugged ftone   305
My couch, my canopy this ftormy cloud,
That rolls ftern winter o'er my fencelefs head ;
'Tis freedom's privilege, nor tribute owes,
Nor tribute pays to Heav'n's defpotic King.

 Thus whilft he fpake, the Savior of mankind,   310
New ris'n from pray'r, drew nigh ; whereat the fiend,

Or

Or e'er the awful prefence met his eye,
Shivering, as one by fudden fever feiz'd,
Turn'd deadly pale ; then fell to earth convuls'd.
Dire were the yells he vented, fierce the throes   315
That writh'd his tortur'd frame, whilft through the feams
And chinks, that in his jointed armour gap'd,
Blue fulph'rous flames in livid flafhes burft,
So hot the hell within his fuel'd heart,
Which like a furnace fev'n times heated rag'd.   320
Meanwhile the winged Meffenger of Heaven,
GABRIEL, with horror and amazement fix'd,
Stood motionlefs behind his orbed fhield :
Not fo the Savior ; he with look compos'd
And ftedfaft noting the difaftrous plight   325
Of that tormented fiend, thefe words addrefs'd.

    SATAN, thou fee'ft the ferpent's primal curfe
At length falls heavy on thy bruifed head ;
When man loft Paradife, by thee betray'd,
This was thy doom, Deceiver; and although   330
Ages have roll'd on ages fince, yet God,
Who from eternal to eternal lives
Bleffed for evermore, computes not time
As thou, whofe mis'ry makes fhort years feem long.
Yet was the interim thine, and thou, who firft   335
Brought'ft fin into the world, haft reign'd in fin :

                           Thou

BOOK THE FOURTH.

Thou hadft the power of death, but I through death
Am deftin'd to deftroy that power and thee.
And now my hour is come, I go to death,
That all through me may live; therefore begone! 340
Get thee behind me! Thou haft now no part
On earth, thy dwelling is prepar'd in hell:
There when we meet, expect to meet thy doom.

    This faid, the fiend replied not but with groans,
Nor ftaid the Angel longer than to turn 345
One laft fad look upon his proftrate foe,
Then flew to heav'n. The Savior bent his fteps
In fearch of his difciples; them he found
Wrapt as before in fleep.—Sleep on, he cried,
And henceforth take your reft: It is enough: 350
The hour is come. Behold! the Son of man
Into the hands of finners is betray'd:
Rife, let us go! The traitor is at hand.

    And lo! while yet he fpake a mingled crew
Arm'd and unarm'd approach; before them all 355
JUDAS advancing thus befpeaks the throng:
Whom I fhall kifs is He, the CHRIST; Him feize
And in fafe keeping hold.—Upon the word
He gives the trait'rous greeting, and exclaims,
Hail, Mafter!—When at once the fwarming crowd 360
Rufh in a fpace, then ftand in circle round,

                           Like

Like blood-hounds held at bay; their eager eyes
Fix'd on his face, which to behold they rear
Their flaming torches, whilft the profpect round
Glares with the ruddy blaze; a ghaftly troop,   365
Like that dread chorus, which the tragic bard
Pour'd on the fcene, when the Athenian wives
Dropt their abortive burthens with affright,
To fee their fnaky locks and fiery brands
Kindled in Phlegethon's fulphureous waves: 370
So glares that haggard crew; in front they fee
JESUS in confcious majefty unmov'd,
Behind him to fome little fpace withdrawn
PETER and JAMES and JOHN, the chofen Three,
Small band, but in their Leader's power a hoft   375
Invincible, 'gainft whom whole armies leagu'd
Were but as chaff before the whirlwind's blaft,
Had he fo will'd; but now with accent firm,
Whom feek ye? he demands: They anfwer make,
JESUS of Nazareth.—I am the man,   380
JESUS replies; He, whom ye feek, is found.
His air, his utterance and that voice divine,
Which could have arm'd Heav'n's legions in his caufe,
Or gulph'd them to the center at a word,
Swift as the vollied thunder fmote their hearts,   385
And hurl'd them to the ground: Headlong they fell

With

With hideous crafh, nor ever thence had ris'n,
Had not his gracious purpofe fo decreed
For man's redemption : Up they rife from earth,
And in like manner to the fame demand   390
A fecond time make anfwer ; he repeats—
I told you, and ye heard, that I am He :
If therefore me ye feek, let thefe depart.
Then burft the chidden zeal of PETER forth,
Arm'd with a fword he rufh'd upon the throng   395
And at the foremoft aim'd a random blow,
That gafh'd the caitiff's head, but mifs'd the life.

    Put up thy fword, rafh man ! the Savior cries,
Did I want refcue, would I afk of thee,
With all my Father's Angels at command ?   400
No ! let me do His will and drink His cup :
And you, that here encompafs me about,
As 'twere a felon ye came out to take,
With fwords and ftaves, fuffer thus far, behold !
The wound his weapon makes my touch fhall heal : 405
'Tis done ! Know all, that they, who take the fword,
Shall perifh by the fword. What needs this ftir,
This midnight plotting and this traitor's kifs,
Thefe ftaves, thefe torches and this arm'd array
To make one harmlefs peaceful man your prize ?   410
You faw me daily in my public walks,

                   S   Freely

Freely we commun'd, for you harm'd me not;
You heard me in the Temple; for I taught
In very zeal the fimple way of truth,
Lab'ring full hard to turn your hearts to God: 415
If this were my offence, why not arreft
Your Preacher in the act, and drag to death.
Him, who would fain have train'd you in the road
To life eternal? Never on the poor
Turn'd I my back; I courted not the rich;   420
Were this my fault, in the broad face of day
Ye might have fmitten me and earn'd the praife
Of the proud Pharifee and braggart Scribe:
I fed the hungry and I heal'd your fick,
I fuccour'd the tormented and poffeft;   425
Are thefe the heinous acts for which I die?
In field, in city, in frequented ways
The wretched flock'd around, if thefe be crimes,
Why is their punifhment fo long referv'd
To this dark hour of night? The fun himfelf   430
Witnefs'd my doings, fo might he my death.
But fee! my followers are difpers'd and fled,
And I ftand in your peril here alone:
No need to fear him, who makes no defence;
Conduct me to my doom: God's will be done!   435
    This faid, their facrilegious hands they laid

Upon

Upon his sacred person : He in' the midst
With meek composure and submitted look
March'd slowly onward, as they led the way
To the proud dome of CAIAPHAS, high-priest   440
Of MOLOCH than of God more fitly call'd.

    Oh! ye hard hearts, was this the Paschal Lamb,
Ye worse than pagan butchers, whom ye cull'd
Pure and unspotted for your bloody feast?
Well did your lawgiver decree this day   445
A record and memorial to be kept
Throughout your generations to all time;
A memorable day, a noted feast
Your stubborn incredulity hath made it.
To you a day of darkness and disgrace;   450
To us Salvation's glorious dawn, to us
By our great Captain led, the Lord of Life,
Who through the darksome avenue of death
And depths mysterious of the mazy grave,
Holding the clue of prophecy in hand,   455
Unravell'd all the ways of Providence
And to our view set ope the golden gates
Of Paradise regain'd, whence light and life
And bliss eternal beam on all mankind;
For all, who with their lips confess the Lord,   460

And

And in their hearts believe that from the dead
God in his pow'r hath rais'd him, fhall be fav'd.

  Meanwhile the prince of hell, whom Christ had left
- Rolling in torments on the ftony rock,
Mad as leviathan, when tempeft-wreck'd   465
Flound'ring he lies upon the fhoaly beach,
Now to one laft and defperate effort driv'n, .
Straining each nerve with many a dolorous groan
Half his huge length had rear'd. His right hand grafp'd
His fpear, the other on his buckler propp'd   470
Pillow'd his head, raging with pain and thoughts
Black as the night around him : To arife
And ftand furpafs'd his power ; in vain he fpread
His feathery vans to raife him in the air ;
About him all the ground with azure plumes   475
Beat from his fhatter'd pinions was beftrewn :
Defpair now feiz'd him, now too late he rued
His blafphemies and bold rebellious taunts
'Gainft Heav'n's Omnipotent, his Judge incens'd :
Hopelefs of mercy now he curs'd his doom   480.
Of immortality, and as he roll'd
His haggard eyes in night, hell's flaming gulph,
Terrific vifion, feem'd to burft upon him
With treble horrors charg'd ; then with a figh,

           That

That ftrain'd his heaving cors'let, he breath'd forth   485
In murmuring lamentations thefe fad words.
    Ah ! who will lift me from this iron bed,
On which Prometheus-like for ever link'd
And rivetted by dire neceffity
I'm doom'd to lie, and wail the cruel boon   490
Of immortality, my baneful fate ?
O earth, earth, earth ! Cannot my groans pervade
Thy ftony heart to' embowel me alive
Under this rock, before to-morrow's fun
Find me here weltering in the fordid duft,   495
A fpeétacle of fcorn to all my hoft,
Wont to behold in me their kingly chief ?
Will not fome pitying earthquake gulph me down
To where the everlafting fountains fleep,
That in thofe wat'ry caverns I might flake   500
Thefe fires, that fhrivel my parch'd finews up ?
Ah ! whither fhall I turn ? who will unbrace
This fcalding mail, that burns my tortur'd breaft
Worfe than the fhirt of Neffus ? Oh ! for pity,
Grant me a moment's interval of eafe,   505
Avenging, angry Deity ! Draw back
Thy red right hand, that with the light'ning arm'd
Thruft to my heart makes all my boiling blood
Hifs in my veins ; or if thou wilt deftroy

§   Whom

Whom thou haft vanquifh'd, terminate thefe feuds   510

'Twixt good and evil, thee and me, reduce

This incorruptible to mould'ring duft,

Make Death a parricide, and fo conclude

Me and my fufferings and my fins at once.

But 'twill not be.   Happy I might have been,   515

Immortal I muft be: God can create

Nothing but blifs; I made the pains I feel:

Sorrow had no exiftence, Death no name

'Till I loft heav'n; to be was to be bleft,

And beings bleft could never ceafe to be.   520

This earth and man its habitant were good,

Till envy, pride, rebellion, in my heart

Engend'ring, marr'd God's perfect work with fin ;

And but for fin the univerfe were heav'n :

So am I author of the hell within me,   525

And thefe tormenting fires God cannot quench ;

For that would be to turn from what he is,

Parent of good, and to become like me

Patron and friend of evil.   Reas'ning thus

I muft renounce all hope of future peace,   530

And wage eternal enmity with God,

Whom longer to oppofe I now defpair,

And under whofe ftrong hand weigh'd down to earth

Proftrate, confounded, I can rife no more.

2   Muft

Muſt I be ever thus? Muſt theſe fierce pangs, 535
Or worſe, if worſe can be, torment me ever?
Are there no means to make a truce with Heav'n?
Submiſſion, penitence, atonement, pray'rs
And interceſſions—Oh! fallacious, vain,
Impracticable terms! Can pride ſhed tears, 540
Falſehood keep faith, or perjury paſs it's oath
Upon that Judge, to whom all hearts are known?
It cannot be. Ages of ſin have roll'd
'Twixt me and pardon, gulph impaſſable.
Man's loſs of Paradiſe, a delug'd world, 545
Sin paramount on earth, the nations turn'd
From God to idols, ſcarce a remnant left
Of this his choſen race, corruption ſpread
Ev'n to' the heart of Judah', and from this Mount,
Sad witneſs of my overthrow and ſhame, 550
Scene of my triumphs once, his ſtandard torn
And hell's proud banners flanting in it's place;
Theſe and a countleſs multitude of wrongs
Cry in the catalogue ſo loud againſt me,
That ſhould the thunder of God's vengeance ſleep, 555
Mercy herſelf would ſeize th' uplifted bolt
And ſpeed the ling'ring blow. What is my hope,
If ſuch the taſk to purchaſe peace for man,
Man ſo ſubordinate in ſin to me,

The

The ſpring and fountain-head of that foul ſtream,   560
Which he at diſtance drank ? If CHRIST muſt die
For man, if nothing leſs than God's own Son
Can ſtand betwixt the Father's wrath and man,
What mediator can be found for me ?
None, and no wonder if his wrath, withdrawn   565
From man now pardon'd, fall with worſe recoil
On my devoted head : Ev'n now it falls.
Me like an eagle in my tow'ring flight,
From the proud zenith of the ſun's bright ſphere
Headlong he hurls to earth with ſhatter'd wing   570
And plumes diſhevell'd grov'ling in the duſt :
Me, the ſole mover of man's foul revolt,
He marks for tenfold vengeance ; for if CHRIST,
The patient meek Redeemer, groans in pain,
What ſhall the Tempter feel ? If on the rack   575
Of agony his guiltleſs brow ſweats blood,
Well may this body' of ſin burſt out in flames,
A conflagration horrible to ſight,
And blazing beacon to th' aſtoniſh'd world.
And what is this vile JUDAS, who ſeduc'd   580
By wily MAMMON ſells his Maſter's life ?
What PETER's ſelf, whom, had not JESUS pray'd,
I'd ſifted into chaff? Theſe purblind prieſts,
Who with their half-ſhut eyes aſkance behold

                                        Their

Their own Meffias in his wond'rous acts, 585
Yet give thofe wonders to the powers of hell,
And trembling for their craft complot his death,
What are they ? Whence but from myfelf their lyes ?
'Tis I in them, and not they of themfelves,
That kill the Prince of Peace ; his guiltlefs blood 590
Sprinkles their hands, but in a flood-gate tide
Redder than fcarlet whelms my finking foul.

He ceas'd, and in his mantle hid his face
For fhame and forrow to be thus furpriz'd ;
For MAMMON, ever on the foot by night, 595
Had fpied him through the gloom, and thus began.

What ails thee, Prince of air, that here thou lieft
On the dull earth, not refting it fhould feem
From victory, but vanquifh'd and o'erthrown ?

Vanquifh'd, alas ! and in the duft o'erthrown 600
By God's all-pow'rful Son, SATAN replied,
Too fure I am ; and how it wrings this heart
So to be found of thee words cannot fpeak.
Yet thou of all the fpirits heav'n hath loft
Art he, of whom my pride hath leaft to fear ; 605
For thou wilt not as others gall my fpleen
With fcorn and taunting : Thou, a friendly chief,
Haft pity for the forrows of a friend ;
To thee my valor and deferts are known,

T

For

For thou wert ever neareft where I fought   610
In front of danger on the battle's edge ;
Thou know'ft the hazard and the chance of war,
And with what malice fortune thwarts our beft,
Our braveft efforts : Scarr'd thyfelf with wounds,
Thou from the wounded wilt not turn afide ;   615
Therefore, O MAMMON, as my hand to thee
Were prefent, didft thou need it, fo to me,
Thy fovereign in diftrefs, reach forth thine hand,
And, if thou canft, upraife me from this fall ;
If thou canft not, let not my armies know   620
Their leader's fate, be mindful of my fame,
And bury this fad fecret in thy breaft.

     He faid, nor need had he of further fuit,
For MAMMON now had put forth all his ftrength
To raife him from the ground ; in his ftrong grafp   625
He feiz'd his giant limbs in armour clad
Of adamant and gold, a ponderous wreck :
Earth trembled with the fhock ; dire were the groans
Hell's Monarch vented, horrible the pains,
That rack'd his ftiffen'd joints ; yet on he toil'd   630
Till by Heav'n's fufferance rather than by aid
Of arm angelic once again he rear'd
His huge Titanian ftature to the fkies,
And ftood ; yet not as late with look erect

                                                      And

And lofty mien : Ruin was in his face ;   635
Sordid and foil'd with ignominious duſt
His robe imperial, and his azure wings
And gloſſy locks, that o'er his ſhoulders curl'd,
Diſhevell'd now, and in like tatter'd trim
With veſſel tempeſt-torn or by the force   640
Of engines weigh'd from bottom of the deep,
Founder'd in creek or harbor, where ſhe lay
Gulph'd in the ſlimy ooze ; when MAMMON thus.
      Joy to our gallant Leader ! Once again
With firm foot planted on the ſubjeċt earth   645
We ſtand as ſpi'rits by our own ſtrength redeem'd
Ereċt and dauntleſs.   Wherefore droops that eye,
As it would root itſelf into the ſoil,
From which with vigor new reſtor'd you riſe
Antæus-like indignant of defeat ?   650
Oft, when in ſearch of gold or ſilver ore
In earth's metallic veins, I've labor'd long
And hard, in damp and darkſome caverns pent,
Mining the ſolid rock, at length to light
And the free air emerg'd, I've found my limbs   655
Stiffen'd with cramps, or with cold ague numb'd :
Yet never did my patient courage droop
Or ſlack it's gainful toil.   I am not apt,
When wealth or glory can be bought with pain,

T 2

To

To ftagger at the terms; and if it pleafe   660
Heav'n's Monarch in his vengeance to attach
To this eternal be'ing eternal pain,
Good hope, as poifons may be fheath'd by ufe,
So long familiarity with pain
May draw it's fting, and habitude convert   665
It's hoftile property to friendly eafe.
But thy great heart perhaps is rent with grief,
Of pain difdainful as of leffer ill:
And wherefore grieve? Our joys were loft with heaven,
Our paffions all revers'd, our natures chang'd,   670
Virtues tq vices, amity to hate;
Deeds, that in heav'n had been our fhame, in hell
Become our glory'; and whilft the world endures,
Whilft evil is to good oppos'd, we keep
The fight at doubtful iffue, oft-times win   675
The glorious field and triumph over God.
Why did I tempt ISCARIOT to betray
His guiltlefs Mafter? 'Twas not that I lov'd
The traitor, no, the treafon was my joy;
I laugh at fools in their own folly caught: 680
The wretch I tempted, him I fhall deftroy,
And like a worn-out weapon caft him by;
He fhall not live to fee his Mafter's fall,
And for the forry purchafe of his fin

                                                        He

He fhall but touch the adder's fting and die :   685
So much for JUDAS! Thus at once I flay
Two victims and refine upon revenge.

    To whom with clouded brow and nothing cheer'd
By this difcourfe hell's gloomy Power replied.

    MAMMON, you well defcribe the rueful change   690
Wrought in us by our overthrow from heav'n,
And for fuch folace as in thought you find
Pondering the fad eternity of pain,
My argument fhall never be employ'd
To make that little lefs; but when you vaunt   695
ISCARIOT's treafon and th' impending fall
Of that juft Perfon, now before the bar
Of envious judges, who fhall doom his death,
You vaunt a deed, which, though the' elect of hell
Jointly with me advis'd, brings on us all   700
Ruin with lofs of empire, and all hope
So quenches, nought can ftand us now in ftead
But patience and your reconciling rules
To wont our natures to eternal pain.
My potency you know, and can you think,   705
Lefs than the hand of God could hurl me down
To mifery like this? It muft be God,
Who fpeaks in CHRIST, the Father in the Son :
Though meek, Almighty he controuls the world

                                And

And me the world's late mafter; he deftroys   710
Sin my begotten and Sin's offspring Death.
Oh ! that I never had approach'd him more,
Foil'd in my firft temptation.   Now, ev'n now,
I feel a nature in me, not mine own,
That is my mafter and againft my will   715
Enforces truths prophetic from my tongue,
Making me rev'rence whom in heart I hate :
I feel that now, though lifted from the ground,
I ftand or move or fpeak but as he wills,
By influence not by freedom : I perceive   720
Thefe exhalations, that the night breathes on me,
Are loaded with the vaporous fteams of hell ;
I fcent them in the air, and well I know
The angel of deftruction is abroad.
I cannot fly from fate ; the man foredoom'd   725
To bruife my head is Christ, the time is come,
The prophecy is full ; exil'd from hence,
As firft from heav'n, my reign on earth is o'er,
And my laft care is for thofe haplefs friends,
The partners of my fall, when I am gone   730
Left like a headlefs trunk.   Warn them to fly
Impending ruin ; fure I am, when Christ
Breathes forth his facred fpi'rit into the air,
His dying gafp fhall blow them like a fpell

                                        To

To the four winds of heav'n : Let them be gone 735
In time and ply the wing ; there's fhelter yet
In this wide world for them : Though I muft hence,
They may abide, and though their names be loft,
Their altars levell'd and their idols maim'd,
Yet fhall their arts and offices endure, 740
Their influences ftill fhall draw the hearts
Of many ; fin fhall not at once fecede
From earth, nor darknefs wholly yield to light.
To thee, aufpicious fpi'rit, whofe potent arm
Hath rais'd me from the ground, I can affure 745
A longer term of refidence and power :
Thy empire in earth's inmoft centre roots,
Thy influence circulates through all her veins ;
Nor earth alone, but ocean wafts to thee
Continual tribute ; commerce hails thy name ; 750
In thee war triumphs, thee fair peace adores
And gilds the feathers of her dove with gold
To dedicate to thee her worldly god,
Thee, the laft foe whom Christ fhall chafe from earth.

So fpake the parting fiend in his laft hour 755
Prophetic, father though he were of lyes :
To him the inferior dæmon anfwer none
Attempted, but in ghaftly filence ftood
Gazing with horror on his chieftain's face,

8. That

That chang'd all hues by fits, as when the north,   760
With nitrous vapors charg'd, convulsive shoots
It's fiery darts athwart the trembling pole,
Making heav'n's vault a canopy of blood ;
So o'er the visage of the exorcis'd fiend
Alternate gleams like meteors came and went ;   765
And ever and anon he beat his breast,
That quick and short with lab'ring pulses heav'd.
One piteous look he upward turn'd, one sigh
From his sad heart he fain had sent to heav'n,
But ere the hopeless messenger could leave   · 770
His quiv'ring lips, by sudden impulse seiz'd
He finds himself uplifted from the earth ;
His azure wings, to sooty black now chang'd,
In wide expanse from either shoulder stretch
For flight involuntary : Up he springs   775
Whirl'd in a fiery vortex round and round ;
As when the Lybian wilderness caught up
In sandy pillar by the eddying winds.
Moves horrible, the grave of man and beast ;
Him thus ascending the fork'd light'ning smites   780
With sidelong volley, whilst loud thunders rock
Heav'n's echoing vault, when all at once, behold !
Caught in the stream of an impetuous gust
High in mid-air, swift on the level wing

Northward he fhoots and like a comet leaves   785
Long fiery track behind, fpeeding his courfe
Strait to the realms of Chaos and old Night,
Hell-bound and to Tartarean darknefs doom'd.
　　His fad affociate, left on earth, look'd up
And with like confcious terror ey'd his flight,   790
As when the merchant trembling for his freight
Looks feaward from fome promontory's top,
And thence defcries his gallant bark a wreck
Driving at mercy of the winds and waves
Full on the rocky fhoal, her certain grave;   795
Then having bid farewell to all his hope
In this one bottom ftor'd, now loft to fight,
Turns with a figh afide, and o'er the ftrand
With heavy heart takes homeward his flow way.
　　So figh'd the fiend, and for his own fad fate   8co
Trembling yet fearful to attempt the wing,
Slunk cow'ring off veil'd in the fhades of night.

ＥND OF THE FOURTH BOOK.

U

CALVARY;

OR

THE DEATH OF CHRIST.

BOOK V.

THE ARGUMENT OF THE FIFTH BOOK.

This Book, proposing to treat of the trial and condemnation of Christ, opens with an invocation to the Evangelists, the sacred historians of that event.——Christ, brought before the priests and elders in council, accused by the witnesses, interrogated by Caiaphas, persists in keeping silence, till being solemnly called upon to declare himself, he answers by an affirmation of the truth. Instantly all voices are let loose upon him, accusing him of blasphemy and pronouncing him worthy of death : He is delivered over to mockery and insult. The Jews resolve to arraign him before Pilate on the following morning. He turns and looks upon Peter, who according to prediction had three several times denied him. The sorrow and contrition of that Disciple is described; he retires apart to bewail his crime and supplicate forgiveness. His prayer and confession in the temple-porch. The council of the Jews resort to Pilate next morning and appeal against Christ. He informs them that by the Roman law no judgment can be given till the accused is confronted with his accusers, and heard in his defence. Now commences the trial of Christ before Pilate, who, finding nothing worthy of death in that just person, refers him to Herod as belonging to his jurisdiction. Herod, after mocking him, arrays him in a gorgeous robe, and in that apparel sends him back to Pilate. He again appears in the judgment hall before Pilate, who after many fruitless efforts to save him, the Jews still urging him by their clamorous importunity to crucify him, finding no other way to prevent a tumult of the people, after declaring himself innocent of the blood of Jesus by the ceremony of washing his hands before the multitude, delivers him to be crucified.

C A L V A R Y.

BOOK V.

THE CONDEMNATION OF CHRIST.

YE ſacred Guides, whoſe plain unvarniſh'd page,
    Penn'd by the hand of Truth, records the ſcene,
Where CHRIST before the bar of impious men,
Patient of all their ſcorn, arraign'd, betray'd
And of his own abandon'd, ſilent ſtands,   5
You I invoke; ſo from the ſame pure ſource,
Whence my faith flows, ſhall alſo flow my ſong,
Not idly babbling, like that ſhallow rill
Trickling at foot of the Parnaſſian Mount,
But deep, ſerene, to hallow'd airs attun'd: 10
Aid me from Heav'n, where now before God's throne
In evangelic attributes ye ſtand
Six-wing'd and thick beſpangled o'er with eyes,
Ranging all points before you and behind,
Seraphic minſtrels, chanting day and night   15

Your

Your ceafelefs hallelujahs to the name
Of Him, who was and is and is to come.
Led by your hand with trembling ftep I prefs
The facred ground, which my Redeemer trode,
Now like a lamb to flaughter led, and now   20
Pendent, Oh horror! on the bloody tree;
And whilft to tell his facrifice of love,
His foul-diffolving agonies I ftrive,
My heart melts into forrows deep as thofe,
When the fad daughters of Jerufalem.   25
Water'd his paffage to the crofs with tears.

   Mufing my pious theme, as fits a bard
Far onward in the wint'ry track of age,
I fhun the Mufes haunts, nor dalliance hold
With fancy by the way, but travel on   30
My mournful road, a pilgrim grey with years;
One that finds little favor with the world,
Yet thankful for it's leaft benevolence
And patient of it's taunts; for never yet
Lur'd I the popu'lar ear with gibing tales,   35
Or facrific'd the modefty of fong,
Harping lewd madrigals at drunken feafts
To make the vulgar fport and win their fhout.
Me rather the ftill voice delights, the praife
Whifper'd, not publifh'd by fame's braying trump: 40

Be

Be thou my herald, Nature! Let me pleafe
The facred few, let my remembrance live
Embofom'd by the virtuous and the wife;
Make me, O Heav'n! by thofe, who love thee, lov'd:
So when the widow's and the children's tears   45
Shall fprinkle the cold duft, in which I fleep
Pomplefs and from a fcornful world withdrawn,
The laurel, which it's malice rent, fhall fhoot
So water'd into life, and mantling throw
It's verdant honors o'er my graffy tomb.   50

    Here in mid-way of my unfinifh'd courfe,
Doubtful of future time whilft now I paufe
To fetch new breath and trim my waining lamp,
Fountain of Life, if I have ftill ador'd
Thy mercy and remember'd Thee with awe   55
Ev'n in my mirth, in the gay prime of youth—
So confcience witneffes, the mental fcribe,
That regifters my errors, quits me here—
Propitious Pow'r, fupport me! and if death,
Near at the fartheft, meditates the blow   60
To cut me fhort in my prevented tafk,
Spare me a little, and put by the ftroke,
Till I recount his overthrow and hail
Thy Son victorious rifing from the grave.

                           Now

Now to that difmal fcene return, my thoughts !   65
Where CHRIST in midft of an irreverent crew,
Ufher'd by torches through the darkling ftreets,
And now at fummit of the holy Mount
Arriv'd, before the pontiff's lofty gate,
Waiting the call of impious pride, attends.   70
The halls and lobbies vomit forth a fwarm
Of faucy fervitors with ideot ftare
Gazing the wond'rous Man, and venting loud
Their coward mockeries : He ftands unmov'd.
Great is the ftir within, and on the poft   75
Through all the palace runs the buzzing news
Of this great Prophet's capture, circling round
With ever new enlargement of ftrange fights
And fearful doings in the garden feen
Of thofe who took him.   CAIAPHAS meanwhile   80
Summons the Temple-chiefs, elders and fcribes,
A hafty Sanhedrim : No longer now
With ftately ftep in meafur'd pace they march ;
Huddled together by their fears they flock,
They clufter in a throng, fafeft fo deem'd,   85
And fill the council feats. In fpeech abrupt
And brief their hierarch the caufe expounds
Of their fo fudden meeting—CHRIST is feiz'd,

The

The Prophet, whom they dreaded, is in hold,
Th'Enchanter, who by league with Belzebub   90
Scar'd them with magic fpells, is at their door;
Now is the time to put his art to proof,
Now is the moment to decide if thus
Their unreveal'd Meffias fhall appear
After long promife in this abject ftate   95
A fhackled pris'ner, or a conquering king.
Admit him! with faint voice fome two or three
Of the leaft timorous cry.—Behold, he comes!
The rabble throng rufh in, and at the bar
Of the immur'd divan prefent him bound   100
With cords, his raiment foil'd with hands profane,
His head uncover'd and his facred locks
By the rude winds and ruder men defpoil'd
Of their propriety, difhevell'd, fpread
Like fhatter'd fragments on the branching top   105
Of piny Lebanon after a ftorm.

    Silence now reign'd, the roar of tongues was hufh'd,
And expectation with fufpended breath
Sate watchful when fome fign or word of power
Should in a miracle break forth upon them.   110
None fuch that patient Sufferer vouchfaf'd,
Nor menace nor complaint his eye befpake,
But meek ferene compofure. Noting this,

As

As cowards out of danger loudeft vaunt,
The council now took heart : Then foon were heard   115
The lying tongues of witneffes fuborn'd
Various and loud ; but thefe no order kept ;
Falfhood with falfhood clafh'd, and each to each
Irreconcileable, as all to truth :
Shame held the council mute; for vileft hearts,   120
Cloak'd in the robes of judgment, will affect
Some outward fhew of what they ought to be,
Then moft malicious when moft feeming juft.
Confufion now enfu'd and perjury
In it's own labyrinth had loft itfelf,   125
When fome of graver note within the pale
Of juftice feated, but far thence remov'd
In confcience and in heart, ftarted new charge,
Averring they had heard the Pris'ner fay—
I will deftroy this temple made with hands,   130
And within three days will another build
Made without hands.—The charge was gravely urg'd,
And, colour'd to the femblance of a plot,
Breath'd facrilegious menace to God's houfe,
Fit matter for defcant pontifical :   135
When CAIAPHAS, as foremoft in degree
So firft to found forth danger and affix
Solemnity to malice, from his ftate

                                        With

With magisterial dignity arose,
And sternly fixing on the face divine   140
His eye inquisitorial, thus began.
    Hear'st thou what these alledge? The words in charge
Stand witness'd by these present: Face to face
Th' accusers they and thou th' accused meet:
Justice is open.   What is thy defence?   145
Answerest thou nothing?—Nothing answer'd he,
But as a lamb before it's shearers mute
He open'd not his mouth; the mystery couch'd
Under those words, prophetic of his death
And following resurrection, to expound   150
To their perverted minds beseem'd not him,
Searcher of hearts and Savior of mankind:
Silent not pertinacious he endur'd
Their scorn, nor did his meek demeanour shew
More than the dignity of conscious truth,   155
Which knows itself prejudg'd and scorns a plea.
    But CAIAPHAS, who brook'd not this repulse,
And still occasion sought from his own lips
By subtlety to' ensnare him, thus re-urg'd
Question with solemn adjuration back'd.   160
Hear me, thou man accus'd, and answer make
I do adjure thee by the living God
To what I now demand.   Art thou the CHRIST,

                The

The very Christ, Son of th' eternal God,
Or art thou not? Refolve us who thou art!   165
 Then Jesus by this folemn adjuration urg'd,
Lifting his eyes to heav'n in mute appeal,
Whilft all his Father's virtue in his face
Effulgent beam'd, thefe glorious words pronounc'd;
Hear them, O heav'n, and Oh! record them, earth,   170
Write them, ye mortals, on your hearts—I am,
I am the Christ; all that you afk I am;
And ye fhall fee me coming in the clouds
Of heav'n, enthron'd at the right hand of Power.
 As when on rapine bent a favage horde   175
Arab or Indian, in fome fandy dell
Or by the fedgy lake in ambufh lodg'd,
Upon the watch-word by their leader giv'n
Leap from their treach'rous lair with fudden yell
And bloody weapons waving to furprize: 180
And overpower th' unguarded traveller,
Fatally trapp'd into their murderous fnare;
So at the fignal of their prieftly chief
Uprofe the dire divan with rufhing found,
Like roar of diftant waters. Terror-ftruck,   185
Frantic as Bromius, with furious hands
Th' enthufiaftic hierarch feiz'd his robes,
And into tatters like a cancell'd fcroll

         Tore

Tore them, exclaiming vehement and loud
That all might hear—What need of further proof?   190
Ye have heard his blafphemy.. How think ye, firs?
What may fuch crime deferve?—Th' infuriate priefts
Seiz'd by like phrenfy with one voice pronounce—
Death be his fentence!—Death through all the hall
Rebounding echoes back th' accurs'd decree.   195.
Horrible fentence! Murder hatch'd in hell;
Libation for the fiends! Dæmons, on you
And on your generations to all time
His righteous blood fhall reft.   Now uproar wild
And horrid din fucceeds: The fcoffing crowd   200
Rufh to the bar, fo privileg'd, and there
With fcurril taunts and blafphemies revile
The patient Son of God. Oh thought of horror!
The Savior of mankind revil'd by man,
The Juft by th' unjuft! Others more profane   205
Vent their vile rheum upon his facred face,
Or fmite him with their palms, then gibing cry—
Tell us who fmote thee; prophefy, thou CHRIST!
    Monfters, that CHRIST hath prophefied, your doom
Already by that Prophet is pronounc'd,   210
The lips you ftrike have utter'd it: Behold!
Jerufalem is fall'n, her towers are duft,
Your city fmokes in ruin: Lo! what piles

                                            Of

Of mangled carcafes; what horrid fcenes
Of violated matrons: Hark ! what fcreams   215
Of infants butcher'd in their mothers arms;
And look ! your temple blazes to the fky;
It's beams of cedar overlaid with gold,
It's fretted roof with carvings rich embofs'd,
And all it's glorious fplendor feeds the flames   220
Infatiate ; mark how high their ferpent fpires
Hiffing afcend : God fans them in his ire:
Thither the wild beafts of the defart hie,
There carrion owls by midnight haunt, there dwells
The dragon, and the fatyrs dance : 'Tis done !   225
That prophecy is feal'd.   There yet remains
An awful confummation unreveal'd,
Till God fhall gather up your fcatter'd race
Still vagrant o'er th' inhofpitable earth.
Ah ! wretched people, broken and difpers'd,   230
Did ye preferve the oracles of God
But to convict your own obduracy ?
Sad nation, on whofe neck the iron yoke
Of perfecution hard, too hard, hath lain,
And yet lies heavy, will ye not accept   235
A High Prieft, holy, harmlefs, undefil'd,
From finners fep'rate and exalted high
Above the heavens ? And do ye not perceive

The

The word of JESUS in yourfelves fulfill'd ?
Rue then the prophecy, which you provok'd, 240
Of faithlefs fathers ye ftill faithlefs fons !
Whilft fhuddering I recount the impious taunts
Of that blafpheming rout : But neither taunts
Nor violence could fhake the Savior's peace ;
He in his own pure fpi'rit collected ftood, 245
Nor of their bafe revilings took account.

    'Twas now that CHRIST, knowing himfelf denied
Three times of PETER, turn'd and look'd upon him.
He from the garden, where his Lord was feiz'd,
Following at diftance JUDAS and his band, 250
Had kept his eye upon their moving fires,
And up the facred mount purfued their track,
Till at the palace-door he ftood and fought
Admiffion with the crowd ; when there behold !
A damfel at the portal fcans him o'er 255
With fcrutinizing eye and ftrait exclaims—
Thou too wert in this Galilean's train ;
Thou art of JESUS.—Sudden to his heart
The coward tremor runs and there fuggefts
The fear-conceived lye ; before them all 260
With confidence to falfehood ill applied—
I know not what thou fay'ft—he ftrait avers,
And to the porch goes forth : There in his ear

    I   The

The cock his firſt ſhrill warning gives and ſings
The knell of conſtancy's predicted breach,   265
Of conſtancy, alas ! too ſtrongly vouch'd
By him in raſh and over-weening zeal,
Boaſting like martyrdom with CHRIST himſelf,
Sole ſacrifice appointed for mankind.
But he, though of preſumption warn'd, by fear   270
Still haunted and the guilty dread of death,
Strait to a ſecond queſtioner replies—
I do not know the man—and to engage
Belief, binds down the falſehood with an oath.
Fatal appeal to Heav'n ! inſult to God   275
And His all-righteous ears ! Is this the man,
Who with ſuch glowing ardor ſelf-aſſur'd—
Though all ſhall be offended, I will not—
Proudly averr'd, and for that pride reprov'd—
Though I ſhould die with thee, dauntleſs rejoin'd,   280
Yet will I not deny thee—? Man, weak man,
Pride was not made for thee. If PETER fell
Preſuming, who ſhall ſay, Behold ! I ſtand
In my own ſtrength nor aſk ſupport of God?
And now, as if devoted to his ſhame,   285
Curious to pry, yet fearful to be ſeen,
He mixes with the throng that crowd the hall ;
And there once more is challeng'd for his ſpeech,

As

As favo'ring of the Galilean phrafe;
Then with reiterated oaths abjures   290
His Mafter the third time; when hark! again
The cock's loud fignal echoes back the lye
In his convicted ear; the prophet bird
Strains his recording throat, and up to heav'n
Trumpets the trebled perjury and claps   295
His wings in triumph o'er prefumption's fall.

   Oh! fall'n how low, is this thy promis'd faith,
Favor'd of CHRIST fo highly? Know'ft thou not,
Difciple, thine own Lord? or know'ft him only
In fafety, in profperity, in power,   300
For thine own felfifh ends, a fummer gueft,
Prone to defert him in the wint'ry hour
Of tribulation, poverty and woe?
Is thy frail memory of that flippery ftuff,
That a friend's forrow wafhes out all trace   305
Of a friend's features? Look upon his eyes!
Behold, they turn on thee: Them doft thou know?
Their language canft thou read and from them draw
The confcious reminifcence thou difown'ft?
Mark, is their fweetnefs loft? Ah! no; they beam   310
Celeftial grace, a fanctity of foul
So melting foft with pity, fuch a gleam
Of love divine attemp'ring mild reproof,

            Y   Where

Where is the man, that to obtain that eye
Of mercy on his fins would not forego   315
Life's deareft comforts to embrace fuch hope?
O death, death! where would be thy fting, or where
Thefe awful tremblings, which thy coming ftirs
In my too confcious breaft, might I afpire
To hope my Judge would greet me with that look?   320
      Vaunt not yourfelves, ye fcorners, nor exult
In this recital of a good man's fall,
Faithful hiftorian of his own offence:
But rather let it phyfic your proud fpleen
To mark how mean, prevaricating, falfe   325
And defpicable a vain-glorious man.
PETER's denial, David's heinous fin,
And all the guilty lapfes of man's heart;
Though fumm'd together into one account,
Each fpot and blemifh malice can fearch out   330
To tarnifh the fair luftre of a name,
Stand but as leffons of humility,
Warnings of frailty to o'er-weening man;
And if our mournful page hath now fet forth
The fall of virtue, let it next record   335
It's glorious refurrection: We have fhewn
The' offender in his fhame, what now remains
But to difplay the penitent? Behold!

Abafh'd

Abafh'd he ftands bath'd in remorfeful tears :
One glance from his beloved Mafter's eye,   340
Like Nathan's parable, hath rous'd from fleep
His drowfy confcience.   Mark, where he retires
To weep in folitude and purge his heart
By forrowful repentance of it's guilt.
O PETER, could my verfe fit offering make,   345
That verfe fhould be beftow'd upon thy tears.
    Now the affembled elders and their chief,
After fhort confultation had, refolve
With the next dawn of morning to arraign
Their Prifoner at the prætorian bar   350
Of PILATE, procurator for the ftate
Imperial of Rome and Cæfar; he
Held judgment fovereign of life and death
In tributary Jewry, judge corrupt,
And like Rome's venal emiffaries prone   355
To every fordid purpofe ; train'd in blood
And for tribunal bloody therefore fit.
    Meanwhile forth iffuing from the fatal hall,
Scene of his fhame, the fad Difciple took
His penfive way acrofs the temple-court   360
Silent and folitary, feeking where
To' unbofom his full forrows and give up
His foul to pray'r, and pardon feek of God

Y 2   For

For his revolt.   Pale through night's curtain gleam'd
By fits the lunar intermittent ray,   365
That quiv'ring ferv'd to light his lonely fteps
To the fair gate call'd Beautiful, whofe porch
High over-arch'd, on writhed columns propp'd
Of fpiral brafs convolv'd, was for it's fhade
Of CHRIST and his Difciples much in queft.   370

    Hither he came, and falling on his knees,
Like the' humble publican fmote on his breaft,
And this confeffion felf-accufing made.

    Here let me fall and in repentant tears
Weep out my foul upon thefe piti'lefs ftones,   375
Made facred by His fteps, whofe awful name
Thrice blafphem'd, thrice abjur'd, I dare not fpeak,
Though in my fupplication.   Can I fay,
Spare me, O God of mercy? Can I afk
Pardon of God, unpardon'd of myfelf?   380
Oh! wretched recreant creature as I am,
What fhall redeem me from this mifery,
And reconcile my confcience to itfelf,
A perjur'd confcience? Never more can peace
Dwell in this bofom; never can my foul   385
Afcend out of the duft, or lift a thought
In hope tow'rds heav'n. With JUDAS let me dwell,
Colleague in treafon; with his fin my fin

                                    In

In the' execration of all time be link'd.
Or fhall I venture to look up and fay, 390
O God, behold a wretch, who dares not fue
For mercy but for mitigated wrath,
For punifhment proportion'd to my bearing,
Protracted, not too fudden, left it take
My fenfes from me and with them all power 395
Of meditation, penance and atonement?
Spare me a little to abhor myfelf;
And if the arrow, which my confcience drives
Into this guilty heart, draws not enough
Of it's vile blood to purify what's left, 400
Let the ftrong hand of juftice force it home
And finifh me at once. Was I not warn'd
Of my prefumption, and a fignal fet
To number my denials, when I fwore
Never to fwerve but follow him to death? 405
Mine, like Iscariot's, was predicted fin :
I fpar'd not him, I call'd his wilful guilt,
Obftinate malice ; and can I now urge
Neceffity my plea? All things are known
To Christ ; the evil motions of my will 410
He faw, not over-rul'd : I might have pray'd
For grace, fupport, prevention ; I pray'd not,
But heedlefs of the prophecy and blind

Rufh'd

Rush'd into sin prepense, self-will'd, self-loft.
What fascination seiz'd me to draw forth   415
The sword in rash defence of Him, whose word
Legions of Angels could have call'd from heav'n?
And what prevaricating dæmon breath'd
The lye into my lips, when the same night,
Nay, the same hour, that saw me prompt to' oppose   420
My life to danger, saw me meanly shrink
From what I courted, and behind a lye
Three times repeated like a coward sculk?
And did I not know CHRIST whom I denied?
Did I not know the Master whom I serv'd,   425
Who call'd me to him, pour'd into my heart
His heav'nly doctrines, rais'd my lowly thoughts
From the mean drudgery of a fisher's trade,
And taught me in the energy of faith
To walk upon that sea, in which ere-while   430
I dragg'd the net and toil'd for daily bread?
O memory, once my glory, now my curse,
To what sad purpose do I call thee home,
Absent in danger, present in despair?
Is there a wonder done of CHRIST on earth   435
I have not witnefs'd? Did I not behold
Dead Lazarus revive at his command?
What shall I say to him, whom I saw die,

                                                   When

When living he arraigns me face to face?
What anfwer make to thofe, whom I have ferv'd   440
From one fmall wallet with the bread of thoufands?
The very blind, ere they receiv'd their fight,
Saw more than I, and hail'd him LORD and CHRIST.
Who fhall believe when I renounce belief?
The very dev'ils own Him whom I denied.   445
Can I call thefe accurft, whofe impious cry
Dooms him to death; who fmite him with their palms
Blafpheming? Harder than their hands my heart.
Wretch, 'twas my falfe tongue train'd them on to murder;
On me, me only all their fin rebounds: 450
I ftand condemn'd; they free. Can I forget
How oft my lips confefs'd him Son of God?
Perifh that tongue, which could revoke it's faith,
Difown confeffion and belie my heart.
Denied of me on earth, when in the clouds   455
Of heav'n he comes at the right hand of Pow'r,
And fends his Angels with the trumpet's found
To gather his elect from the four winds,
When, as a fhepherd culling out his flock,
To feparate all nations and divide   460
The good from evil he proceeds, Ah! then,
Then will he not retort the fatal words
Firft us'd of me, I know thee not! Depart,

Thou

Thou wicked fervant, into outer darknefs,
There weep and gnafh thy teeth in fires prepar'd   465
For SATAN and his outcaft crew accurft?

    Thus he all night with deep remorfe o'erwhelm'd,
Mournfully kneeling at God's temple-gate,
Bewail'd his crime and fupplication made
For pardon ; and let after-times atteft   470
How full a portion of God's fpi'rit abode
In this bleft Penitent, when with the found
Of rufhing mighty winds it was pour'd down
On him and on his fellows, thence inftall'd
Apoftles, and with gifted tongues infpir'd   475
To fpeak all languages and preach the Word
Of CHRIST throughout the whole converted world.
Here in this very fpot, where now he kneels
Repentant, fill'd ere long with pow'r divine,
He bade the cripple in the name of CHRIST   480
Rife up and walk; He at the word in fight
Of all the people rofe and ftood and walk'd
And in the temple gave loud praife to God.
Then let not his offence, pardon'd of God,
By man but for example's fake be nam'd,   485
And once more, hail, thou renovated Saint !
Made brighter by repentance : Enter thou
Into thy Mafter's joy once more ; refume

                        Thine

Thine apoftolic primacy, and feed,
Shepherd of CHRIST deputed, feed his flock.   490
Nor fhall thy faith once faulter, nor thy zeal
Shrink from the teft of martyrdom, referv'd
To glorify thy Mafter on the crofs.

    Now morning from her cloudy barrier forth
Advancing crimfon'd all the flecker'd Eaft,   495
As blufhing to lead on the guilty day.
With the firft dawn the wakeful elders meet,
Short council hold, for little time fuffic'd
To take their voices, whofe relentlefs minds
In the fame bloody league were banded all;   500
And now unanimous with their high prieft
In ftately grave proceffion forth they march
To find their heathen judge, and at his bar
Arraign the Holy One.—But check, my heart,
Thine indignation; let the verfe proceed !—   505
Him in his feat of judgment high enthron'd,
With axes and with lictors round embay'd
In martial ftate, with reverence they falute,
And lowly ftoop their tributary heads
To his vice-gerent majefty : With fmile   510
Of condefcending favor he accepts
Their abject greeting, and to his right hand
Their chief advances; others in their ranks

              Z   And

And orders he difpofes ; then with feign'd
Solicitude, as if to feek the caufe   515
Of this concerted meeting, he begins.

     What caufe fo weighty brings JEHOVAH's prieft
With thefe wife elders and time-honor'd fcribes
Thus early to feek juftice at my bar ?
Appeal fo reverend, with fuch leader grac'd   520
And by fuch followers witnefs'd, well demands
Of Cæfar's fervant his moft equal ear.

     Whereto the' high prieft, fecond to none in craft,
With folemn accent and demeanor grave
Mafking his bafe collufion, thus replies.   525

     When he, whofe hand the fword of juftice fways,
Her balance alfo holds in equal poife
Over this realm provincial, we have caufe
To thank the mafter of our liberties,
Who by fuch delegation of his power   530
Makes light that yoke, which elfe would gall our necks,
Though Cæfar lays it on us : Then let praife
Be giv'n to Cæfar for the love we bear
To PONTIUS PILATE. Have I leave to fay,
That we your fervants, a peculiar race,   535
Pay worfhip to one God and hold at heart
As facred that commandment handed down
From our forefathers, which for ever makes.

                                    His

His undivided Unity the creed
Of all our nation; and whoe'er blafphemes   540
His name and controverts our holy faith,
Dies by our law? This fentence we have pafs'd,
But execution ftaid, fo bound in duty,
Upon a certain Nazarite, by name
Jesus, obfcure of birth, but of our peace   545
No flight difturber; for the common herd,
A monfter as you know with many heads,
And every head with twice as many ears
Itching for novelties, have rais'd this man
To dang'rous eminence; and for he cheats   550
Their grofs credulity with juggling fleights,
Which they call miracles, have blown his pride
To fuch a monftrous bulk, he now fcales heaven,
There feats himfelf—Oh! where fhall I find words
To fpeak his blafphemy?—at God's right hand,   555
His Son, his equal, fharer of his throne,
Judge of the world. If this be not a crime
For death to expiate we are flaves indeed,
And every ftatute, ordinance and law
Rome leaves inviolate, Jesus fhall break   560
Unpunifh'd: Nor is this, dread fir, the whole
Of his prefumption; mark, I pray, the heighth
To which his phrenfy rages, mark his threat!

He

He will put down this temple in three days
And in like time with hands invifible   565
Erect another.—Patron of our laws,
Fountain of juftice ! ought this man to live ?
Such madnefs breath'd into our peoples minds
Will fpur them to the deed, break every band
That ties, them down to order, and turn loofe.   570
Their fury not on us alone but Rome,
Not on our temple only but perhaps
On this tribunal, which Heav'n guard ! And now
Take the whole matter of our charge at once :
This Jesus hath pronounc'd himfelf a king,   575
Our king, your mafter's rival : You beft know
If your great empe'ror abdicates his right
To our allegiance, which we fain would hold,
Where we have vow'd it, to imperial Cæfar,
Not to this mean mechanic, Jofeph's fon.   580
This is our plea, O Pontius, why we claim
Juftice againft the pris'ner, who now waits
Your fentence under guard and bound, as fits
Delinquent fo atrocious : I have faid.

    To him the Roman—Be it known to all,   585
The fentence, which you urge againft the life
Of your now abfent pris'ner, cannot pafs
By practice of our law, till face to face

                                            With

With his accufers he fhall ftand at bar,
And licence have to anfwer for himfelf   590
Touching the crime in charge ; therefore thefe words,
Which you have largely fpent, are fpent in air,
Elfe might the ear of juftice be foreftall'd
By the empleader's charge, and fo perchance
Let fall the axe upon the guiltlefs head.   595
Much knowledge of your laws I cannot boaft,
Nor with thefe learned fcribes hold argument ;
For fo much therefore as to them pertains
I on the part of Cæfar am no judge ;
His tributes, his fupremacy and rights   600
Difputed or oppos'd I fhall uphold
'Gainft all offenders.   Let th' accus'd appear !
   This faid, behold the bleffed Son of God
Dragg'd to a pagan bar ! There whilft he ftood
A fpectacle of pity, patient, meek,   605
Submitted to his fate, PILATE, who knew
Him innocent and his accufers falfe,
Envious and cruel, ey'd him o'er and o'er;
And as he ponder'd in his mind how bafe
The fentence he was now requir'd to give,   610
Some fparks of Roman virtue, not quite dead
Though faintly felt in his degene'rate breaft,
Revolted from the deed : Soft was the touch,

                                        Though

Though ineffectual, which fweet pity gave
To his ftern heart : He wifh'd, yet knew not how, 615
To' unfold the gates of mercy, and through them
Let pafs the refcued Innocent to life ;
The fon of Epicurus could no more.
Upon the Sufferer's brow ferene he faw
Where innocence and fanctity enthron'd 620
Sate vifible and claim'd his juft award :
He turn'd him to th' accufers and beheld
Such malice, as brought up to view a groupe
Of his own furies from their fabled hell ;
Then with a frown he cries—What law is your's, 625
Which makes this man a culprit ere he's tried ?
Unmanacle his limbs ! A Roman judge
Hears no man plead in fhackles ; he, who fpeaks
In life's defence hath call for every aid
That Nature can beftow, free ufe of limbs, 630
Action and utterance to grace his caufe,
And hold him up againft the world's contempt :
I will not hear a man that pleads in bonds.
Cut thofe vile cords afunder : Set him loofe !

 And now our bleffed Lord, his arms releas'd 635
From the harfh thongs, which the malignant Jews
Had bound about them, 'gan to re-compofe
His decent vefture and with calm furvey

To

To note his perfecutors, thofe dire priefts
And cruel hypocrites that bay'd him round.   640
In every breaft tranfparent to his eye
Malice and craft and envy he difcern'd :
In PILATE's face the fhifting hues befpoke
Internal ftrife of paffions all in arms,
Combat 'twixt good and evil: In his hand   645
He held a fcroll, which with intentive eye
And thoughtful brow deep pondering he perus'd :
The writing well he knew, but the contents,
Thus worded, much perplex'd his wav'ring thoughts.

   " O Pilate, if thy wife was ever held   650
" In honor, love or truft, I do adjure thee
" This once take warning from her voice infpir'd
" To fnatch thee from deftruction. Oh ! withhold
" Thine hand from that juft perfon, harm not him,
" That holy JESUS, who now ftands before thee ;   655
" Touch not his facred life, or on thine head
" A fearful judgment thou fhalt elfe pull down :
" A mighty Pow'r protects him, what I know not,
" But mightier fure than all the Gods of Rome ;
" For I have feen his glory in a dream,   660
" And dreams defcend from heav'n. Pilate, beware !"
   Such was the warning fcroll he now perus'd,
Ev'n on the judgment feat, by timely hand

9   Sent

Sent for his refcue : Happy ! had he turn'd
His heart fo warn'd to juftice, and obey'd   665
The vifitation of the fpi'rit vouchfaf'd :
But he, like Cæfar, deem'd his manhood pledg'd
To make flight 'count of a weak woman's dream :
Yet much confus'd, uncertain and perplex'd
He look'd around, and faw all eyes upon him :   670
The Jews impatient, JESUS at the bar
Prepar'd for trial : What fhall he refolve ?
Break up the court and judgment put afide
For a mere vapor, for no better plea
Than to indulge a woman's fond caprice,   675
And bid the law ftand ftill and wait the time
" Till PILATE's wife fhall meet with better dreams ?"—
Such fcorn he dar'd not to provoke, and now
Loud murmurs fill'd his ear : Compell'd to rife,
Though uncollected and in mind difturb'd,   680
He thus addrefs'd the LORD.—Art thou a king,
And of this nation, who accufe thee to me,
King of the Jews ?—Thou fay'ft it, JESUS cried :
But fay'ft thou of thyfelf this thing, or taught
Of others art thou prompted fo to fpeak ?—   685
Am I a Jew ? the fault'ring judge replied ;
Not I, but thefe, who if thou wert a king
Were thine own fubjects, elders, priefts and fcribes,

                                        Thefe

Thefe have accus'd thee.   Not of them am I ;
Nor in this bufinefs covet further fhare,   690
Than on the part of juftice to demand,
What haft thou done ? How anfwer'ft thou their charge ?

 Of this world were my kingdom, faid our LORD,
My fervants would defend their King, and fight
To fave me from my' oppreffors : But I reign   695
Not on this earth, nor is my pow'r from hence.

 Art thou a king then ?—interpos'd the judge :—
Thou fay'ft, cried JESUS, that I am a king ;
And truly to this purpofe was I born,
And for this caufe came I into the world,   700
That I fhould witnefs bear unto the Truth ;
And all, that to the Truth belong, hear me.—
What is the Truth ? faid PILATE, but his voice
Now falter'd and his thoughts unfettled, wild
And driv'n at random like a wreck, could grafp   705
No helm of reafon ; only this he knew
There was no fault before him : This aloud
To all he publifh'd and pronounc'd him clear.

 Whereat with rage and difappointment ftung,
Furious as wolves defrauded of their prey,   710
Uprofe the priefts appellant, and afrefh
Urge o'er and o'er their aggravating charge,
Forging new falfehoods and re-forging old :

A a

The

The Preacher of forbearance, peace and love
Perverter of the nation now they call,   715
Fomenter of fedition, fpreading wide
From Galilee, the cradle of his birth,
Throughout all Jewry to the capital;
Where now affuming to himfelf the name,
Prerogative and ftate of King and CHRIST,   720
He ftirreth up the people to revolt,
Forbidding them to pay their rightful dues
Of tribute to Rome's emperor, himfelf
Exalting above Cæfar.   This and more
In the like ftrain of virulence, with lips   725
In afpic venom fteep'd they now depofe;
Nor had they brought their malice to a paufe,
When PILATE, hoping he had now found plea
To fhift the dreaded fentence from himfelf,
Thus interpofing check'd their clam'rous fpleen.   730

    Break off, and let your tongues take reft awhile:
It is not at this bar you muft emplead
This man, a Galilean as it feems;
Whom, being fuch, it is not mine to hear
But HEROD's: Let his fpecial tetrarch judge   735
'Twixt him and you: Thither remit your fuit.

    This faid, he rofe preventing all reply,
Whilft they, though by procraftination gall'd,

                                                    Yet

Yet of their tetrarch confident, fubmit :
But nor with HEROD could their malice fpeed   740
To it's main purpofe : Little care had he .
For all their prieftly clamor ; in his thoughts
Religion had no intereft, truth no weight :
For prophets and for prophecies no ear
Had he, alike regardlefs how CHRIST preach'd,   745
Or they complain'd ; yet much he wifh'd to fee
Some fplendid miracle of him perform'd,
Something to ftrike his fenfes with furprize
And fatisfy a wanton curiofity,
Made eager by the fame of thofe great works,   750
Whereof he much had heard and nothing feen.
But when our LORD to all his queftions mute
Nor word nor fign vouchfaf'd, to wrath impell'd,
What by enticements he had fail'd to gain
By taunts he hop'd to' extort ; and now his fpleen   755
To impious fcorn and mockery gave the rein :
Forthwith his Pris'ner in a gorgeous robe
Apparel'd as a king, to all his court
Held up for fport and laughter, he expos'd.
Loud was the roar of blafphemy the whilft,   760
And wild the revels of the fcoffing throng
As the lewd orgies of the frantic god,
Or clamor of that facrilegious rout,

A a 2

When

When their mad rage the Thracian minftrel tore,
Whofe wonder-working harp could charm the ear   765
Of hell and call dead nature into life.
The priefts look'd on and grinn'd malicious joy ;
Yet would not HEROD execution doom ;
Or willing to appeafe the jealoufy
Of PILATE, or content to mark his fcorn   770
Of JESUS by this arrogant difplay
Of mercy, as not dreading whom he fpar'd.
   Now once again at PILATE's bar he ftands,
Not as before like malefactor tied
And round begirt with cords, but overlaid   775
With a rich load of fumptuous mockery ;
A lamb compell'd to carry the proud fpoils
And guilty trappings of the ty'rannous wolf.
Again the judge with flow unwilling ftep
To his tribunal mounts and thus he fpeaks.   780
   You ftill perfift to bring this man to me
As a perverter of your nation's faith
And loyalty : Your witneffes I've heard,
Ponder'd their depofitions and throughout
Examin'd ev'ry tittle of your charge :   785
Him too I've queftion'd in the ears of all
Here prefent, and no fhadow of offence
Can I difcern to warrant your appeal

                                 For

For execution, and pafs judgment on him:
No, nor yet HEROD, for to him I fent   790
You and your pris'ner, and behold him freed,
Nothing is done unto him worthy death:
I will chaftife him therefore and relcafe;
Yet this chaftifement rather to allay
Your anger, than fo merited of him,   795
I fhall inflict.   Remember this your feaft
Hath the long plea of cuftom to be mark'd
With pardon and forbearance: To reprieve
One culprit from his fentence I am bound
No lefs by inclination than by rule   800
And ufage immemorial: Make your choice!
But let it fall on innocence not guilt.

   Inftant all voices echo'd forth a cry—
Hence with this man! away with him to death!
Give us the murd'rer, fet Barabbas free: 805
Let JESUS perifh!—Wherefore; for what crime?
PILATE exclaim'd: What evil hath he done?
No caufe of death in JESUS can I find,
Be witnefs for me, juftice, none in him;
But for that wretch, on whom ye would beftow   810
Pardon mifplac'd, fo various are his crimes,
So black their quality, ye cannot name
A death more terrible than he deferves.

                                   Take

'Take of the guiltlefs blood what ftripes can draw
To fatisfy your longing, but forbear   815
To take the life, if not for pity's fake,
In honor of yourfelves, that ye may fay,
There was one prophet, whom ye did not kill.

 Loud as the winds that lafh the raging feas
And all as deaf, redoubling now the roar,   820
Th' infuriate Jews rend their blafpheming throats,
Howling for blood; 'till deafen'd with the din
Of, Crucify him! crucify him! dreadful cry,
PILATE, who 'twixt their tumult and the death
Of that juft Perfon faw no middle courfe,   825
By which t' efcape, one folemn act prepar'd,
By expiatory wafhing of his hands
In prefence of the multitude, to purge
His foul, and thereof God alone is judge,
From the pure blood of that devoted Lamb.   830

 Behold! he cries, I pour this water forth,
And therein make ablution of my foul
From all participation in your crime,
By wafhing of my hands from every ftain
Of this inhuman facrifice, each fpot   835
And fprinkling of this guiltlefs Victim's blood.
Reft on your heads the murder! I am clean.

 This faid, he turn'd and fix'd a pitying look

        Upon

Upon the LORD ; then figh'd and gave the word :
Eager as hounds, when flipp'd upon their prey,   840
In rufh the throng, and foon the hiffing fcourge
Whirl'd with impetuous fwing aloud refounds
Gafhing that facred flefh, whofe bleeding ftripes
Heal'd our fin-wounded fouls; upon his brow
A thorny crown they fix, whofe tortu'ring fpikes,   845
Thruft rudely in by facrilegious hands,
Furrow his temples and with crimfon ftreams
Cover his face divine : Him thus abus'd,
Mangled with ftripes and all o'er bath'd in blood,
In purple robe they fcornfully array   850
And drag to public view.—Behold the man !—
PILATE proclaim'd with horror in his voice
And out-ftretch'd arm, that pointed to a fight,
Which had to pity mov'd their fteely hearts,
Had they not been of metal forg'd by fiends   855
And temper'd in the fterneft fires of hell.
Dry-ey'd, as rock of adamant unmov'd,
Obdurate to his forrows they look'd on,
Nor from their crucifying clamor ceas'd,
Till PILATE, now all hope for JESUS loft,   860
Yielding to their tumultuous fury, cried.

    Take him and do your bloody work yourfelves :
Impofe it not on me; I find no caufe

5.   Of

Of death, no fault in Jesus.   Take ye him
And crucify him! Of his guiltlefs blood   865
- Lo! I am innocent; fee ye to that!
     On us and on our children be his blood!—
Then anfwer'd all the Jews.   Tremendous words,
Tremendoufly fulfill'd! And now afrefh
They clamor for the crofs; when thus the judge—   870
Would you that I fhould crucify your king?—
We have no king but Cæfar, they rejoin,
Nor art thou Cæfar's friend to fpare this man.—
'Twas paft; to that dread name the Roman bow'd
Obedient, and from his fad heart figh'd forth   875
Th''extorted doom—Death to the Lord of Life!

END OF THE FIFTH BOOK.

C A L V A R Y;

O R

THE DEATH OF CHRIST.

B O O K VI.

B b

The ARGUMENT of the SIXTH BOOK.

Judas Iscariot seized with remorse returns the thirty pieces of silver to the priests and departs: Mammon reassumes the habit of a Levite, and meeting Judas after he had returned the money to the priests, instigates him to destroy himself. That evil spirit now takes wing and repairs to the wilderness, convenes the dæmons from all parts of Palestine, and informing them of Satan's expulsion from earth, warns them by his command to betake themselves to flight before the hour of Christ's crucifixion: This is no sooner announced than the whole infernal host breaks up in disorder and disperses to various parts of the world therein described.—The subject of the Crucifixion is now brought forward: The procession sets out for Mount Calvary; Christ bearing his cross is bewailed by the spectators as he passes: He is seen by Gabriel and the angels with him from the mount, on which they were stationed: He addresses himself to the daughters of Jerusalem: The executioners nail his hands and feet to the cross; the priests revile him and call upon him to come down; one of the malefactors crucified with him casts the same in his teeth; he is reproved by the other, whose penitence is rewarded by the promise of immediate salvation and glory: Christ from the cross recommends his mother to John the beloved disciple: Christ dies: The sun is darkened, the earth quakes, the rocks are rent, and the bodies of the saints and prophets are raised from the dead and appear upon earth: The priests and elders, alarmed by these prodigies, resort to Pilate and demand a guard of Romans to defend the sepulchre, lest the disciples should take away the body of Christ and pretend that he was risen: Pilate replies, that they have a watch; bids them see to it themselves and dismisses them.

C A L V A R Y.

B O O K VI.

THE CRUCIFIXION.

" ON us and on our children be his blood !"—
    Such was your imprecation, O ye Jews,
When in your fight the world's Redeemer ftood.
Gafh'd o'er with wounds, and emptying ev'ry vein.
For man's redemption; and behold ! it flows,   5
It whelms upon you in a flood-gate tide ;
Steep'd to the lips ye are in all the blood
Of all the righteous fhed upon the earth,
From blood of righteous Abel to the blood
Of Zechariah, whom your fathers fton'd   10
Betwixt the altar and the houfe of God.
Ye have enough ; the mark is on your race ;
Ye have drawn down the judgment ye provok'd,
It refts upon you : Yet for you no reft,
No ftation, no abiding-place is found ;   15

Strangers and weary wand'rers upon earth,
If in the duft of your Jerufalem
With foot profcrib'd ye dare to tread, ye die;
A favage race ufurps your facred mount,
And Jordan echoes an unhallow'd name;   20
Should ye but ftop to fhed a filial tear
Upon the foil where your forefathers fleep,
Woe to the circumcis'd that fo is found!
Oh! flow of heart, when will ye underftand,
That thus afflicted, fcatter'd and difpers'd   25
Through every clime and kingdom of the world
Ye are fent forth to publifh, as ye pafs,
How truly CHRIST predicted of your fate;
And though your lips deny, your fufferings prove
That prophet JESUS, whom your fathers flew,   30
Was Savior, Chrift, Meffias, Son of God.

    Amidft the throng that fill'd the judgment-hall
Stood JUDAS; he upon the watch to' avoid
The Mafter's eye with caution took his poft;
Yet was his ear to all that JESUS fpake   35
Still prefent, and, though few the words, yet ftrong
And potent of thofe few the' impreffive truth.
There was a magic fweetnefs in his voice,
A note that feem'd to fhiver every nerve
Entwin'd about his heart, though now corrupt,   40

Debas'd

Debas'd and harden'd. Ill could he abide,
Murderer although he were, the dying tones
Of him, whom he had murder'd : 'Twas the voice
As of a fpirit in the air by night
Heard in the meditation of fome crime,   45
Or fleep-created in the troubled ear
Of confcience, crying out, Beware ! It fmote
Upon the foul, for it was CHRIST who fpake,
Well then might JUDAS tremble ; 'twas the traitor
Liftning the plea of innocence betray'd,   50
Well might that plea awaken his remorfe.
When the perverting witneffes depos'd
To crimes, of which he knew his Mafter free,
The refutation quiver'd on his lips,
And hard he ftruggled to bring forth the words,   55
Yet could not, tongue-ty'd with defpair and fhame.
But if his hearing fo alarm'd his heart,
What were his feelings, when at times his eye
Glanc'd on the facred perfon of his Lord,
Bound like a felon, his defencelefs hands   60
In manacles confin'd behind his back,
His cheeks with blows fufflated, and his face,
Oh, piteous ! with blafpheming flaver ftain'd ;
Then ftripp'd, transform'd, in purple ftole array'd,
Saluted with the infolent All-hail,   65
                                                          King

King of the Jews ! a fpectacle of fport
And merriment to all the fcoffing crowd ?
Could heart of man bear this, who had beheld
His miracles, his mercies ; prov'd his love,
His patience, his forbearance ; fhar'd his cares,   70
His labors and his watchings ; heard his voice,
When tempeft-toft, rebuke the elements,
Though filent now amidft the roar of tongues ?
'Twas all that prieftly malice could inflict,
But more than MAMMON's convert could fupport.   75
Yet worfe had thefe tormentors in referve
To agonize his foul, another fcene
To fhift new horrors on that bloody ftage :
The torturing fcourge now founded in his ears,
The mangled flefh flew off in tatter'd ftripes,   80
The crimfon ftream ran down, the pavement drank
Libation of his immolated blood :
The hall rebellow'd with the echoing cry
Of monfters, who applauded every ftroke,
Wolves, vultures, Oh, for words to fpeak them worfe !   85
Men turn'd to dæmons.   Traitor though he were,
Son of perdition, this was all too much.

     Take hence, he cried, take back your bribe accurft,
Damn'd price of damning deed ! Tell o'er your coin ;
Count out your thirty pieces, for each piece   90

                                                   Is

Is thirty thousand daggers to my heart :
Burthen'd too much already with my sins,
I should but into worse damnation sink
Under this mercenary load oppreſt.
I have betray'd the innocent ; too late   95
For pardon, I am paſt redemption loſt ;
Ye may redeem the time, if ye recall
Your fatal condemnation and atone
To that juſt perſon ye have doom'd to death ;
If not, ye crucify the Lord of Life.   100
    This ſaid, he threw the thirty pieces down
And ſtrait departed ; they to his retort
Short anſwer made remorſeleſs and malign.
And now diſburthen'd of his filthy bribe,
It ſeem'd as though his conſcience would permit   105
A momentary pauſe for one ſhort gleam
Of hope to viſit his benighted ſoul :
'Twas ſomething like atonement, 'twas one ſtep
Turn'd backward from the precipice of ſin
And pointed tow'rds repentance ; 'twas the laſt   110
Faint effort that reluctant nature made
To ſtruggle 'gainſt ſelf-murder ; but how vain !
For MAMMON, once the tyrant of man's heart,
Ill brooks expulſion thence, from youth to age,
From age to life's extremeſt hour he holds   115

5   Abſolute

Abfolute empire, nor does hell contain
Spirit fo jealous of ufurp'd command.
He in the bofoms of thofe impious priefts
Held high pre-eminence, and them amidft,
Himfelf unfeen, had noted all that pafs'd ;   120
And much indignant to be now abjur'd
Of that compunctious traitor, fwift as thought,
Such was his power of motion, took the form
And habit of that Levite firft affum'd,.
And him clofe following to the outward hall,   125
There with thefe taunting words affail'd his ear.

    A lofing game, friend JUDAS, thou haft play'd
To fet thy foul upon a defperate caft,
And after pay the ftake on either fide.
What folly is it to be knave by halves !   130
Who would ftrike virtue in the face, and then
Afk pardon for the blow ; fall off from truth,
Enlift with falfehood and take pay for treafon,
Then by a paltry plea of reftitution
Think to compound one trefpafs by another,   135
Defertion by defertion ? Get thee hence,
Thou fhame to manhood ! wring out the fad dregs
Of thy detefted life in hopelefs tears,
For thou haft thrown away both worlds at once ;
All gain in this, all glory in the next.   140

                          And

And what art thou, cried JUDAS, fo to gall
A wounded fpirit, wounded by thy arts,
Tempter accurft? Human thou canft not be,
Elfe thou wouldft find fome pity in thy heart
For wretch like me.   Who but thyfelf feduc'd   145
My loyalty from CHRIST ? Who fapp'd my faith ?
Who fix'd this adder to my breaft but thou ?
Thou, dæmon as thou art, haft hurl'd me down
From my high hope to fathomlefs abyfs
Of mifery and defpair, from heav'n to hell.   150

    Rail not on me, quoth MAMMON, but thyfelf
And thine own folly; there the charge were juft.
Didft thou not fell thy Mafter for a bribe?
My part was faithfully perform'd ; the price
Condition'd for was paid.   What wouldft thou more ?   155
I needed treafon, and I fought out thee
As fitteft for my purpofe : Envious, proud,
Luftful of pelf, a villain ready-made
And ripe for mifchief, fuch I mark'd thee down;
Nay, and yet better; for I thought thee whole   160
And perfeft villain with no rotten part
Of penitence to mar thee; but, behold,
Thou haft deceiv'd me vilely, and haft got
A blinking vice about thee, a perverfe

C c

And

And retrograde depravity of foul,   165
That makes thee hateful to my fight : Begone!
That thou art wicked put not me to blame ;
Hadft thou been conftant I had made thee rich,
And riches would have fav'd thee from contempt ;
Now thou art poor and loathfome.   Hence ; avaunt!   170
One remedy I'll give thee for defpair,
This cord, a remnant of thy Mafter's bonds ;
A legacy moft opportunely left
To heal thy cares and recompence thy love :
Take, and apply it to it's proper ufe ;   175
It tied his limbs : Let it encafe thy throat.

    He faid, and ftooping, from the pavement took
The cord there left, and hurling it with fcorn
To the defponding traitor difappear'd :
Nor did that wretch the fatal gift reject,   180
But eager feiz'd the inftrument of death,
And foon within a darkfome vault beneath
The judgment-hall fit folitude he found
And beam appropriate to his defperate ufe ;
Whereto appendent he breath'd out his foul,   185
Not daring to put up one prayer for peace
At his dark journey's end ; but trembling, wild,
Confus'd, of reafon as of hope bereft,

                                                    With

With heaving breaſt and ghaſtly ſtaring eyes
There betwixt heav'n and earth, of both renounc'd,   190
Hung terrible to ſight, a bloated corpſe.
   Oh ! how ſhall raſh and ignorant man preſume
To judge for God, and on his narrow ſcale
Think to mete out by limits and degrees
Immeaſurable mercy ? Who can tell   195
How high the ſorrows of man's ſuffering heart
Aſcend tow'rds heav'n, how ſwift contrition flies,
What words find paſſage to the throne of grace,
What in mid-way are loſt, diſpers'd in air
And ſcatter'd to the winds? Oh ! that my harp   200
Could ſound that happy note, which ſtirs the ſtring
Reſponſive, that kind Nature hath entwin'd
About the human heart, and by whoſe clue
Repentance, heav'nly monitreſs, reclaims
The youthful wanderer from his dang'rous maze   205
To tread her peaceful paths and ſeek his God :
So could my fervent my effectual verſe
Avail, poſterity ſhould then engrave
That verſe upon my tomb to tell the world
I did not live in vain. But heedleſs man,   210
Deaf to the muſic of the moral ſong,
By Mammon or by Belial led from ſin
To ſin, runs onward in his mad career,

C c 2

Nor

Nor once takes warning of his better guide,,
Till at the barrier of life's little span   215
Arriv'd, he ſtops: Death opens to his view
A hideous gulph; in vain he looks around:
For the loſt ſeraph Hope;, beſide him ſtands,
The tyrant fiend and urges to the brink;;
Behind him black deſpair with threat'ning frown   220
And gorgon ſhield, whoſe interpoſed orb
Bars all retreat, and with it's ſhade involves
Life's brighter proſpects in one hideous night..
So JUDAS fell; ſo like him every wretch,
By the ſame filthy Mammon lur'd, ſhall fall..   225

     Meanwhile the vengeful dæmon unappeas'd,,
Pond'ring the warning of his Stygian Lord
Late driv'n from earth, and mindful that the charge
And conduct of hell's hoſt on him devolv'd .
Now claim'd his warieſt thought, upon the wing   230
Sets forth full ſail to ſummon his compeers,
As many' as in that quarter might be found,,
And them apprize of their foul loſs incurr'd
By their great captain's fall; and what diſpatch
Behoves them now put forth timely to 'ſcape   235
Impending danger of their chief foreſeen,
If CHRIST's death-hour ſhould unawares ſurprize
Them idly ſtation'd, or with curious gaze

                                 Hovering

Hovering about his crofs. So forth he goes :
But firft to fpy the land he wheels his flight   240
Athwart Mount Calvary, and there on guard
A file of heav'nly warriors he defcries
Covering the facred hill, and at their head
GABRIEL in golden panoply array'd,
Arm'd at all points, commander of the band;   245
The fate of SATAN and the recent fight
Of CHEMOS' ghaftly wound, with guilty fears
Haunting his coward fancy, warn'd him fly
Beyond the range of that ftrong fpear, from which
Spirit more warlike than himfelf had fled.   250
    As when a pirate galley on the fcout,
Roving the feas of fome ftrong-guarded coaft,
In bay or inlet moor'd under the lea
Of headland promontory' at anchor fpies
A warlike fleet, whofe tow'ring mafts and fails   255
Unbent for fea befpeak their ready trim,
Down goes the helm at once, the felon crew
Beftir all hands and veer the veffel round
To feaward, then ply oars and fails for life :
So at the fight of that angelic band   260
The Stygian fcout wheel'd round and fped his flight
Sheer to the wildernefs on fwifteft wing.
There on the watch AZAZEL haply found.

                                        He

He bade found forth the loud Satanic trump,
Heard through all Paleftine, at call whereof   265
Spi'rits, to whatever element affix'd,
In troops fwift-pofting on the charmed winds,
Came from all parts; from Sidon and from Tyre
New ris'n amidft the waves; from Gaza's coaft,
Meridian limit, to the fnow-capt mounts   270
Hermon and Libanus, and them beyond
From Epidaphne on Orontes' ftream,
Fam'd for it's grove prophetic; from the banks
Of Pharphar and Abana, Rimmon's haunts;
From Byblus, where Aftarte's wanton train   275
Howl for the death of Thammuz, yearly loft
And found as oft by the love-frantic dames.
Thefe on the defart heath alighting ftand
Obedient to the fignal; all around
Expectant of their arch-angelic chief   280
They caft an anxious look, but look in vain:
Him in far other region they fhall find
In chains faft bound amidft eternal fires,
His difmal dwelling, for them alfo' referv'd
In God's appointed time. To whom the fiend.   285

    I mufe not, warriors, that ye ftand amaz'd
To fee yourfelves in abfence of our chief
Here fummon'd by his arch-angelic trump,

Which

Which other breath than his before ne'er fill'd;

But public danger urges this bold ſtep, 290

In me preſumptuous, had I not to plead

Your ſafety for my warrant, and withal

His laſt ſad mandate earneſtly bequeath'd

At parting, when ſole witneſs I beheld

His utter loſs, diſcomfiture and flight. 295

Ah, friends! how ſympathetic with my ſoul

Is that deep general groan, which now I hear!

Full cauſe, immortal mourners, have we all

To groan and beat our breaſts, nor I the leaſt,

Whoſe melancholy taſk it is to pour 300

Theſe heavy tidings in your grieved ears.

But let us yet remember what we are,

And be not therefore heartleſs, though bereft

Of him, who was the head and brain of all.

Many and mighty are the chiefs yet left, 305

Though he prime chief no longer ſhall review

This widow'd hoſt. Of SATAN the return

Is deſp'rate, ſuch a whirlwind caught him up,

So ſtrong a ſouthern blaſt at CHRIST's command

Blew him beyond the ſtretch of angel ken 310

Right onward to the realm of antient Night

Impetuous through the empyrean void

Sheer on the level wing. Of him the fate

Is

Is worfe than doubtful; of his Victor's power
And Godhead irrefiftible what proof   315
Greater than this fad downfall can we need,
Or after fuch example what provoke?
Behoves us now prepare for inftant flight;
This our late chief, prophetic in his fall,
With his laft words enjoin'd me to propound   320
To thefe our legions fcatter'd o'er the coafts
Of Paleftine, whom elfe the coming hour
Of CHRIST's myfterious paffion fhall involve
In like difgrace and ruin with your prince,
Who to his lateft moment upon earth   325
Was ftudious of your fafety.   I have now
In words unworthy of my charge, yet fuch
As heart o'erwhelm'd with forrow can fupply,
Surrender'd to your ears my painful truft.
But whither to repair, whom to elect   -   330
As captain and conductor of this hoft,
Now headlefs, confcious that fuch high command
With none but with the worthieft fhould be lodg'd,
I, as becomes me, to your wifer thoughts
Submit, and with the general choice fhall clofe.   335
     No more, for now with fudden panic feiz'd,
The Stygian hoft, no voice imperial heard
Nor rule nor order kept, uprofe at once

                           Difbanded,

Difbanded, lawlefs; dreadful was the yell
.Of that infernal rout, a fwarm as thick   340
As locufts, making horrid night beneath
Their wings, that with like clangor beat the air,
As of a flock of cormorants difturb'd
From fome lone ifland on the rocky coaft
Of Chili, where they haunt; fo they with cry   345
More hideous mount, there hover for a while,
Then to all points difperfe, as chance falls out,
Or fhort confult prefcribes.   Some to the South
With Ifis and Ofiris at their head
To Memphis, Thin and Tamis take their flight;   350
There with the beftial deities to herd,
Birds, ferpents, reptiles, monfters of the Nile,
Gods that would half unfurnifh Noah's ark :
Some with Melcartus, demi-god of Tyre,
Light fhort, and in his temple refuge take,   355
Where arm'd with maffy club and lion hide
His huge athletic idol frowning ftands :
Others with Rimmon eaftward wing their way
To fam'd Damafcus; there in bow'ring fhades
By rilling fountains on the flowery turf   360
To doze away the foft oblivious hours,
A flumb'ring fynod: Some the golden fpires
Of Nineveh attract and Nifroc's fane,

D d   Stain'd

Stain'd with Sennacherib's impérial blood,
There by the parricidal princes fhed :   365
To Byblus and Belitus others fpeed,
Light feathery wantons by Aftarte led
With loofe love-ditties and foft fmiles lur'd on
To page her pride and deck her amorous fports :
But of the reft far greater part repair   370
To high Olympus, where prefides the power
Of thundering Baäl ; he that ftation keeps
Pre-eminent o'er all the idol gods,
And in his feftive hall rich nectar quaffs
With purple lips, and midnight revels holds   375
Luxurious, fenfual, lewd, in vice immers'd :
Yet fome there were and of no vulgar note,
Who, grief to tell ! to the biforked mount
Flew off, and there with the Parnaffian maids
Held fhameful dalliance, from whofe lewd embrace   380
Defcended a whole family of bards
Corruptive, illegitimate and bafe ;
A fpurious breed of wickednefs and wit ;
A Mufe's genius with a Dæmon's heart :
MAMMON meanwhile, a folitary fprite,   385
Selfifh, morofe and ev'n by dev'ils abhorr'd,
Hied him alone, on fordid thoughts intent,
To rummage in Pactolus' fands for gold ;

None

None join'd, nor fought he partner in his flight,
His fole ambition to engrofs and hoard.   390
   Now came the awful confummation on,
The hour of promife, dimly fhadow'd out
By types and prophecies, when from the womb
Of myftery, long travailing in pains
And groanings, now in ripe time fhould fpring forth   395
Her full form'd revelation to difpel
Th' Obfcure of antient days and ufher in
Twin birth of Immortality and Life.
Now God by the' off'ring of his only Son
The type of Abraham's facrifice fulfill'd,   400
Who, though unconfcious of that type, by faith
Righteous, was of the promifes made heir.
And now, as Mofes in the wildernefs
Lifted the ferpent, fo the Son of man
Exalted on the crofs fhall heal the world   405
Of fin, and expiate the wide-wafting plague.
Now the peace-offering of the fpotlefs Lamb
By one conclufive Paffover fhall rend
The law's fymbolic veil, and all abfolve,
Whofe confciences are fprinkled with his blood,   410
From punifhment entail'd upon the world
By man's firft difobedience.   Forth He comes

From

From condemnation : Ye too from your tombs
Come forth, ye prophets !—Son of Amoz, thou
Prepare for refurrection : Come and fee,   415
Not darkly' as in a glafs, but face to face,
The object of thy vifion ; Him, the man
Of forrows ; Him, who like a lamb is brought
To flaughter : Mark the travail of his foul ;
Witnefs how he is ftricken for our fins,   420
Witnefs how we are healed by his ftripes,
And by the note and comment of his death
Conftrue thine own predictions.   Forth he comes
From condemnation under Roman guard,
Bearing his crofs : Upon his bleeding brow,   425
Enfign alike of royalty and woe,
A thorny crown ; no friendly hand is found
To wipe away the tear mingled with blood,
That hangs upon his cheek : The foldiers cry,
Room for the criminal ! and reft their pikes   430
To keep the crowd aloof ; ftaggering beneath
The ponderous burthen of his crofs he faints
And finks to earth o'erfpent, till one is found,
A fturdy ftranger of Cyrenean birth,
On whom to lay the venerable load.   435
Hail, SIMON ! bleffed above men wert thou,
If faith in Him that fuffer'd on that crofs

                                                    Glow'd

Glow'd in thy heart and furnifh'd thee with zeal
To render this laft fervice to thy Lord.

    Without the city walls there was a mount   440
Call'd CALVARY : The common grave it was
Of malefactors ; there to plant his crofs
It was decreed : Long was the way to death,
And like th' afcent to glory hard to climb.
Upon the fummit ftood the Angel troop   445
Of MAMMON feen, though to man's filmed eye
Invifible : Here GABRIEL from the heighth
Noting the fad proceffion, had efpied
The fuffering Son of God amidft the throng
Dragg'd flowly on by rude and ruffian hands   450
To fhameful execution : Horror-ftruck,
Pierc'd to the heart th' indignant Seraph fhook
His threat'ning fpear, and with the other hand
Smote on his thigh in agony of foul
For man's ingratitude ; glift'ning with tears   455
His eyes, whence late celeftial fweetnefs beam'd,
Now fhot a fiery glance on them below,
Then, raifing them to heav'n, he thus exclaim'd.
    Oh ! that the Everlafting would permit
His Angels to chaftife thefe impious men,   460
And from their hands his holy Son redeem,
Whom in the heav'n of heav'ns we have beheld
                                             Beloved

Beloved of the Father, ever bleft,
At the right hand of Pow'r in glory thron'd !
But this for purpofes beyond our reach   465
God ever wife forbids, and who againſt
God's interdict ſhall ſtir ? Therefore retire,
Stand off and wait the time ! If CHRIST commands,
We are his miniſters to do his will,
Be it to lift this mountain from it's baſe   470
And whelm it on his murderers ; if not,
Patient ſpectators we muſt here abide
And let the ſacrilegious work proceed ;
Knowing that God hath ſaid, I will revenge :
Vengeance belongeth to the Lord alone.   475
    Now on the news of their great Prophet's fate
Each heart with fearfulneſs and trembling ſeiz'd,
Through all Jeruſalem the tumult ran ;
Native or ſtranger, aged or infirm,
None in the Holy City now kept houſe :   480
Where'er the Savior paſs'd his preſence drew
Thouſands to gaze ; and many' an aching heart
Heav'd ſilent the laſt tributary ſigh
In memory of his mercies ; zealous ſome
Ruſh'd in the grateful bleſſing to beſtow   485
For health or limbs or life itſelf reſtor'd :
But theſe the ſoldiers rudely thruſt aſide,

And fome with brutal violence they fmote,
Thick'ning their files to hem their Pris'ner clofe,
As fearful of a refcue.   Loud the cry   490
Of women, whofe foft fex to pity prone
Melts at thofe fcenes, which flinty-hearted man
Dry-ey'd contemplates : Mothers in their arms
Held up their infants, and with fhrill acclaim
Begg'd a laft bleffing for thofe innocents,   495
Whofe fweet fimplicity fo well he lov'd,
And ever as he met them laid his hands
Upon their harmlefs heads with gentle love
And gracious benediction, breathing heav'n
Into their hearts.   Oh ! happy babes, fo bleft !   500
    Fenc'd in with fhields and fpears and compafs'd round
With Roman guards the perfecuting priefts,
Elders and fcribes follow'd their Victim's fteps
Amidft the fcoffs and hiffings of the crowd ;
And ftill as CHRIST approach'd the fatal fpot   505
Loud and more loud the fad lamentings grew,
Till at the foot of the funereal mount
Arriv'd he ftopt, and, turning to the group
Of mourners, thefe prophetic words addrefs'd.
    Daughters of Solyma, weep not for me,   510
Weep rather for yourfelves and for your babes ;
For lo ! the dawn of forrows is at hand ;

                                           The

The dread prediction preſſes to the birth,
When through Jeruſalem a voice ſhall cry—
Give thanks, ye childleſs matrons, and confeſs   515
A barren bed, your worſt misfortune deem'd,
Now your beſt bleſſing : Break forth into joy,
Ye, at whoſe breaſts no infant ever hung,
For ye have none to mourn.   Now to the clefts
And caverns of the mountains they ſhall ſay,   520
Fall on us, cover us, ye rocky vaults,
And hide us from this wrath ! For if with us
Already it begins, what ſhall the end
Of the ungodly and the ſinner be ?
If the green tree cannot abide the ſtorm,   525
How ſhall the dry eſcape ?—And now no more :
Upon the ſummit of Mount CALVARY
They rear his croſs ; conſpicuous there it ſtands
An enſign of ſalvation to the world.
Kneel, all ye Chriſtian nations ! bow your hearts   530
And worſhip your Redeemer, in whoſe death
Ye live, and from whoſe iſſuing wounds flows life,
By his blood purchas'd ; hope's beſt promiſe flows
Of joys immortal for the juſt reſerv'd.

    The ſoldiers, now by their centurion form'd   535
In hollow orb around the croſs, begin
Their horrid prelude to the murd'rous ſcene ;

                                        And

And firſt his veſture, their accuſtom'd ſpoil
And perquiſite, they part; but for his coat
From top to bottom woven without ſeam,   540
That they rend not, but on it caſt their lots
Whoſe it ſhall be entire.   Upon his croſs
In Hebrew, Greek and Latin they inſcribe,
So PILATE will'd though by the prieſts oppos'd,
" JESUS OF NAZARETH, KING OF THE JEWS !"   545
This title, in three ſeveral tongues diſplay'd,
Read all thoſe crucifiers of their King
And murmur'd as they read; hard to the laſt,
Obdurate, unbelieving.   Now began
The executioners to ſpread his arms   550
Upon the beam tranſverſe, and through his palms,
Monſters of cruelty ! and through his feet
They drove their ſpiked nails ; whilſt at the clang
Of thoſe dire engines every feeling heart
Utter'd a groan, that with the mingled ſhrieks   555
Of mothers and of children pierc'd the air.
The prieſts and elders gnaſh'd their teeth for rage
And rancorous ſpite to hear him ſo bewail'd :
Women dropt down convuls'd and on the ſpot
Let fall their burthens immature for birth.   560
Words fail to paint the horrors of that ſcene :
The very ſoldiers paus'd and ſtood aghaſt,

E e

Muſing

Mufing what thefe lamentings might portend;
Scarce dar'd they to purfue the dreadful work
Awe-ftruck and gazing on the face divine   565
Of the fufpended Savior.   He, though ftretch'd
Upon the rack of agony, to heav'n
Raifing his eyes—Father of mercy, cried,
Forgive them, for they know not what they do !

    O ruthlefs murderers ! could ye hear thefe words   570
And yet perfift ? Blafphemers ! can ye read
And not adore ? The people ftand at gaze :
The rulers eager to provoke anew
Their quailing refolution with one voice
Cry out amain—Ah ! thou, that on the crofs   575
Now hangeft, thou, that boaftedft to deftroy
Our temple and rebuild it in three days,
Where art thou ? If thou be the very CHRIST,
The King of Ifrael, now come down, defcend
And fave thyfelf; this feeing, we will then   580
Confefs thee and believe.   But 'tis in vain ;
He hears not, he replies not, he expires :
Others he fav'd ; himfelf he cannot fave.

    Peace, peace, revilers ! nor expect reply :
Think not that CHRIST, thus dying for mankind,   585
Will from his great commiffion turn afide
And ftop the facrifice and quit the crofs,

                              On

On which his body offer'd up for fin
As on an altar lies. Your taunts he hears;
Yet will he not defcend call'd down by you,   590
Nor at the door of death fhrink back and leave
Short of perfection his all-glorious work.
But wait the time and greater fign than this
Ye fhall behold, when rifing from the dead
And incorruptible he fhall return   595
On earth triumphant o'er the crofs and death.
Yet, fuch is the perverfenefs of your hearts,
Him nor defcending would ye now believe,
Nor re-afcending will ye then confefs.

    And now behold ! on either fide the crofs   600
Of CHRIST a wretched malefactor hung
Groaning and writhing in the pangs of death :
When one of thefe, encourag'd by the taunts
Of the reviling priefts, fcornful exclaims—
Hear'ft thou not what they fay ? If thou be CHRIST,   605
Why art thou in this torture ? Save thyfelf,
And us thy fellows from this crofs redeem—
This when his penitent companion heard,
New horrors fmote his heart, his fault'ring voice
He rais'd and thus the blafphemy rebuk'd.   610

    Haft thou no fear of God, expiring wretch ?
Stretch'd as thou art upon the tree of death,

Haft

Haft thou no terror for the wrath to come?
And truly we the merited reward
Of our ill deeds receive, but this juft Man,   615
What hath he done? In him no fault is found.

　　This faid, the penitent with faith infpir'd
Upon the Savior turn'd his dying eyes,
And—Lord! he cried with fupplicating voice,
When to thy heav'nly kingdom thou fhalt come,   620
Oh then remember me!—To him the LORD—
I tell thee of a truth this very day
Thou fhalt be found in Paradife with me.

　　Oh! words of joy, that breathe into the ear
Of the expiring penitent the pledge   625
Of pardon and acceptance: Words, that waft
The foul yet hovering on the lips of faith
Into the heav'n of heav'ns, with grateful heart
We hail the glorious promife, which unfolds
The gates of blifs and prefent entrance gives   630
To the repentant finner.　Now no more
Conjecture ponders on the life to come;
Our dying Savior draws afide the veil,
Through which dim reafon caught a doubtful glimpfe
Of fhadowy realms, that ftretch'd beyond the grave,   635
Elyfian fcenes in clouds and mift involv'd.
Yet with this comfort take the caution too;

　　　　　　　　　　　　　　　　　　　　For

For who fhall fay what penitence was his,
That earn'd this promife? Fatally he errs,
Whofe hope fore-runs repentance, who prefumes   640
That God will pardon when he's tir'd of fin
And like a ftale companion cafts it off.
Oh! arrogant, delufive, impious thought,
To meditate commodious truce with Heaven,
When death's fwift arrow fmites him unprepar'd,   645
And that protracted moment never comes,
Or comes too late: Turn then, prefumptuous man,
Turn to the other finner on the crofs,
Who died reviling, there behold thy doom!

    Thou too, the Virgin Mother of our Lord,   650
By the angelic falutation hail'd
Bleft above women, thou amidft the group
Of fympathifing mourners at that hour
Waft prefent, when th' incarnate Virtue, born
Of thine immac'ulate womb, impregn'd of Heav'n,   655
Hung on the crofs expiring: He from thence
On thee difconfolate a dying look
Of tendereft pity caft, and at thy fide
Noting the meek difciple whom he lov'd,
Thus both addrefs'd—Woman, behold thy fon;   660
Son, look upon thy mother!—Sacred charge,
And pioufly fulfill'd.——Now darknefs fell.

                                                         On

On all the region round; the fhrowded fun
From the impen'itent earth withdrew his light :
I thirft !—the Savior cried, and lifting up   665
His eyes in agony—My God, my God !
Ah ! why haft thou forfaken me ?—exclaim'd.

    Yet deem him not forfaken of his God :
Beware that error : 'Twas the mortal part
Of his compounded nature breathing forth   670
It's laft fad agony, that fo complain'd :
Doubt not that veil of forrow was withdrawn,
And heav'nly comfort to his foul vouchfaf'd,
Ere thus he cried—Father ! into thy hands
My fpirit I commend :—Then bow'd his head   675
And died.   Now GABRIEL and his heav'nly choir
Of minift'ring angels hov'ring o'er the crofs
Receiv'd his fpi'rit, at length from mortal pangs
And flefhly pris'on fet free, and bore it thence
Upon their wings rejoicing. Then behold   680
A prodigy, that to the world announc'd
A new religion and diffolv'd the old :
The temple's facred vail was rent in twain
From top to bottom 'midft th' attefting fhocks
Of earthquake and the rending up of graves :   685
Now thofe myfterious fymbols, heretofore
Curtain'd from vulgar eyes and holieft deem'd

                              Of

Of holies, were difplay'd to public view :
The mercy-feat with its cherubic wings
O'erfhadow'd and the golden ark beneath   690
Covering the teftimony now through the rent
Of that diffever'd vail firft faw the light.
A world redeem'd had now no further need
Of types and emblems, dimly fhadowing forth
An angry Deity withdrawn from fight   695
And canopied in clouds : Him face to face
Now in full light reveal'd the dying breath
Of his dear Son appeas'd, and purchas'd peace
And reconcilement for offending man.
Thus the partition wall, by Mofes built,   700
By CHRIST was level'd, and the Gentile world
Enter'd the breach by their great Captain led
Up to the throne of grace, opening himfelf
Through his own flefh a new and living way.
Then were the oracles of God made known   705
To all the nations, fprinkled by the blood
Of JESUS and baptiz'd into his death ;
So was the birth-right of the elder-born,
Heirs of the promife, forfeited ; whilft they,
Whom fin had erft in bondage held, made free   710
From fin and fervants of the living God,
Now gain'd the gift of God, eternal life.

Soon

Soon as thefe figns and prodigies were feen
Of thofe who watch'd the crofs, conviction fmote
Their fear-ftruck hearts: The fun at noon-day dark, 715
The earth convulfive underneath their feet,
And the firm rocks in fhiver'd fragments rent
Rous'd them at once to tremble and believe.
Then was our Lord by heathen lips confefs'd,
When the centurion cried—In very truth 720
This righteous perfon was the Son of God—
The reft in heart affenting ftood abafh'd,
Watching in filence the tremendous fcene:
The recollection of his gracious acts,
His dying pray'rs and their own impious taunts 725
Now rofe in fad review; too late they wifh'd
The deed undone and fighing fmote their breafts.
    Strait from God's prefence went that Angel forth,
Whofe trumpet fhall call up the fleeping dead
At the laft day, and bade the Saints arife 730
And come on earth to hail this promis'd hour,
The day-fpring of Salvation. Forth they came
From their dark tenements, their fhadowy forms
Made vifible as in their flefhly ftate,
And through the Holy City here and there 735
Frequent they gleam'd, by night, by day with fear
And wonder feen of many: Holy feers,

Prophets

Prophets and martyrs from the grave fet free,
And the firft-fruits of the redeemed dead.
They, who with CHRIST transfigur'd on the mount 740
Were feen of his difciples in a cloud
Of dazzling glory, now in form diftinct
Mingling amidft the public haunts of men,
Struck terror to all hearts : Ezekiel there,
The captive feer, to whom on Chebar's banks 745
The heav'ns were open'd and the fatal roll
Held forth with dire denunciations fill'd
Of lamentation, mourning and of woe,
Now falling faft on Ifrael's wretched race :
He too was there, Hilkiah's holy fon, 750
With loins clofe girt and glowing lips of fire
By God's own finger touch'd : There might be feen
The youthful prophet, Beltefhazzar nam'd
Of the Chaldees, interpreter of dreams,
Knowledge of God beftow'd, in vifions fkill'd 755
And fair and learn'd and wife : The Baptift here
Girt in his hairy mantle frowning ftalk'd,
And, pointing to his ghaftly wound, exclaim'd—
  Ye vipers ! whom my warning could not move
Timely to flee from the impending wrath, 760
Now fallen on your heads ; whom I indeed
     F f   With

With water, CHRIST 'hath now with fire baptiz'd :
Barren ye were of fruits, which I prefcrib'd
Meet for repentance, and behold ! the axe
Is laid to the unprofitable root
Of every faplefs tree, hewn down, condemn'd   765
And caft into the fire.   Lo ! thefe are they,
Thefe fhadowy forms now floating in your fight,
Thefe are the harbingers of antient days,
Who witnefs'd the Meffias and announc'd   770
His coming upon earth.   Mark with what fcorn
Silent they pafs you by : Them had ye heard,
Them had ye noted with a patient mind,
Ye had not crucified the LORD OF LIFE :
He of thefe ftones to Abraham fhall raife up   775
Children, than you more worthy of his flock ;
And now his winnowing fan is in his hand,
With which he'll purge his floor, and having ftor'd
The precious grain in garners, will confume
With fire unquenchable the refufe chaff.   780

    Thus the terrific Vifion in the ears
Of the aftonifh'd multitude declaim'd
With threat'ning voice, and wrung their confcious hearts ;
Whilft the blafpheming priefts, who in their fcorn
Triumphant faw the Savior of the world   785
       8   Expiring

Expiring on the crofs and deem'd him loft,
Now by the refurrection of the faints,
Ufher'd on earth with prodigies and figns,
Confounded and amaz'd, began to doubt
If yet the fepulchre had power to keep   790
It's crucified Poffeffor fafe in hold,
And with thefe thoughts perplex'd, mafking their fears
Under pretence of caution, they repair
To PILATE and demand a Roman guard
To watch the tomb of CHRIST, and then they add—   795
For we remember that Deceiver faid,
Whilft he was yet alive, after three days
I will again arife; therefore we pray
Command the fepulchre to be made fure
Till the third day, left his difciples come   800
By night and craftily remove him thence;
So the laft error fhall outgo the firft.

    But PILATE, whofe unrighteous judgment ftill
Sate heavy on his heart, had little care
For what might them befall, and to their fuit   805
Briefly reply'd—Why do ye afk of me
That cuftody, which in yourfelves ye have?
Take your own watch and to their charge commit
The fafeguard of that body, which, though dead,

Keeps

Keeps yet alive your fears : 'Tis your own caufe,   810
As fuch I leave it with you ; fo begone !

   He faid and turn'd afide, nor did they tempt
Further difcourfe, but murm'ring went their way.

END OF THE SIXTH BOOK.

CALVARY;

OR

THE DEATH OF CHRIST.

BOOK VII.

THE ARGUMENT OF THE SEVENTH BOOK.

This Book opens with the scene of Mount Calvary at the coming on of evening; Christ still hanging dead upon the cross, the disciples standing apart and the holy women watching, amongst whom is the Blessed Virgin supported by St. John, Christ having bequeathed her to his care: His address to her on this subject, and her reply. The soldiers come and break the legs of the two malefactors, but finding Christ already dead, they pierce his heart with a spear and blood and water issues from the wound: They take him down from the cross and lay him in the sepulchre. His spirit in the meanwhile is conveyed by the angels into the region of Death; that region described, and the distant prospect of the bottomless pit, where the souls of the wicked are in torment: Christ points out these scenes to Gabriel and instructs him as to the future objects of his descent into this gloomy region. Satan expelled from earth falls prostrate at the foot of the throne of Death: He makes suit to that power for protection: Death rejects his intercessions: The person and palace of the King of Terrors described: The triumphant entry of Christ: Satan is hurled into the bottomless pit and there bound by the strong angel; the horrors of that dreadful abode are represented: Death humbles himself before the Redeemer of mankind, and conscious that his power is overthrown, tenders his crown to Christ as to his conqueror: He lays the key at his feet, which sets free the souls of the Saints, who are destined to be partakers of the first resurrection: This key is given to Gabriel with instructions for their release: Christ in his reply to Death forewarns him of his doom, but signifies to him that the dissolution of his power will not be immediate. The approach of the Saints concludes the Book.

C A L V A R Y.

BOOK VII.

THE DESCENT INTO HELL.

NOW Hefperus renew'd his evening lamp
    And hung it forth amid the turbid fky
To mark the clofe of this portentous day:
The lab'ring fun, in his mid-courfe eclips'd,
Darkling at length had reach'd his weftern goal;   5
And now it feem'd as if all Nature flept
O'erfpent and wearied with convulfive throes.
Upon his crofs the martyr'd Savior hung;
Pale through the twilight gleam'd his breathlefs corpfe
And filvery white, as when the moon-beam plays   10
On the fmooth furface of the glaffy lake;
His thorn-crown'd head upon his breaft reclin'd;
His arms were wide out-fpread, as if in act
To' embrace and welcome the converted world:
So were they late expanded, when he cried—   15

Come

Come all ye heavy laden, come to me,
And I will give you reft ! Death had not dar'd
To rob thofe features of one heav'nly grace,
Nor had the worm authority to taint
That incorruptible and hallow'd fhrine,   20
Wherein his purity had deign'd to dwell.
The living faints here mingling with the dead
Stood round in penfive meditation rapt,
Silent fpectators of the awful fcene:
There his difciples in a group apart,   25
Like frighted fheep that clufter in a ftorm,
Throng'd each on other interchanging looks
Of forrow and defpair; no voice was heard,
No utterance but of fighs ; though all had need
Of comfort, none had comfort to beftow.   30
But PETER, in whofe felf-accufing breaft
Grief roll'd in tempefts, had the whilft chos'n out
A folitary fpot, where at his length
Outftretch'd with face incumbent on the ground
He lay like one, whom fortune had caft off,   35
Of all hope 'reft, moft wretched and forlorn.

    There too the holy Mother might be feen,
Like Rizpah, watching o'er her murder'd fon,
Rooted in earth, a monument of woe.
Befide her, bath'd in fympathifing tears,   40

Firſt in his Maſter's love, as meek of ſoul,
Stood JOHN, adopted by his dying Lord
Son and ſupporter of that mournful Saint.
At length with reverend love he turn'd his eyes
Upon the Virgin Mother and thus ſpake.   45
  Oh thou! participant with God himſelf
In his incarnate Offspring, if I claim
The glorious title, which my dying Lord
On me, thy ſervant ever, now thy ſon,
Gracious bequeath'd, let not my words offend.   50
High honor and a truſt than life more dear
Hath CHRIST by this adoption deign'd to caſt
On me unmeriting; yet well I heard
Thoſe ſacred words—Mother, behold thy ſon;
Son, look upon thy mother!—Yes, I heard,   55
And treaſuring in my heart the rich bequeſt,
Bow'd and obéy'd : Ev'n then my zeal had ſpoke
The dictates of devotion, had I dar'd
To break the awful ſilence of that hour,
Or ſacrilegiouſly divert the ear   60
Of mute attention, whilſt thoſe lips divine,
Thoſe living oracles, had breath to move;
Now mute, alas! for He is now no more,
Who had the words of life : Our hope is quench'd,
Our glory vaniſh'd. See! the deed is done: 65

     G g   Thoſe

Thofe murderers have kill'd the Prince of Peace,
Cold on the crofs and ftiff'ning in the wind
To the rude elements his corpfe is left;
Nor is there found, who fhall provide a grave
For the fad reliques of the Son of God.   70
But lo! the heav'ns, that three long hours have mourn'd
In darknefs, now throw off their fable fhroud:
The earth no longer quakes beneath our feet,
The fhatter'd rocks fubfide; Nature is calm,
The fun unmafks and through difparted clouds   75
With ruddy twilight ftreaks the weftern fky.
And may not we, fince God hath now withdrawn
His terrors and affwag'd the wrathful fky,
May not we hope, that as his light revives
At the third hour, fo of his bleffed Son   80
The promis'd refurrection to new life
At the third day fhall alfo come to pafs?
When, as the fun emerging from eclipfe
Darknefs difpells, fo CHRIST from out the grave
Arifing fhall difpell our dark defpair?   85

     To him the holy Mother thus replied:
Thou meek Difciple, in thy Mafter's love
Pre-eminently bleft, fince He, whofe will
Should govern, fo decrees it, from this hour
Henceforth I lodge thee in a mother's heart   90

*

And

And hold thee as my fon; for I perceive
CHRIST from his human nature is withdrawn,
And to mortality hath render'd back
All that from me a mortal he receiv'd:
His Incorruptible now lives with God, 95
And in that glory I no part muft claim;
Flefh cannot fhare with fpirit. Henceforth thou,
Thou art my fon adopted in the place
Of that incarnate Virtue, of whofe birth
Miraculous the eaftern ftar gave fign, 100
And Angels witnefs'd him the Son of God.
And now behold! what wonders mark his death:
Whence are thefe prodigies? What but the hand
Of God can fhake the pillars of the earth,
Seal up the fun and rend thefe rocks in twain, 105
Turn day to night, tear down the temple vail,
Break up the graves and bid the faints come forth?
Lo, where they pafs as fenfible to fight
As in broad day fubftantial man to man.
And can we afk if He be very CHRIST, 110
Whom ftars and Angels ufher'd into birth?
Can we doubt Him on whom the Spi'rit of God
Dove-like defcended? Can we ftop our ears
Againft a voice from heav'n? Are we fo blind,
Dull and infenfible not to behold 115

G g 2 That

That sun emergent and thefe moving fhapes,
That to revifit earth have left their graves,
Awaken'd as from fleep? If thefe can rife,
If thefe, whofe bones are moulder'd into duft,
On whom the worm hath fed for ages, men   120
As mortal as ourfelves can re-afcend
Out of the pit, do not thefe figns befpeak
His fecond coming, who is LORD and CHRIST?
He fhall, He fhall return upon the earth
Victorious over death, and we, though now   125
Humbled in heart and for a feafon fad,
Yet wavering not in faith and holding faft
The anchor of our hope, fhall yet again
Behold his glory, and as now his death
Turns day to night, his refurrection then   130
Shall into joy convert our prefent gloom.
But fee, where PETER proftrate on the earth
Is loft in forrow: Hafte and bid him rife;
Tell him the day's at hand when he muft work.
Hath he not heard the fervant fhall not fleep   135
In his Lord's abfence? Strengthen thou his heart!
     So fpake thefe Saints, and each to other gave
Alternate folace; faith infpiring hope,
And hope affwaging woe. At PETER's fide
Behold the meek difciple—Up! he cries,   140
                          Awake

Awake and put on ftrength : The Virgin Saint,
The Mother of our Lord, bids thee awake.
Unprofitable grief availeth nought,
But godly forrow is approv'd in works
Meet for repentance.   Up ! for CHRIST, though dead,   145
Yet fpeaketh, and fhall come again on earth :
Woe to that fervant therefore, whom his Lord
Shall find thus fleeping ; great fhall be his wrath.

 This faid, he reach'd his hand and rais'd him up :
He ftood and fpake—Servant, of CHRIST approv'd,   150
Thee and thy bleffed Sender I obey :
Yet doth my heart, by deep remorfe fubdued,
Prefs downward to the duft.   A wretch I am,
Who hath denied his Lord : What can I do,
A miferable man ? O righteous JOHN,   155
When thou fhalt fpread abroad, as fure thou wilt,
The direful doings of this fatal day,
And publifh to mankind the wond'rous love
Of CHRIST thus dying for them, I conjure thee
Be faithful to the truth, fcreen not my crime,   160
Foul though it be, but let the nations know
PETER, who vaunted of himfelf, was falfe,
So fhall they reap inftruction from my fhame,
And by defpifing me correct themfelves.

          Thus

Thus fpake the contrite Saint, when now the prieſts, 165
Whoſe cuſtom was upon this folemn eve
To purge their Golgotha from human blood,
Send forth. their guard official to remove
CHRIST and the flaves convict before the dawn
Of that great day, too hallow'd to permit   170
Their bodies feſt'ring on th' ill-omen'd croſs.
And lo ! the foldiers fo encharg'd arrive,
Survey the victims and begin the work :
But firſt the pond'rous ſledge with horrid craſh
Defcending breaks the knees and ankle joints   175
Of thefe two criminals ; for ſtubborn life
Still hover'd on their lips, and now and then
Their heaving boſoms fetch'd a deep-drawn ſigh,
Like the flow ſwell of feas without a wind.
But when the Savior's body they approach'd   180
And faw there needed not a fecond blow
To make his death fecure, the word of God
Prophetic mov'd their elfe obdurate hearts
To break no limb ; yet one, fo deſtin'd, thruſt
His fpear into his fide and forthwith flow'd   185
Water and blood from the heart-piercing wound :
So deep the ſtab, that to life's citadel,
Had life remain'd, the mortal point had reach'd

                                                        And

And there had finifh'd it.   Meanwhile behold !
JOSEPH arrives; a counfellor was he,   190
But not for death, and rich and juft withal ;
In Ramoth born, where Samuel firft drew breath,
And as his heart in righteoufnefs and faith
Stood firm with CHRIST whilft living, fo his zeal
An honour'able interment to beftow   195
On his dead Mafter prompted him to make
Bold fuit to PILATE for the lifelefs corpfe,
Nor fail'd he of his fuit ; therefore he came,
So favor'd, to receive the precious charge
Of thofe dear reliques and with decent rites   200
Commit them to the grave : Spear'd to the heart,
And death with double diligence enfur'd,
The body they take down ; the hands and feet
Pierc'd through with nails and all befmear'd with blood,
O piteous fpectacle ! which to behold   205
Bathes every angel face in heav'n with tears !
Accurfed Deicides ! the time comes on,
When every mark your facrilegious hands
Have printed on that corpfe fhall be a feal
To teftify againft you, every gafh   210
Unclos'd fhall with it's living lips proclaim
CHRIST in his human attributes renew'd,
Corporeal yet immortal : Then the hand.

Of

Of him who doubts ſhall probe thoſe gaping wounds,

And by the evidence of ſenſe compel   215

The faithleſs and reluctant to believe.

And now they place the body on the bier,

Cleans'd of the blood and wrapt in ſeemly cloths :

Then under guard convey it to the vault

Hewn in the rock, where never corpſe was laid,   220

And there conſign it to it's dark abode,

Rolling a maſſy fragment to the door,

Unwieldy, vaſt ; and having ſeal'd the ſtone,

They poſt their centinels, and ſo depart.

   Meanwhile the' unhouſed ſpirit of CHRIST, ſet free   225

From groſs communion with his earthly clay,

Borne with the meteor's ſpeed upon the wings

Of mightieſt Cherubim had now approach'd

The dark confines of Death's engulph'd domain :

Here at the barrier of that vaſt profound   230

On the firm adamant, from whence uproſe

The tow'ring ſtructure of hell's ebon gate,

The heav'nly Viſitant deſcending bade

His cherub bearers ſtoop their wings, on which

As in a plumey chariot he rode;   235

And now alighted on the dreadful brink

The Savior paus'd and downward caſt his eye

O'er that immeaſurable blank, the grave

Of

Of univerfal Nature, founded then
And charter'd to the gloomy powers of Sin   240
And Death Sin-born, when the primæval pair
Loft immortality and fell from God.
The ftarry lamps of heav'n here loft their light,
No fun-beam ever reach'd this difmal realm :
Yet in CHRIST's fpi'rit divine that living light,   245
Which from the Father of creation flow'd
Before all time, inherently fupplied
Self-furnifh'd vifion to explore the bounds
Of that oblivious pit, in whofe dark womb
Myriads of unredeemed fouls were plung'd ;   250
All who of human birth had pafs'd that gate
From righteous Abel, the firft-fruit of death,
To him, whofe heart had newly ceas'd to beat,
Were in that gulph immers'd.   At fartheft end
Of that Obfcure a pillary cloud arofe   255
Of fulph'rous fmoke, that from hell's crater fteam'd;
Whence here and there by intermittent gleams
Blue flafhing fires burft forth, that fparkling blaz'd
Up to the iron roof, whofe echoing vault
Refounded ever with the dolorous groans   260
Of the fad crew beneath : Thence might be heard
The wailing fuicide's remorfeful plaint ;
The murd'rer's yelling fcream, and the loud cry

Of

Of tyrants in that fiery furnace hurl'd,

Vain cry ! th' unmitigated furies urge   265

Their ruthlefs tafk and to the cauldron's edge

With ceafelefs toil huge blocks of fulphur roll,

Pil'd mountains high to feed the greedy flames :

All thefe, th' accurfed brood of Sin, were once

The guilty pleafures, the falfe joys, that lur'd   270

Their fenfual vota'rifts to th' infernal pit :

Them their fell mother, watchful o'er the work,

With eye that fleep ne'er clos'd and fnaky fcourge

Still waving o'er their heads, for ever plies

To keep the fiery deluge at it's height ;   275

And ftops her ears againft the clam'rous din

Of thofe tormented, who for mercy call

Age after age implor'd and ftill denied.

    Thefe when th' all-prefent Spirit of CHRIST defcried

At diftance toffing in the fulph'rous lake,   280

And heard their difmal groans, the confcious fenfe

Of human weaknefs by experience earn'd

In his own mortal body now put off,

And recollection that Himfelf of late

In his fublunar pilgrimage had prov'd   285

Temptations like to their's, drew from his foul

A figh of nat'ral pity, as from man

To man although in merited diftrefs :

                                                  But

But when his human fympathy gave place
To judgment better weigh'd and riper thoughts   290
Congenial with the Godhead reaffum'd,
The juftice of their doom, th' abhorrence due
To their vile deeds by voluntary act
Of will, left free, committed in defpight
Of confcience moving them to better thoughts,   295
Turn'd him indignant from the loathed fight
Of thefe impenitents; when, after paufe,
To GABRIEL, chief of the cherubic hoft
And late his ftrength'ning angel, thus he fpake.

   GABRIEL, or e'er from this high fteep we launch   300
With prone defcent into this gloomy vaft,
This fhadowy dark inane, the realm of Death,
After fo fwift a race through all the fpheres
From earth to this hell's portal, it behoves
Thee and thy plumed cohort to recruit   305
The vigor of your wings; for fure I am
That in this fubterranean we fhall find
No breeze from heav'n's pure æther to give aid
To motion, or uphold in fteady poife
Your feath'ry vans outftretch'd; nor may we look   310
For ftar or planet or one ftraggling ray
From circumlucent fun to guide our courfe
Through this obfcure domain of Night and Death.

Nor

Nor lefs behoves thee, gentle as thou art,

Friendlieft to man of all heav'n's angel hoft   315

And for each tafk of mercy and of love

Firft in the choice of God, to arm thy heart

For the fad fpectacles, the difmal fcenes,

Which we muft needs encounter in this gulph

Of human mifery, this world of woes,.   320

Fit refidence for SATAN and his crew

Of outcaft angels ; fad reverfe to thee

Inhabitant of heav'n : And now, behold !

Where hell's infernal pit with horrid glare

Flames through the difmal gloom, there, but that God   325.

In mercy films thine arch-angelic eye,

Such myriads in that ever-burning lake

Of fouls tormented thou wouldft elfe difcern,,

As would appal thy nature; but thefe fcenes

From thee, a fpi'rit fo loving to mankind,   330

So melting foft to pity, are with-held :.

No mercy can I meditate for them

Impenitent, no embaffy of peace

Have I in charge, no refpite, till the trump

Of general refurrection calls them up   335

At the laft day of judgment, then to hear

Their crimes rehears'd, their blafphemies expos'd,

Their envyings, frauds, revilings, treach'ries, plot¬

9   And

And ev'ry fecret of their hearts unmafk'd
By an all-righteous Judge, who fhall pronounce 340
Their final condemnation and decree
Their prefent pains perpetual. We meanwhile
To other regions fhall divert our courfe
From them and from their torments far apart,
Regions of night and filence, where the fouls 345
Of righteous men in their oblivious caves
Sleep out the time till their Deliverer comes
To wake them from their trance, diffolve the fpell
Of their enchanter Death and fet them free
To range the fields of Paradife, where flows, 350
As from a fountain by God's prefence fed,
Beatitude furpaffing human thought,
Pleafures unfeen, unnumber'd, unconceiv'd.

   This faid, from thofe high battlements the Dove
Of Peace upon Redemption's errand fent, 355
Borne on the wings of his cherubic choir,
Defcended fwift, and through the drowfy void
To Death's terrific palace fteer'd his flight.

   Here the Arch-foe of man, from earth expell'd
By man's Redeemer, newly had arriv'd, 360
But fear-ftruck and in like difaftrous trim
With war-worn Sifera, when in his flight
From the victorious Naphthalite he came

                         To

To afk protection at falfe Jael's tent,
And ruin found inftead.   The whirlwind's blaft   365
Had fhatter'd his proud form ; now fcorch'd by fires,
Now driv'n to regions of perpetual froft
Beyond extremeft Saturn's wint'ry fphere,
No middle courfe kept he, nor had his feet
From their aërial journey once found reft,   370
Till at the threfhold of Death's gloomy throne
Down on the folid adamant he fell
Precipitate at once, and lay entranc'd
Of arch-angelic majefty the wreck.

   Scar'd at the hideous crafh and all aghaft   375
Death fcream'd amain, then wrapt himfelf in clouds,
And in his dark pavilion trembling fate
Mantled in night.   And now the proftrate fiend
Rear'd his terrific head with lightnings fcorch'd
And furrow'd deep with fcars of livid hue ;   380
Then ftood erect and roll'd his blood-fhot eyes
To find the ghaftly vifion of grim Death,
Who at the fudden downfal of his fire
Startled, and of his own deftruction warn'd,
Had fhrunk from fight, and to a mifty cloud   385
Diffolv'd hung lowring o'er his fhrouded throne.
When SATAN, whofe laft hope was now at ftake,
Impatient for the interview exclaim'd.

                                        Where

Where art thou, Death? Why hide thyfelf from him,
Of whom thou art? Come forth, thou grifly king;   390
And though to fuitor of immortal mould
Thy refuge be denied, yet at my call,
Thy father's call, come forth and comfort me,
Thou gaunt anatomy, with one fhort glimpfe
Of thofe dry bones, in which alone is peace   395
And that oblivious fleep, for which I figh.

He faid, and now a deep and hollow groan,
Like roar of diftant thunders, fhook the hall,
And from before the cloud-envelop'd throne
The adamantine pàvement burft in twain   400
With hideous crafh felf-open'd, and difplay'd
A fubterranean chafm, whofe yawning vault,
Deep as the pit of Acheron, forbade
All nearer accefs to the fhado'wy king.
Whereat the imprifon'd winds, that in it's womb   405
Were cavern'd, 'gan to heave their yeafty waves
In bubbling exhalations, till at once
Their eddying vapors working upwards burft
From the broad vent enfranchis'd, when, behold!
The cloud that late around the throne had pour'd   410
More than Egyptian darknefs, now began
To lift it's fleecy fkirts, till through the mift
The' imperial Phantom gleam'd; monfter deform'd,

Enormous,

Enormous, terrible, from heel to fcalp
One dire anatomy ; his giant bones   415
Star'd through the fhrivell'd fkin, that loofely hung
On his fepulchral carcafe ; round his brows
A cyprefs wreath tiara-like he wore
With nightfhade and cold hemlock intertwin'd ;
Behind him hung his quiver'd ftore of darts   420
Wing'd with the raven's plume ; his fatal bow
Of deadly yew, tall as Goliah's fpear,
Propp'd his unerring arm ; about his throne,
If throne it might be called, which was compos'd
Of human bones, as in a charnel pil'd,   425
A hideous group of dire difeafes ftood,
Sorrows and pains and agonizing plagues,
His ghaftly fatellites, and, ev'n than thefe
More terrible, ambition's flaught'ring fons,
Heroes and conquerors ftil'd on earth, but here   430
Doom'd to ignoble drudgery, employ'd
To do his errands in the loathfome vault,
And tend corruption's never-dying worm,
To haunt the catacombs and ranfack graves,
Where fome late popu'lous city is laid wafte   435
By the deftroying peftilence, or ftorm'd
By murdering Rufs or Tartar blood-befmear'd
And furious in the defp'rate breach to plant

                                  His

His eagle or his crefcent on the piles
Of mangled multitudes and flout the fky   440
With his victorious banners.   Now a troop
Of fhrowded ghofts upon a fignal given
By their terrific Monarch ftart to fight,
Each with a torch funereal in his grafp,
That o'er the hall diffus'd a dying light,   445
Than darknefs' felf more horrible: The walls
Of that vaft cenotaph, hung round with fpears,
Falchions and pole-axes and plumed helms,
Shew'd like the arm'ory of fome warlike ftate:
There every mortal weapon might be feen,   450
Each implement of old or new device,
Which favage nature or inventive art
Furnifh'd to arm the ruffian hand of war
And deal to man the life-deftroying ftroke:
And them betwixt at intervals were plac'd   455
The crowned fkeletons of mighty kings,
Cæfars and Caliphs and barbarian Chiefs,
Monfters, whofe fwords had made creation fhrink
And frighted peace and fcience from the earth.

    Pondering the fcene in mute amazement rapt   460
The loft Arch-angel ftood, when foon the voice
Of Death as from the tombs low-murmuring thus
Befpoke attention—What uncivil caufe,

Prince

Prince of the air, provokes thee to offend
Againſt the peaceful charter of theſe realms   465
By voice thus rude and clamo'rous ? Know'ſt thou not
I reign by privilege, though ſon not ſlave
Of thee heav'n-exil'd ? Here no place haſt thou,
For here is peace ; no part in this domain
To.thee and to thy rebel hoſt belongs :   470
They in the flames of Tartarus, but we
Dwell with the ſilent worm : The pow'r we have
O'er man's corruptible and mortal part
Ends with the body ; here the bones may ſleep,
For theſe anatomies diſturb us not :   475
But for the ſpark unquenchable, the ſoul
Immortal, which ſurvives the fleeting breath,
Of that we take no charge ; that muſt abide
In other regions it's appointed lot
Of miſery or bliſs.   What then hath Death   480
To do with SATAN ? Can the ſon, who drew
Exiſtence from the father, quench that ſpi'rit,
Which God decreed eternal ? Will thoſe fires
Ceaſe at my word ? Hell will not hear my voice,
Nor can the howlings of th' infernal pit   485
Enter my ears.   Aſk not repoſe of me,
Tormented fiend : There is no grave for ſin,
No ſleep for SATAN ;. fall'n from heav'n thou art,

                                  There

There thou haft no abode ; fall'n now from earth,
Where is thy lodging ? Where, but in thofe flames ?   490
Pafs on then in thy courfe, nor loiter here,
For hell expects thee : Wert thou here to ftay,
Death in deftroying thee himfelf deftroys.

    Whereto th' unwelcome vifitant replied—
Inhofpitable Pow'r ! and is it thus   495
Thou greet'ft a father in his extreme need
Suppliant for leave to draw a moment's breath
In thy pale prefence, till this furious blaft,
That follow'd me from earth, fhall fpend it's rage
And ceafe to howl through the profound of hell ?   500
If in thy heartlefs trunk no mem'ory dwells
Of what I was; Oh ! teach me to forget
What now I am and make my fenfes dull
To pain, as thine to gratitude are loft :
But if thy mind be prefent to record   505
My fall from blifs, will it not alfo ferve
To put thee in remembrance how that fall
Beftow'd on thee a ftation and a name ?
Had I not fall'n from heav'n man had not loft
The joys of Paradife, immortal joys   510
Till I deftroy'd them; who then but myfelf,
Exil'd from God, brought Death into the world,
Gave thee the fepulchre for thy domain,

And

And every mortal body for thy prey ?
Whofe hand but SATAN's, thanklefs as thou art,   515
Plac'd that victorious wreath upon thy brow,
Arm'd thee for war and bade thee be a king ?
And what doth SATAN now demand of Death ?
What, but a moment's refpite, the fmall boon
Of hofpitable fhelter, where to lay   520
My aching head and reft my weary wing ?
This to the father can the fon refufe ?
I afk no more.   If CHRIST, from whom I fly,
Purfues me to this pit, and into hell
Defcending fhall repafs her gloomy gates   525
Guarded by Sin, that barrier loft, farewell.
To all thy greatnefs ! Where fhall be thy fting,
O Death, and where thy victory, O Grave ?
Then to have harbor'd SATAN fhall not add
One feather to the balance of thy fate :   530
All muft be loft together ; I to flames
Confign'd, thou, Phantom, into air diffolv'd.

    No more of this vain arguing, Death replied ;
My peace and my repofe I can but deal
As God decrees, and as he wills withhold :   535
Thus wrangling to the lateft hour of time.
Nothing, O SATAN, could'ft thou wring from me
But the fame anfwer and the fame defpair :

                                        I with

I with mortality alone confer,
Thou art a deathlefs fpirit : If my pow'r   540
Cannot annihilate the foul of man,
How then of angel ? Guilty thou haft been,
Confcious muft ever be, and therefore curft.
Of me complaining thou condemn'ft thyfelf,
The righteous ever are at peace with Death ;   545
Thou art not of their number.   Spi'rit unbleft,
Author of man's revolt and all things ill,
The hell which thou haft peopled, is thine own.
Earth thou haft made a ruin, men by thee
Perverted turn to monfters, Heav'n itfelf,   550
Difturb'd by thy rebellion, for a while
Suffer'd convulfion, and her thrones befieg'd
Echo'd the din of battle ; the fair bloom
Of Paradife was blafted by thy fpells,
And man driv'n forth to till th' unthankful earth   555
And toil and fweat for a precarious meal,
Degraded from his origin, at length
To me and to corruption was confign'd.
Thefe were thy doings, this was my defcent,
And my inheritance the loathfome worm,   560
The throne funereal and this yawning gulph
Impaffable, which I am yet to thank
For that it holds thee at a diftance from me :

This

This is thy bounty.   Look upon thefe bones,
Survey this dread anatomy, and fay.   565
If fon fo fafhion'd owes his father thanks :
Proportion'd to thy goodnefs I accord
My gratitude by bidding thee avaunt ;
Hence from my fight, intruder ! Thruft from earth
As heretofore from heav'n, and tempeft-torn   570
With bruifed head and fhatter'd flagging wing
Hither thou com'ft a fugitive from Him,
Whom in the wildernefs for forty days
Tempting thou didft annoy : Dull, doating fpirit !
Blind to thine own deftruction, not to fee   575
God's pow'r in CHRIST, nor underftand that He,
Who foil'd thy cunning, might defy thy ftrength :
But neither ftrength nor cunning fhall prevail
To draw me forth upon a lofing fide,
And fet this empire on a defp'rate caft :   580
I lack prefumption to oppofe that Power,
Which puts hell's monarch to inglorious flight.
What fhelter can'ft thou find behind a fhade,
An airy phantom ? Such thou fay'ft I am,
Such let me be ! That phantom will not tempt   585
The furious blaft of God's avenging breath,
Nor mov'd to pity by thy treacherous plaints
Tender oblivion's boon to foul accurft :

                                     Such

Such favor when thou wouldſt extort from Death,
That phantom will be adamant to thee.   590
Now learn a truth: CHRIST in the fleſh is dead;
Yet long I cannot hold him in the grave;
His body interdicted to the worm
For ſome myſterious purpoſe is reſerv'd
From all corruption free, and ſure I am   595
He will not leave his enemy at large
In this obſcure domain, where ſleep the ſouls
Of righteous men; fly then, whilſt yet the hour
Serves thee for flight—And hark! the angel trump
Sounds his approach. Now tremble, thou accurſt!   600
    No more; encanopied beneath the wings
Of mighty Cherubim with ſounding trump
And joyful chaunt the LORD OF LIFE came on—
Lift up your heads, the heav'nly chorus ſung,
Lift up your heads, ye everlaſting gates,   605
And CHRIST the King of Glory ſhall come in—
Bright as the ſun his preſence; darkneſs fled.
Down to the center; SATAN on the earth
Fell motionleſs; Death trembled on his throne,
And call'd his ſhadowy guards, they with loud ſhrieks   610
Vaniſh'd in air, whilſt from the gulph profound
Blue lightnings flaſh'd and deep-mouth'd thunders roar'd;

5   When

When CHRIST with eye fevere on SATAN turn'd
Bade the ftorm ceafe and thus addrefs'd the fiend.

 Well art thou found, thou ferpent, on the brink 615
Of thy laft home, this horrible abyfs,
For thee and for thine impious crew prepar'd.
Man from his God by thy corruption turn'd
Is by my death receiv'd into the peace
Of his offended Maker, and if faith 620
Opens his way to heav'n in righteoufnefs
And true converfion, Death cannot retain
His foul in darknefs, nor thy crafty wiles
Puzzle his path and damp his glowing zeal; --
But thou prefumptuous, who haft had the world 625
To range at will, and from God's altars pluck'd
Their confecrated honors, falfely view'd
Thofe fpoils, by fufferance yielded, as the prize
Of thine own proper victory. Behold!
Thefe are thy triumphs; in this pit receive 630
Thy folly's confutation and the doom
Of woe eternal on thy fin denounc'd.

 He faid, nor other anfwer SATAN gave
Than one deep groan rent from his lab'ring breaft.
The ftrong vindictive Angel, to whofe charge 635
The key of that infernal pit belong'd,

          Now

Now feiz'd him in his grafp and from the ground
Lifting his pond'rous bulk, fuch vigor dwelt
In arm celeftial, headlong down at once
Down hurl'd him to the bottom of the gulph,   640
Then follow'd on the wing: His yelling cries
Death heard, whilft terror fhiver'd every bone:
Not fo the choir cherubic; they with joy
Beheld Redemption's triumph in the fall
Of that Great Dragon, enemy of man,   645
That antient Serpent, now with bruifed head
And fting-bereft hurl'd down into the pit:
Whereat in heav'nly concert they begin
To raife their tuneful voices and fing forth
Praife to the Lamb of God, and joyful ftrain   650
Of gratulation to the Saints redeem'd——
     Now is falvation come and ftrength and power,
The kingdom of our God and of his CHRIST:
Now is that railing and malignant foe
Caft down into the pit, which day and night   655
Accus'd our righteous brethren to their God:
Now are they made victorious by the blood
Of the Redeeming Lamb, and in the word
Of Truth, their fearlefs witnefs, through the world
Go forth againft the anarchy of Sin   660
A hoft of martyrs faithful unto death;

                    K k   Therefore

Therefore rejoice, ye heav'ns, and ye of earth
Inhabitants, awake to joy and hail
The day-fpring of Salvation from on high.

    SATAN meanwhile ten thoufand fathoms deep   665
At bottom of the pit, a mangled mafs
With fhatter'd brain and broken limbs outfpread,
Lay groaning on the adamantine rock :
Him the ftrong Angel with ethereal touch
Made whole in form, but not to ftrength reftor'd,   670
Rather to pain and the acuter fenfe
Of fhame and torment; hideous was the glare
Of his blood-ftreaming eyes and loud he yell'd
For very agony, whilft on his limbs
The maffy fetters, fuch as hell alone   675
Could forge in hotteft fulphur, were infix'd
And rivetted in the perpetual ftone :
Upon his back he lay extended, huge,
A hideous ruin ; not a word vouchfaf'd
That vengeful Angel, but with quick difpatch   680
Plied his commiffion'd tafk, then ftretch'd the wing
And upward flew ; for now th' infernal cave
Through all it's vaft circumference had giv'n
The dreadful warning, and began to clofe
It's rocky ribs upon th' imprifon'd fiend :   685
Fierce and more fierce as it approach'd became

    2   The

The flaming concave; thus compreſt, the vault
Red as metallic furnace glow'd intenſe
With heat, that had the hideous den been leſs
Than adamant it had become a flood,   690
Or SATAN other than he was in ſin
And arch-angelic ſtrength pre-eminent,
He neither could have ſuffer'd nor deſerv'd :
Panting he roll'd in ſtreams of ſcalding ſweat,
Parch'd with intolerable thirſt, one drop   695
Of water then to cool his raging tongue
Had been a boon worth all his golden ſhrines :
Vain wiſh ! for now the pit had clos'd it's mouth,
Nor other light remain'd than what the glare
Of thoſe reverberating fires beſtow'd :   700
Then all the dungeon round was thick beſet
With horrid faces, threat'ning as they glar'd
Their haggard eyes upon him ; from hell's lake
Flocking they came, whole legions of the damn'd,
His worſhippers on earth, ſenſual, profane,   705
Abominable in their lives, monſters of vice,
Blood-ſtained murderers, apoſtate kings,
And crowned tyrants ſome, tormented now
For their paſt crimes and into furies turn'd,
Accuſing their betrayer : Curſes dire,   710
Hiſſings and tauntings now from every ſide

Aſſail'd

Aſſail'd his ear, on him, on him alone,
From Cain firſt murderer to ISCARIOT all,
All with loud voices charg'd on him their ſins,
Their agonies, with imprecations urg'd   715
For treble vengeance on his head accurſt,
Founder of hell, ſole author of their woe,
And enemy avow'd of all mankind.

   Now when the King of Terrors had perceiv'd
The pow'r of his new Viſitant and ſaw   720
SATAN engulph'd and the devouring pit,
Beſt barrier of his throne, for ever clos'd,
Deſcending from his ſtate with heart abaſh'd,
Conſcious that pride would ill befriend him now
In preſence of his Conqueror, at the feet   725
Of CHRIST with low obeiſance he put off
The trophies of his brow, and on the knee,
Stooping his vaſſal head, low homage paid,
And ſuppliant thus his humble ſuit preferr'd.

   Immortal King ! all glorious and all good,   730
At whoſe great name befits that every knee
In heav'n or earth or in theſe realms beneath
Should bend adoring, let thy will prevail
Here, as wherever elſe ! And ſure I am
'Tis not my pow'r but thine own wond'rous love,   735
Conſenting to the deed, hath brought thee here

                                    In

In pity to mankind to tafte the cup
Of agony and vifit thefe fad fhades,
Though deathlefs; thence to re-afcend, as foon
Thou fhalt, victorious to the realms of light.   740
I know thee for the CHRIST the Son of God,
Meffias of the prophets long forefeen,
Yet of the unbelieving Jews defpis'd,
Rejected, for thou cam'ft not in the pomp
Of tempo'ral majefty and only great   745
In patience, in humility, in love
And miracles of mercy.   At thy feet
This head uncrown'd thus ftooping, I refign
All empire; not on me let fall thy wrath
As on that bruifed Serpent.   What am I?   750
What is the fword, what is the peftilence,
And all my hoft of mortal minifters,
But fervants of thy providence, a fcourge
And rod of vengeance, wherewith to chaftife
Prefumptuous, guilty pride? Whofe hand but mine   755
Strikes terror to the atheift's harden'd heart?
Who plucks the tyrant from his bloody car
And rolls him in the duft? or at a blow
Strangles the curfe in the blafphemer's throat?
If on the martyr's head my axe defcends,   760
The fame hand plants a crown of glory there;

And

And if in my dark caves the righteous fleep, ·
Peaceful they fleep; I break not their repofe,
For filence dwells with me and night and reft.
Behold the key inviolate that guards   765
Their hallow'd flumbers; never did I yield,
Though oft folicited, this facred pledge
To SATAN or his fin-defiled crew;
Faithful I've kept it ever, faithful now
To thee their Savior I refign my charge.   770
    This faid, the golden badge of his command,
Rich and of heav'nly workmanfhip with gems
Of azure, green and purple thick embofs'd,
Humbly he laid at the REDEEMER's feet:
He to the zeal of GABRIEL ftrait confign'd   775
Th' enlargement of thofe fpi'rits to blifs preferr'd,
Fit minifter for office fo benign:
Whereat he bade found forth the fignal trump
Of the Firft Refurrection, heard of none
Save of thofe holy Saints elect of God,   780
Martyrs and prophets, call'd to live with CHRIST
In antecedent glory till the day
Of general Refurrection fhall awaken
And fummon into judgment all mankind.
Swift hied that friendly Angel on the wing,   785
Swifter, for that, on gracious errand fent,

                                                        Joy

Joy urg'd him to put forth his utmoſt ſpeed ;
Meanwhile the heav'nly Viſitant of Death
Upon that ghaſtly Viſion turn'd his eyes,
And thus in accent mild addreſs'd the Shade.'   790
  That I came down from heav'n and am the CHRIST,
Rightly, O Death, thou haſt pronounc'd ; yet here
I come not to deſtroy thy power at once,
But to ſet free the Saints thou hold'ſt in thrall,
And call them to my peace ; but ev'n of theſe   795
Part till my ſecond coming muſt abide :
Of thee and all things of corruption bred
The term is fix'd ; God muſt be all in all :
But time, as man computes, hath yet to roll
Through numerous ages ere the final trump   800
Shall ſound thy knell. I brought not upon earth
Peace, but the ſword ; the goſpel I have preach'd
Man will corrupt, miſconſtrue and pervert ;
Nor ſhall my Church be only drench'd with blood
Of it's own martyrs, zealots ſhall ariſe   805
Aliens to my humility and peace,
With more than pagan enmity enflam'd
Each againſt other ; then ſhall ruthleſs war
And perſecution and fierce civil rage
Ravage the Chriſtian world ; intole'rant pride,   810
Uſurping pow'r infallible, ſhall ſend

It's

It's heralds forth with curfing in their mouths
And fetters for man's confcience in their hands ;
They in the battle's front fhall plant the Crofs
And bid the unconverted nations kneel   815
Under their conqu'ring ftandard and adopt
The creed of murderers, who, in the place
Of the pure bond of charity, prefent
A forged fcroll blurr'd and defac'd with lies,
And impioufly infcribe it with my Name.   820
Thefe are religion's traitors, and from them
An ample harveft fhalt thou reap, O Death ;
Suffice it thee to know that for a while
Thou fhalt be fpar'd : And now no more ; Behold !
GABRIEL leads on the congregated Saints.   825
Vanifh, pale Phantom ! Give the ranfom'd place.

END OF THE SEVENTH BOOK.

CALVARY;

OR

THE DEATH OF CHRIST.

BOOK VIII.

The ARGUMENT of the EIGHTH BOOK.

*Chrift, having clofed his interview with Death, prepares to receive the
Saints of the Firft Refurrection now approaching under the conduct of
the angel Gabriel, and having afcended a mount in the midft of the
congregation appears to them in glory: They pay homage to their Redeemer in a hymn of praife and thankfgiving: He addreffes them in
reply, and affures them of the bleffings of immortal life beftowed upon
them by the Father as the reward of righteoufnefs: The patriarch
Abraham enters into conference with Chrift, in the conclufion of which
the Savior of the world fhews him the glorious vifion of the heavenly
Jerufalem, the holy city, as defcribed in the Apocalypfe: When this
beatific vifion is paffed away, Chrift reafcends to earth in view of the
whole affembly of Saints: The angel Gabriel, who is left behind, addreffes them from the mount and expounds the purpofes of the Savior's
refurrection from the dead and return to earth: Mofes recapitulates
the events of his life, inftances the frequent rebellions of the Lord's un-
faithful people, and laments their future impenitence and incredulity:
Gabriel replies, and from the nature of man's free will explains the origin
and neceffity of evil, from which he deduces the benefits of Chrift's
death and redemption: And now the Spirit of God defcending on the
hearts of the righteous, infpires them with all underftanding and knowledge, fitted to their happy condition: A Paradife arifes within the
regions of Death; Gabriel addreffes them for the laft time, and upon
his departure the Poem concludes.*

C A L V A R Y.

B O O K   VIII.

THE RESURRECTION FROM THE DEAD.

NOW had the Savior by the word of power
    Wafted the magic Phantom into air,
And all the horrors of the fcene difpell'd:
Swift as the ftroke of his own winged dart,
Or flitting fhadows by the moon-beam chas'd,   5
Death on the inftant vanifh'd: What had feem'd
A citadel of proud and martial port
With baftions fenc'd and tow'rs impregnable
Of adamant compos'd and lofty dome,
Covering the throne imperial, now was air;   10
And, far as eye could reach, a level plain,
In the intermin'able horizon loft,
Unfolded it's vaft champain to the view.
Darknefs twin-born with Death had fled; the rays,
That from the Savior's fun-crown'd temples beam'd,   15

     With

With dazzling luftre brighten'd all the fcene.
There juft emerging to the diftant view,
And glitt'ring white, a multitude appear'd,
Stretch'd eaft and weft in orderly array,
Swift marching underneath the mighty wings   20
Of the protecting Angel, who in air
Soar'd imminent, and with the broad expanfe
From flank to flank envelop'd all the hoft:
He with the blaft of the awak'ning trump
Gave note of their advance.   In the mid-plain   25
There was a mount; thither the Savior hied
With his cherubic guard, and there in view
Of the affembled myriads ftood fublime.
The Saints in order form'd themfelves around,
Orb within orb, each in his proper fphere   30
Inftinctively arrang'd; then all at once,
As by one foul infpir'd, with bended knee
And forehead proftrate on the earth they paid
Joint homage and ador'd.   Oh ! who fhall dare
With bold conjecture to compute the lift   35
Of that bleft multitude, or fay, who firft,
Who laft, receiv'd the glorious All-hail,
Ye bleffed of my Father? Yet perchance,
So warranted by fcripture and fo taught
By moral fage experience, we may doubt   40

                                                   If

If many rich, if many great or learn'd
Were of that righteous company ; be sure
The lover of this world had there no place,
He barter'd it for gold, he pafs'd it off
To Belial for a perifhable toy,   45
He fold it to a wanton : There the proud
Were brought down, and the meek and lowly rais'd :
The conque'ror not of others but himfelf
There found pre-eminence : All joy to him,
Who rear'd the orphan, dried the widow's tears,   50
And fought affliction in her fecret haunts,
Not for the praife of men ; and may not we,
Born in an age when mild philanthropy
Hath taught a better leffon to the heart,
May not we fofter a kind hope that fome   55
Of pagan name were call'd, who through the maze
Of dark idolatry took Reafon's clue,
And found a mental avenue to God ?
Here with the Father of the Faithful flood
A hoft of patriarchs, prophets, judges, faints :   60
Noah, who perfect in the time of wrath
And righteous found, was left unto the earth
A remnant, when the waters fell from heav'n,
And was in covenant with the Moft High
That man no more fhould perifh by the flood :   65

Mofes,

Mofes, the faithful fervant of the Lord,
Meckeft, though mightieft, of the fons of men
And glorious in the fight of dreadful kings:
Jofhua, th' avenger of th' Elect of God,
Whofe voice upon mount Gibeon ftaid the fun   70
In the mid-heav'n, and bade the moon ftand ftill
In Ajalon's dark vale, till Ifrael ceas'd
From flaughter and the conqu'ring fword was fheath'd:
Here Samuel in his linen ephod girt,
Thrice call'd of God, amid the foremoft ftood: 75
He, who with Baäl's priefts contending rear'd
His rival altars and brought fire from heav'n
To vindicate his God: The Pfalmift King,
And he, at whofe fick pray'r the fun went back,
And he, furnam'd the Good: Daniel the feer,   80
And they, who in the furnace walk'd unhurt;
All in the facred page recorded juft
And faithful fervants of the living God:
For who can doubt the holy word of truth
Attefting their falvation? Yet there is   85
One, who, by promife facredly affur'd
Of blifs immediate, heard the glorious call,
Whilft hanging on the crofs, by penitence
And faith obtain'd from the all-gracious lips
Of God's own Son expiring at his fide.   90

Hail,

Hail, holy congregation, elder-born
Of righteousnefs and firft-fruits of the grave,
Elect unto falvation ! Hail, bleft Saints,
Now cloathed in white robes, as in your lives
With purity, found forth your praife to God   95
And to the Lamb, in whofe blood ye are wafh'd ;
Wave high your branches of victorious palm,
Hymning the ftrain, which He in Patmos heard,
What time the glorious vifion was reveal'd.

   Hail, Firft and Laft ! th' immortal chorus fung,   100
Of all things the beginning and the end ;
For thou art he, who liveth and waft dead,
And lo ! thou art alive for evermore,
And hold'ft in hand of hell and death the keys.
Salvation to our God and to the Lamb   105
At his right hand, who fitteth on the throne ;
Blefling and glory, wifdom, honor, power,
Might and thankfgiving evermore to God
And to his Christ ! Father, we give thee thanks,
Lord God, which waft and art and art to come,   110
For this thy mighty pow'r in us fulfill'd.
Now are the kingdoms of this world become
The kingdoms of our Lord and of his Christ;
And he fhall reign for ever ; now thy wrath.
On the rebellious nations is let loofe ;   115

  5

Now is the firſt call of the ſleeping ſaints,
And all thy ſervants faithful unto death
Thou haſt rewarded with eternal bliſs.
Henceforth for ever bleſſed are the dead,
Thus dying in the Lord, for they ſhall reſt   120
From labor, and their good works are not loſt!

    Their hymn perform'd, the whole rèdeemed hoſt,
With hands uplifted and all eyes direct
Upon the glorious Preſence, bent the knee
Silent, whilſt thus the LORD OF MERCY ſpake.   125

    Ye bleſſed of my Father, prophets, ſaints
And martyrs; ye of Abraham's faithful ſtock,
And ye, though wild by nature, grafted in
Upon the parent tree and bearing fruits
To life eternal, welcome to my peace!   130
Now are your watchings and your labors paſt,
Your tribulations, ſelf-denials, pains
And mournings recompens'd; never again
Shall ye know thirſt or hunger, nor the ſun
Scorch you by day, nor yet by night the moon;   135
For ye ſhall dwell before the throne of God,
And I will feed you; I will lead you forth
To living founts and wipe away all tears.
Come, enter ye into your Maſter's joy,
Come, for the throne awaits you, take the crown   140

                                         Of

Of glory, take the kingdom from all time
For you prepar'd, poffefs your happy rights,
The earnings of your charity and love :
For I was hungred and ye gave me meat,
Thirfty I was and ye affwag'd my thirft, 145
I was a ftranger and ye took me in,
Naked ye cloath'd me, fick ye vifited,
I was in prifon and ye came unto me.

When Lord, the righteous humbly interpos'd,
When were thefe charities by us perform'd ? 150
How have we merited this praife of thee,
Whom in the flefh we knew not ? Tell us, Lord,
When faw we thee an-hungred and gave food ?
When thirfty and gave drink ? a ftranger when
And took thee in, naked and cloathed thee ; 155
When faw we thee in ficknefs or in prifon
And came unto thee ? When didft thou endure
Thefe hard neceffities, or we relieve ?

Whereto the LORD replied : Truly ye fay
Me in the flefh ye knew not, yet in fpi'rit 160
Ye knew me, for my law was in your hearts ;
And what to thefe my brethren ye have done,
Or to the leaft of thefe, ye did to me,
Patron of mercy and the friend of man.
To every one, but not to all alike, 165

M m   Some

Some talent is in truft, the loan of Heav'n,
To hufband as he may, and he who fpares
From his imparted fund wherewith to help
His neighbor's fcantier dole, improves the loan
And makes his Lord his debtor.   Firft and laft,   170
Ere Abraham was I am.   Open your ears!
Hear, mark and underftand : The world by fin
Original had fallen off from God;
Man was become corrupt, idolatrous,
Abominable; SATAN reign'd on earth.   175
Ye are of various ages; all have flept,
And fome from earlieft times or e'er the flood
Swallow'd the nations, yet with one accord
All in your feveral periods have bewail'd
Degenerated man : Noah can tell   180
How all the earth with violence was fill'd,
Or e'er the fountains of the vafty deep
Were broken up : Mofes can well declare
How hard and to rebellion prone the hearts
Of thofe, whom he led forth : Samuel beheld   185
A ftiff-neck'd generation fpurn the yoke
And kick againft their God; but vain his voice,
Vain all the prophets voices, which foretold
My coming, without whom the world were loft.
Now is falvation come; I've drank the cup   190

5

Of

Of bitternefs and died the death for man :
My peace I've left on earth ; the living world,
They have the word of truth and by that word
Through faith they fhall be fav'd; from them I came
To vifit thefe dark regions and redeem   195
The faints who flept ; behold ! ye are alive :
Death hath no more dominion ; SATAN, chain'd
For ages, fhall abide his time to come :
Meanwhile in glory ye fhall dwell with me ;
By refurrection purchas'd with my blood   200
Ye are the firft-fruits of immortal life.

   Now ABRAHAM, father of the faithful band
And firft in ftation neareft to the mount,
His eyes uplifted to the face divine
Of the effulgent Virtue, and thus fpake.   205

   Yet once more, as aforetime in the days
Of Sodom, fuffer me to plead for man,
And afk of thee his Savior if thefe few,
Few not in numbers, yet for heav'n too few
And for heav'n's mercy, feeing there are paft   210
So many many ages of the world,
Are all that fhall be fav'd : Alas, for man !
If this be the whole remnant, all the ftock
Cull'd from fo many myriads for God's fold.
Where are the nations vanifh'd ? Where the hofts,   215

M m 2

That

That fea, earth, flood and fire have fwallow'd up?
Can hell contain them? Can devouring Death
Find ftomach for them all? Did God make man
For death and hell, or thou endure the crofs
Only for us? Are all the righteous fhrunk   220
To this fmall meafure? And, if thefe be all,
Are they not yet enough to fave the reft,
If heav'nly mercy liften to our prayer?
May not our righteoufnefs fo fave a world
From wrath, as once the righteoufnefs of five   225
Had fav'd a guilty city from it's fate?

    To him the LORD OF MERCY: I have faid
Ye are the firft fruits by my blood obtain'd,
The earneft of redemption: I have bruis'd,
Not crufh'd, the Serpent's head; he fhall arife   230
Out of the pit once more to vex the earth.
Death the laft enemy is not deftroy'd,
Yet is his fceptre fhorten'd, and the key,
That opens into life, now in thofe hands,
Where mercy beft can place it for man's good: 235
Thus of all pow'r though Death is not bereft,
Yet I have fhook his throne, with inroad deep
Pierc'd his dark realm, and, you redeeming thence,
Made tenantlefs your graves, his ftrongeft holds.
With you when from this depth I reafcend,   240

                        And

And through heav'n's golden portal lead my hoft
Of Saints high-waving thefe victorious palms,
Your white robes glitt'ring in God's ftarry courts,
Great fure will be the triumph, loud th' acclaim,
When all my Father's Angels fhall found forth   245
Their joyful halelujahs round his throne.
Enough for victory hath been atchiev'd,
Deftruction is referv'd to that great day,
When the compelling Angel fhall go forth
To gather every atom of man's duft,   250
Which the feas cover or the earth contains :
Then fhall all fouls be judg'd ; if Abraham then,
When of all hearts the fecrets fhall be known,
Then if the Friend of God hath aught to urge
In mitigation of man's guilt, be fure,   255
Ere juftice ftrike, mercy will hear the plea.
Of this no more : The feafons and the times
Are with the Father; the dread hour draws on :
But I muft firft revifit thofe on earth,
Whom I have left in forrow ; for their fakes,   260
I muft again fubmit me to the flefh,
And by the evidence of fenfe confirm
My promis'd refurrection ; this perform'd
And immortality reveal'd to man,
By faith made fure, my gofpel fhall go forth.   265

My

My office then the Comforter will take ;
The weak he shall make strong, the foolish wife,
And by the mouths of sucklings and of babes
He shall confound the wisdom of the world,
And o'er the gates of hell erect my Church.   270

When thus the Patriarch, glowing still with zeal
For man's salvation, further question urg'd.

Lord, will not then the faithless world believe,
When thou return'st with glory ? From the dead
When they behold thee visible on earth   275
And thence to heav'n ascending, can they doubt ?
Such revelation can their eyes resist,
Their ears such truth recorded ? Shall there then
Be left a Gentile idol upon earth
To rival Israel's God ? Shall there not be   280
One Shepherd and one fold for all mankind,
One faith, one baptism, one Lord and Christ ?
But I perhaps too bold offend thine ear
With my rude converse ; Lord, if so, command
My tongue to silence ; yet not in thy wrath,   285
Not in thy wrath, O Lord, reprove my zeal.

Whereto the Savior mildly thus replied.
O Abraham, in whose soul compassion glows
And love, that burns with zeal for all thy sons,
Nor for thy sons alone, but the whole world,   290

Whose

Whofe advocate thou art, think not the tongue,.
That fpeaks for mercy, can offend my ear :
Yet what thy zeal anticipates in time
Is diftant far ; ages muft roll betwixt
Thy hope and its completion ; threat'ning clouds 295
Lour on the glorious profpect ; feas of blood
Muft firft be pafs'd ; long pilgrimage and fad .
My martyrs have to make through vallies dark,
Where ign'rance fhades the fun, through frightful haunts,
Where fuperftition pictures out the fcene 300
In monftrous forms, and worfhips what it dreads :
Painful their march and round befet with fnares ;
Here treach'ry lurks, there perfecution flames,
Before them infidelity, behind
Reproach and flander and the roar of tongues 305
Contentious, urging them to turn from God
And wafte their nobler zeal in vain difpute.
Thus ftep by ftep in righteoufnefs and faith
Arm'd at all points my fervants militant
Shall win their way, and what they earn enjoy. 310
Lowly and meek I came into the world,
And meek and lowly I fhall now return,
Not with that glory rifing from the grave,
Which for my fecond coming is referv'd,
But in that mortal body, which they pierc'd, 315

Shewing

Shewing my wounds, not with the proud difplay
Of one, who courts the voice of public fame,
But communing apart with thofe I left
To be my witneffes, that fo through them
Men may be taught by reafon to difcern   320
Not what they muft, but what they fhould, believe;
Not by the evidence of fenfe to feel,
But by the mind's conviction to perceive
Truth in it's argument, not act, and build
On reafon, not neceffity, their faith,   325
And on their faith and their good works their hope.
God will not always ftruggle with mankind,
Heap proof on proof till incredulity
Though blind muft fee, though deaf of force muft hear;
He will not bring his heav'n upon the earth,   330
Rather will lead man's heart from earthly things
To reach at heavenly; the railing Jews,
Who fix'd me to the crofs, bade me come down
And with the fign of pow'r difpel their doubts:
So had I fruftrated all faith at once,   335
And with all faith all virtue: I was dumb,
I open'd not my mouth to their reproach,
I ftirr'd not from the crofs, I died the death,
Nor to my refcue brought one Angel down,
Though legions waited to obey my call: 340

And

And now none other fign will I vouchfafe
But of the prophet Jonas; for as he
From out the belly of the whale emerg'd
On the third day, fo I from out the tomb
In the fame body will come forth on earth 345
With the third morning's dawn; thus fhall the word
Of prophecy by my difciples heard,
Not underftood, be perfected in me,
And I will breathe my fpi'rit into their hearts
To comprehend all fcriptures, and to preach 350
Me crucified; nor fhall there be a dearth
Of witneffes to publifh and atteft
My refurrection; hundreds fhall behold
My fubftance in the flefh, and he that doubts
Shall touch me and believe. More to expound 355
There needs not; this in all your ears aloud
I now promulgate, that when I am gone
Ye may abide the interim in peace,
By terror or impatience undifturb'd:
And now not many are the days to pafs, 360
Ere to the heav'n of heav'ns I fhall afcend,
And there in bleft communion with my Saints,
Made perfect after death, for ever dwell
At the right hand of Pow'r; meanwhile the feed,
Which I have fown, though of all grains the leaft, 365

Yet

Yet water'd by the Comforter fhall grow
Of herbs the greateft, and become a tree,
Within whofe branches all the birds of air
Shall come and lodge, fo fhall my kingdom rife
From mean beginning into mighty growth,   370
A ftill fmall current, fpreading as it goes ;
For in the arm of man I place no ftrength,
Nor in the battle's thunder can be heard
His voice that preacheth peace ; to ftorm the ear,
Like thofe loud heathen orators, who fhake   375
The forum with their eloquence, ill fuits
The fervants of a Mafter little vers'd
In this world's wifdom and not vain of fpeech :
In love, in calm perfuafion and in peace
My gofpel I have planted : Woe to them,   380
Who in the place of thefe fweet fruits provoke
The baneful growth of perfecution, ftrife
And difcord in my Church, op'ning my wounds
Unheal'd and crucifying me afrefh.

    To him the Patriarch : Lord, we give thee thanks   385
For that thou haft imparted to thy faints
Thefe tidings of great joy, though diftant far
And through fuch clouds of forrow dimly feen ;
And fure we are thy gofpel fhall prevail,
Yet much do we lament for what thy faints   390
                                  And

And martyrs have to fuffer upon earth,
Foil'd by that firft Deceiver of mankind,
Who, though now bruis'd and for awhile enchain'd,
Shall yet come forth to vex thy holy Church,
To conjure up falfe prophets and pervert   395
Thy follo'wers, who are taught to live in peace
And charity with all men : But we know
God did not build this goodly frame of things
For SATAN to deftroy, and he and Death
Shall have an end : Heav'n is man's natural home   400
And righteoufnefs the impulfe of his heart;
Nor will God fail his promife, that in me
And in my feed the whole world fhall be bleft :
Ah! when fhall I behold that promis'd day ?
When fhall I fee the warring world at peace ?   405
When fhall my Ifrael, fcatter'd o'er the earth
And ftraggling wide, hear their good Shepherd's call
And come into his fold ? Sure that bleft voice,
That glorious vifion would be heav'n itfelf.

    That vifion thou fhalt fee, the LORD replied   410
And fmil'd all-gracious on th' enraptur'd Saint,
From this profpective mount with purged eye,
That through the length'ning tract of time difcerns
Futurity remote, thou fhalt behold
Th' Apocalypfe, which to no living eye,   415

Save

Save of my fervant John, I fhall difclofe :
But know ere this bleft period fhall arrive
The elements muft melt with fervent heat,
And earth and fea and heav'n muft pafs away,
Darknefs and fin and death fhall be no more,   420
And a new world fhine forth. Afcend the mount,
And eaftward turning tell me what thou fee'ft.

I fee, the Patriarch cried, an heaven and earth,
Earth without fea and heav'n without a cloud,
All bright and glift'ning from the Maker's hands :   425
I fee defcending from the throne of God
Jerufalem the Holy City, new,
Deck'd like a bride for her celeftial fpoufe :
Order and grace and fymmetry confpire
In all her parts, and with the rich difplay   430
Of vivid gems make glorious her attire :
To the four points of heav'n in equal fpan
She ftretches out her many-colour'd walls,
Celeftial mafonry, whofe meaneft ftone,
More rare and precious than the brighteft gem   435
Of earthly diadems, tranfparent flames,
From the foundations to the topmoft cope
Of mural battlement one dazzling blaze
Of glorious jewelry, and them amidft
On every flank quadrangular three gates,   440

                                                       Each

Each of an orient pearl, to our twelve tribes
By number and by name appropriate,
Stand open, guarded by Cherubic watch ;
Through whofe unfolded portals I defcry
A city all of pureft gold and clear   445
As the unclouded cryftal, on whofe towers
God's all-fufficient glory fheds a flood
Of radiance brighter than the borrow'd beam
Of fhadowy moon or fun oft wrapt in clouds,
Making alternate night and day on earth :   450
But night is here unknown ; day needeth not
To reft in darknefs, nor the eye in fleep;
Nor temple here for worfhip may be found,
The ever-prefent Deity demands
No houfe of pray'r ; in ev'ry heart is built   455
His altar, every voice records his praife,
And every faint his minifter and prieft.
Through the mid-ftreet a cryftal river flows
Pellucid, welling from the throne of God,
It's living fource, upon whofe border fprings   460
The tree of life, bearing ambrofial fruits
Monthly renew'd and varied through the year,
Food for immortals, in whofe balmy gum
And leaves medicinal a virtue dwells
So general and potential, that no pain   465
                                                        Or

Or ailment but here finds it's ready cure :
No tear ſhall wet this conſecrated ſoil,
Nor feud nor clamor nor unholy curſe
Diſturb theſe peaceful echoes, here the ſaints
In ſweet harmonious brotherhood ſhall dwell   470
Serene and perfect in the ſight of God.
And hark ! I hear ſeraphic voices chaunt
To their melodious harps the bridal hymn—
Now is our God eſpouſed to his Church,
And from their heav'nly union are gone forth   475
Bleſſing and peace and joy to all mankind :
Now ſhall his ſaints eternal Sabbath keep
From death and pain and wailing and complaint :
All is made new, the old is paſs'd away,
Time draws aſide the faded ſcene of things   480
And Nature in immortal freſhneſs blooms :
Now to the waters of the fount of life,
Perpetual waters, every ſoul may come,
And he that is athirſt may freely drink :
But fire and brimſtone in the burning lake   485
Shall be their portion, who revolt from God ;
There with the Beaſt in torments they ſhall dwell,
Seal'd in their foreheads with his mark and drink
The cup of indignation to the dregs
Wrung out in anger, whilſt their ceaſeleſs cry   490

Shall

Shall with the fmoke of the infernal pit
Day after day for evermore afcend.

No more; for now the heav'nly vifion clos'd;
Awaken'd from his trance the Patriarch turn'd
With grateful reverence to addrefs the LORD 495
And giver of thefe new-difcover'd joys,
When lo! afcending from the mount he faw
CHRIST in a cloud of glory on the wings
Of mighty Cherubim upborne in air
High-foaring, to this orb terraqueous bound, 500
Seen over-head diminifh'd to a point
Dim and opake amid the blue ferene:
His raiment, whiter than the new-born light
Struck out of chaos by the Maker's hand
In earneft of creation, fparkling blaz'd 505
In it's fwift motion and with fiery track
Mark'd his afcent to earth; the hoft of Saints
With joyful loud hofannas fill'd the air:
Glory to God on high, was all their ftrain,
On the earth peace, good-will to all mankind! 510
Meanwhile th' Arch-angel GABRIEL, who yet kept
His tutelary ftation on the mount,
So bidd'n of CHRIST, with arm outftretch'd and voice
Commanding filence, thus the Saints befpake.

6   Now

Now is your refurrection fure, your joy,   515
Your glory and your triumph over Death
And hell made perfect; for behold where CHRIST
Your firft-fruit is aris'n, and waves on high
The enfign of redemption; now he foars
Up to yon pendent world, that darkling fpeck,   520
Which in the boundlefs empyrean floats
Pois'd on it's whirling axle; there he liv'd
And took your mortal body, there he died
And for your fakes endur'd the painful crofs,
Giving his blood a ranfom for your fins;   525
Thither he goes to re-affume his flefh;
There, when his angel minifters have op'd
The fealed fepulchre, he fhall come forth
And fhew himfelf refurgent from the grave
To thofe whom he hath fanctified and call'd   530
To be his witneffes in all the world,
And of his refurrection after death
Their faithful evidence to feal with blood
Of martyrs and apoftles, warning men
With their laft breath to be baptiz'd and live;   535
So fhall the feed be water'd and increafe,
Till all the Gentile nations fhall come in
And dwell beneath it's branches evermore.

Now are the gates of everlafting life
Set open to mankind, and when the LORD, 540
Captain of their falvation, fhall have liv'd
His promis'd term on earth, and thence to heav'n
Afcending feat himfelf at God's right hand,
Then fhall the Holy Ghoft the Comforter
Bufh like a mighty wind upon the hearts 545
Of his infpir'd apoftles ; tongues of fire
And languages untaught they fhall receive
To fpeak with boldnefs the revealed Word,
Enduring all things for the gofpel's fake;
Troubled on ev'ry fide yet not diftrefs'd, 550
Perplex'd but not furrender'd to defpair,
Afflicted not forfaken they fhall be,
Caft down but not deftroy'd, knowing that God,
Who raifed the LORD JESUS from the dead,
Them alfo into life through him will raife, 555
And that the light affliction of this world,
Which is but for a moment, foon fhall be
O'erpaid by a far more exceeding weight
Of glory' eternal in the life to come.

 He ceas'd, and all were filent, wrapt in awe 560
Of the late glorious vifion, yet in heart
Troubled for what the Angel had reveal'd
Of forrows ftill to come and pains and deaths

O o

To

To be encounter'd by the Saints on earth;
When now that Shepherd, who on Sinai's mount   565
Commun'd with God and heard creation's plan
Expounded by it's Architect, thus fpake.

    Oh thou, whom through the fiery cloud I faw
On Horeb's hill, when tending Jethro's flock,
What time I heard my name twice call'd of God   570
In thunder from amidft the flaming bufh,
Bidding me ftrait go forth to loofe his fheep
From Egypt's captive fold, I do perceive
That I have penn'd the Word of God aright,
And now in CHRIST behold the woman's feed   575
Bruifing that Serpent's head, who wrought the fall
Of our firft parents.   Forty days and nights
On Sinai's top 'midft thund'rings, clouds and fire
Fafting I ftood, and whilft the hallow'd ground
Trembled beneath my bare unfandal'd feet,   580
I heard an awful voice, that bade me write
The glorious record of his fix days work.
Aghaft, confounded, dazzled with the blaze
Of glory, ftill my faithful pen obey'd
The facred dictates of an unfeen God: 585
I wrote, and to an unbelieving world
Publifh'd the wond'rous Code; age after age
Libell'd the tranfcript: With the rod of pow'r

4

I fmote

I fmote the feas afunder; Ifrael pafs'd
Through wat'ry battlements; forty long years   590
In the wafte howling wildernefs I fed
Their murmuring tribes with food miraculous;
They fed but murmur'd ftill: I brought them laws
With God's own finger graven; I came down
Bearing Jehovah's ftatutes in my hand   595
On both fides written; impious noify fhouts,
Lewd triumphs and vile revels fmote mine ear;
The people danc'd around a molten calf,
Monftrous idolatry! Raging with fhame
I dafh'd the ftony tablets on the ground,   600
And fhiver'd them to fragments; God was mock'd;
A ftiff-neck'd and a ftubborn race they were,
Who from the rock of their falvation turn'd
And facrific'd to devils; and behold!
Their fons have crucified the LORD OF LIFE;   605
Therefore his refurrection, which fhall be
Light and redemption to the Gentile world,
To them is darknefs and the fhadow' of death;
For they have flain the very Pafchal Lamb;
That bloody fymbol of their antient law,   610
Which I made facred, they have now made void,
And cancell'd my legation: I perceive
A new commandment is gone forth; I fee

The temple's vail is rent; for the old law,
A carnal fhadow of things fpiritual,   615
Suffic'd not for perfection and the pow'r
Of an eternal life : CHRIST is become
That King of Salem, that immortal Prieft
Of God moft high, whofe miniftry fupreme,
Before all time from heav'n itfelf deriv'd   620
And not from right Levitical, removes
All title from that confecrated tribe,
Where I had fix'd it.   God, who fending me,
Sent but his fervant, now hath giv'n his Son
More worthy of his glory; without fin   625
And fpotlefs He, the great High Prieft, hath pafs'd
Into the heav'ns victorious over Death ;
But I, whofe trefpaffes at Meribah,
Frail finful man, provok'd the Lord to wrath,
Saw but the fkirts of Dan from Pifgah's top,   630
Unworthy deem'd to enter that fair land,
And died upon mount Nebo. But when CHRIST,
Who hath awaken'd us from fleep, fhall rife
And in his mortal flefh a fecond time
Vifit his Saints on earth, who then fhall fay   635
There is no refurrection of the dead?
Faintly I fhadow'd forth a future life ;
I fpake not to men's fenfes, as CHRIST fpeaks;

                                                         God

God gave me no commiffion to reveal
The fecrets of the grave; corruption's worm   640
Spar'd not my flefh, nor came my fpirit back
From Death's dark citadel to give mankind
Conviction ocular of his defeat;
I left him in his power till CHRIST fhould come
To break that fceptre, which had aw'd the world.   645
Much then it moves my wonder, much I grieve
That darknefs fhall not yet be drawn afide
From Ifrael, and that thofe, who would not hear
Me and the prophets, fhall not yet believe
CHRIST their Meffias rifing from the dead.   650

 To whom th' Arch-angel anfwer'd heav'nly mild:
Well may'ft thou mufe that reas'ning man fhould doubt,
And caufe we have to grieve, when he neglects
So great falvation; but when CHRIST hath fhewn
What is the good and true and perfect way,   655
Reafon muft do the reft: When all are free
Some muft be faithlefs, wilful and perverfe.
God could have made his creatures void of fin,
For he can put a mafter in their hearts,
And govern them by inftinct; but to man   660
He gave a nobler faculty, a will,
A fpark of immortality, a foul,
Reafon to counfel that immortal foul,

         And

And confcience to reftrain licentious will.
Grace fhall affift the humble and devout ;   665
A proud man hath no friend in heav'n or earth,
Renounc'd of angels and by men abhorr'd:
Truth muft be fought, it will not be impos'd :
What were that revelation, which fhould leave
No exercife to faith ? All men muft work   670
With fear and trembling their falvation out.
God does not give free will to take away
What he hath giv'n ; if man will fin, he muft :
Nor do we call them good, who cannot err,
Elfe brutes would claim a virtue.   None is good   675
Save God alone ; impute we not to God
The evil which man does, nor him arraign
For not preventing ills which he foreknows :
Angels have finn'd and fome are fall'n from blifs ;
All had their days of error, their degrees   680
Of good and ill, elfe why have we degrees
Ranks and precedencies of blifs in heav'n ?
Call your own lives to mind ; ye have been men,
Your failings many, yet your virtues more ;
Why are ye now rewarded by your God ?   685
Why but becaufe thofe virtues were your own ?
Ye made them what they were, ye rear'd their growth,
Reafon reform'd the wild luxuriant foil,

                                      Pluck'd

Pluck'd up the weeds and nurs'd the glorious fruit.
Is there amongſt you one that hath to boaſt　　690
Human perfection? There is none that will.
A free yet faultleſs creature would be more
Than man, than angel; nor can God create
An equal to himſelf, a rival God.
In Eden's happy groves when man was plac'd,　　695
One interdicted baneful plant there was,
Tempting and rich in fruit; all elſe was good,
Fair to the eye and wholeſome to the taſte;
Yet of that fruit man pluck'd and eat and died;
Tempted he was, but not compell'd to take;　　700
Warn'd to abſtain, no angel ſtopp'd his hand,
No thundering voice deterr'd him from the deed,
For man was free; ſo could he not have been,
Had God's foreknowledge over-rul'd his will.
Thus Sin had origin and Death began　　705
His occupation with the human race,
More terrible for that he came with pangs,
Horrors and doubts on ſin-oppreſſed man,
When conſcience wrung him in the parting hour:
But ſtill the inextinguiſhable ſoul　　710
Mock'd at Death's dart, the body was his own
From the beginning; of the earth 'twas made,
The earth it till'd and from the earth it fed;

A tenement

A tenement of duſt was never form'd
For immortality; and now, behold,   715
Adam the earthy man, in whom all die,
Is buried to the world; redemption brings
The day-ſpring of Salvation from on high,
CHRIST in his glory comes, the LORD from heav'n,
And who in him have faith, in him have life.   720
   He ceas'd, when now th' aſſembly of the Saints,
Who whilſt he ſpake ſtood in their orbs unmov'd
Circling the mount, 'gan feel the Spi'rit of God
Deſcending on their hearts, and, like a ſea
By ſecret currents from it's bottom ſtirr'd,   725
Wav'd to and fro their undulating files
Wide and more wide, as with a mighty wind
The heav'nly inſpiration on them ruſh'd:
This GABRIEL heard and from the mount came down,
Which quak'd beneath his feet, whilſt over-head   730
Loud thunderings announc'd the coming God:
And now a fire, that cover'd all the mount,
Beſpoke him preſent; all the air reſpir'd
Ambroſial odours, amaranth and roſe,
For Nature felt her God, and every flower   735
And every fragrant ſhrub, whoſe honied breath
Perfumes the courts of heav'n, had burſt to life
Blooming, and, in a thouſand colors dy'd,

                                Threw

Threw their gay mantle o'er the naked heath :
Now glow'd the living landſcape ; hill and dale   740
Roſe on the flat, or ſunk as Nature ſhap'd
Her lovelieſt forms and ſwell'd her wavey line,
Leaving unrein'd variety to run
Her wild career amid the ſportive ſcene :
Nor were there wanting trees of ev'ry growth,   745
Umbrageous ſome, making a verdant tent
Under their ſpreading branches, ſome of ſhaft
Majeſtic, tow'ring o'er the ſubject groves :
Bloſſoms and fruits and aromatic gums
Scented the breeze, that fann'd their ruſtling leaves ;   750
And them betwixt a cryſtal river flow'd
O'er golden ſands, meand'ring in it's courſe
Through amaranthine banks with lulling ſound
Of dulcet murmurs breathing ſoft repoſe.

     Thus at the ſight of God ſpontaneous roſe   755
A Paradiſe within the realm of Death,
Where that bleſt congregation might abide
Their LORD's return now viſitant on earth :
And now th' Eternal having breath'd his joy
Into their hearts and giv'n them to diſcern   760
All knowledge, that befitted ſouls ſo bleſt,
Withdrew his preſence from the flaming mount ;

P p

Whereat

Whereat the min'iftring Angel, who beheld
Salvation's work complete, thus parting fpake.

    God, in whofe prefence pleafure ever dwells,   765
Hath for your dear Redeemer's fake beftow'd
Thefe joys, and now his prefence is withdrawn ;
Yet hath he left his fpirit in your hearts.
To teach you all that is and is to be :
Behold, the cloud that veil'd your mortal eyes   770
Is drawn afide, and what as in a glafs
Darkling ye faw now face to face is feen :
Ye now difcern the ways of God how juft,
How true, how wife, how perfect in defign,
And well ye know that man, prefumptuous man,   775
In a vain fhadow walketh ; ye perceive
His boafted mind fufficient for the things,
That to his own falvation appertain ;
Yet when it fcans the myfteries of heaven,
How falfe, how weak, how daringly abfurd !   780
Firm faith, warm charity and humble hope,
Thefe are the Chriftian graces, thefe the guides,
That lead to life eternal ; thoughts perverfe,
Pert quibbling follies, publifh'd in the pride
Of falfe philofophy, are dev'lifh arts,   785
That damn the inftrument, who thus attempts
To hide the light of revelation's beam

    I   From

From weaker eyes, and turn the world from God ;.
Thefe verily fhall have their juft reward :.
And now no more; this Paradife ye fee   790
Is but your paffage to a brighter fcene,.
A refting-place till CHRIST fhall re-afcend
To the right hand of God and call you hence
To fhare his glory in the heav'n of heavens.

    He faid, and fwifter than the meteor's glance,   795
Sprung on the wing to feek his native fphere :
The Saints look'd up, then fung with joint acclaim—
Glory to God and praifes to his CHRIST,
Judge and Redeemer of the quick and dead !   799.

www.ingramcontent.com/pod-product-compliance
Lightning Source LLC
Chambersburg PA
CBHW021038030726
47496CB00006B/1596